Until You Are Dead

WITHDRAWN

Until You Are Dead

JOHN LUTZ

Five Star
Unity, Maine

Five Star Mystery.
Published in conjunction with Tekno-Books and Ed Gorman.

Cover photograph by Jason Johnson.

November 1998
Standard Print Hardcover Edition.

Five Star Standard Print Mystery Series.

The text of this edition is unabridged.

Set in 11 pt. Plantin by Minnie B. Raven.

Printed in the United States on permanent paper.

Library of Congress Cataloging in Publication Data

Lutz, John, 1939–
    Until you are dead / by John Lutz.
      p. cm.
    ISBN 0-7862-1660-3 (hc : alk. paper)
    I. Title.
    PS3562.U854U58   1998
    813'.54—dc21
                                        98-42586

CONTENTS

Introduction

For a writer, culling old work for the best and most lasting can be an unsettling trip into the past. I made the journey with unsuspected reluctance, looking right, looking left. There were my old friends Dr. Mindle the psychiatrist, Ruddy Kane the free-living trucker, Frank Seabold the dual defendant, Thana the curious kidnap victim, O'Hara the terrorist on the run, Snodman the smug cop. How had they held up since the years when my hair was dark and I was stronger and leaner of limb?

Not bad, not bad at all.

Of course a few of the stories are somewhat dated, for which I ask the reader's indulgence. There is the Last Stop Lounge, a hangout for workers rumored to manufacture "a component for the hydrogen bomb." Hit men sure work cheap. And Richard Widmark is still in the wrong place at the wrong time. But for the most part I'm pleased with my journey, and I've tried to bring back the best for you. My old friends haven't aged as much as I have (in fact, not at all), and series characters Nudger and Carver are in a time warp we all should enjoy. Estimable office employee Miss Knickelsworth is sans computer and using an electric typewriter, yet this tale of a light and power company monopoly seems shockingly current.

One reason I believe these stories have held up well is because they are mysteries. That is to say they are *stories*. They are about something. There are problems, and then progressions to logical solutions — or at least conclusions. The beginning, middle and end are here, and, I would like to think, flesh-and-blood characters that are timeless even if their hairdos are bouffant and their lapels are an unstylish width. (There are no leisure suits; I have shame.) But most of all I believe the stories still work because they sprang from my intense desire to express them. Writers who love the short story form are from time to time struck by ideas that must be expressed no other way. There are intriguing concepts which are too spare for novels, or perhaps for commercial reasons they are unpublishable as books or articles. But *Wow!* — we've just gotta share them with somebody, put them into story form. Thousands of years ago folks like us jabbered at fellow brutes squatting around campfires. More years ago we tried to scare the bejibbers out of everyone in the dark shelter of the communal cave. You can't stop us anymore than we can stop ourselves. You can't shut us up. Storytelling is genetic.

Which brings me to another reason my trip into the past was a pleasant one. I enjoyed the devil out of writing each and every story in this collection. Maybe that's why I enjoyed revisiting them, and maybe that's why you'll enjoy reading them. That sort of thing rubs off.

In every language there is a proverb to the effect that we are all born with something, however humble, to offer the world. Be that truth or optimism, I offer the following pages.

Until You Are Dead

The glass jars of enamel added to the colorful formless composition that was being created as one-by-one they exploded against the brick wall. Wilson Benton was smiling as he picked up each jar and hurled it with the conscienceless exuberance of a mischievous seven-year old.

Mrs. Hefferman, whose hobby was the making of ceramic pots, mugs, praying-hand plaques, and the like, kept her brightly colored enamels on a dusty shelf in the garage. Usually the garage door was closed and locked. But not today, when Wilson happened by, spotted the neat row of jars, looked at the wide expanse of brick wall on the other side of the alley, and surrendered to the temptation.

"What do ya think you're doin'?"

The voice belonged to Randy Hefferman, Mrs. Hefferman's twelve-year-old nephew who lived with her. With Randy were Bob Rourke, a gangly boy of ten who was the best ballplayer in the neighborhood, and Frankie Toller, an overweight and overbearing eleven-year-old who nurtured a developing skill at instigating trouble among others while remaining outside the fray.

There wasn't much that Wilson could say to Randy's indignant question. Wilson had, almost literally, been caught red-handed. He stood silently, a frail dark-haired boy with wide and fearful brown eyes that took in the older and heftier Randy with morbid apprehension. The glass jar containing Chinese red dropped from his suddenly sweating hand to shatter at his feet and join the shards of broken

9

glass in the cobblestoned alley.

"He broke the lock on the garage an' got that stuff an' smashed it," Frankie Toller said accusingly.

Wilson swallowed. "I didn't!" he choked.

Randy moved a menacing step closer to him. Wilson could smell his breath; he'd been eating the hot chili his aunt often made. "Didn't what?" Randy asked.

"Break into the garage!"

"Then how'd you get all my aunt's paint jars an' break 'em up?"

"The door was open! It was!"

"She always locks it," Frankie Toller remarked.

Bob Rourke stood silently staring at Wilson. He was only vaguely interested in what was going on, but he would go along with whatever Randy and Frankie decided to do to the trapped and unquestionably guilty Wilson.

Randy moved still nearer and Wilson's throat went dry. A coppery corruption of fear lined the sides of his tongue.

"Ain't no reason to break all that stuff just 'cause the door was open," Randy said. His hand pistoned out, pushing Wilson backward, broken glass crunching loudly beneath the soles of his tennis shoes.

"What we gonna do to him?" Frankie asked eagerly. "Can't let him get away with it."

"Tell your aunt," Bob Rourke suggested to Randy.

"Naw, she won't do nothin'," Frankie said. "Besides, we ain't snitches."

Randy's cool gray eyes flared with sudden inspiration. He placed his fists on his hips. "Take off your shoes," he said to Wilson.

Frankie grinned.

"He cuts up his feet through them socks and we'll get in trouble," Bob Rourke observed.

10

"He's the one in trouble," Randy said fiercely. "This'll teach him not to break into people's garages and bust up their stuff!"

"He'll cut himself," Bob Rourke repeated. "Anyway, he ain't gonna take off his shoes."

"If he don't, we'll make him!"

Wilson's hands were trembling. Frankie and Bob Rourke stepped closer to stand beside Randy. Wilson looked into Bob Rourke's narrowed eyes and knew he could expect no help from that direction.

"Now!" Randy demanded.

Wilson bent and removed his shoes.

"Now walk!" Randy demanded.

Wilson stared down at the glittering multicolored fragments of glass.

"You heard Randy!" Frankie said.

Wilson took a step. Another. He felt the uneven pressure of the glass on the soles of his feet, threatening to break through the dirty cotton of his socks and embed itself in his flesh. Gingerly, fearfully, he took light, carefully aimed steps, almost wishing that the jagged glass would penetrate the bottoms of his feet and create a pain that might alleviate the overpowering sense of shame that was enveloping him.

But finally he reached a clear spot beyond the broken glass. His feet were undamaged; the cotton socks had been enough protection. He stood staring at the three boys on the other side of the expanse of glimmering danger.

"See," Frankie told Bob Rourke, "he didn't even get cut." He sounded disappointed.

Randy was looking at Wilson with something like startled recognition. "He's a coward," he said gravely. "The guy's a coward." It was as if he'd heard about cowards but had never really expected to see one. And now here was

11

one, standing directly in front of him. Not only that — it was someone he knew.

"He's a coward all right," Frankie agreed.

For a moment Wilson felt totally alienated from his world as if it had unexpectedly come to his and everyone's attention that he had webbed feet. With one abrupt stroke he was separated from the rest of humanity.

"I —"

But the rest of humanity was no longer interested in anything he had to say. Its three representatives turned and walked away toward the mouth of the alley. Frankie glanced over his shoulder for just an instant, but no one else looked back. As they rounded the corner and disappeared, Bob Rourke gracefully leaped to slap the bottom of a rusty Coca-Cola sign protruding from the brick building. The metal sign twanged and continued to vibrate loudly.

Wilson stood for a long time, still holding his shoes in his right hand, staring at the bright world beyond the mouth of the alley. Then he shivered. That world would never be the same. He had been, if not a close friend, an occasional companion of the three boys who had just left him. But he was no longer one of them. He could never be one of them again.

Pearl Harbor had been bombed six months ago. When war had been declared, Wilson Benton, now twenty-six years old, had, in a patriotic fervor, attempted to enlist in the Army. A perforated eardrum and weak eyesight had caused him to be turned down and classified 4-F. Not knowing what else to do, he'd returned to his art studies.

Wilson was considerably talented as a painter in oils. His ambition was to be an illustrator; once, the art director of *The Saturday Evening Post* had given him encouragement in

12

a long friendly letter. Nature was Wilson's favorite milieu for his art, so with what savings he'd accumulated he leased a tiny clapboard cabin in a gently rolling lush green area of the Ozark Mountains. He intended to spend the summer and part of the fall at the cabin painting. Then, with what he'd created, he would again approach the world of magazine illustration and try to establish a beachhead.

The cabin was a one-room affair with a sharply peaked roof. Though it wasn't equipped with electricity, it did have a septic tank and indoor plumbing. Wilson slept in a comfortable feather bed, cooked his meals on an old iron wood stove, and sat up nights listening to the Silvertone radio he'd hooked up to two six-volt car batteries.

Once a week he would drive into Colver, the nearest town, in his dented gray '36 Chevy coupe and buy groceries to haul back in the trunk. Sometimes he would pull to the side of the narrow dirt road that led to the alternate highway and survey a particularly beautiful view, returning the next day to sketch or paint there. Primitive, yet with a deceptive, almost feminine loveliness that disguised nature's ongoing life-and-death struggle, the rolling green Ozark country was ideal for Wilson's purpose. He was content with what he was accomplishing.

The cabin had a large window that provided northern light, but often during the day Wilson would set up his easel on the side of the wooden front porch and work outside. It was on one of those days that he heard the racketing bang and clatter of a car approaching the cabin along the seldom traveled dirt road. As he stepped down from the porch, he saw a haze of dust among the high branches of maples near the road's sharp bend; the car was very near.

It was a Model A Ford, rusty, the top cut off, the engine exposed. One of the rear fenders was hanging half off and clanking against the car's body as the tall rubber tires bounced over the deep ruts.

When the driver saw Wilson he hit the brakes and the old Ford pulled to a squealing, rattling halt before the cabin. There were three men and a woman in the car, two of the men in the front seat. The man in the back was slouched sideways, his legs stretched across the woman's lap, his bare feet propped up on the glassless window frame. The cloud of dust raised by the car caught up with it and slowly settled in the brilliant sunlight.

"What you doin' at the Harris cabin?" the driver asked Wilson. He had blond hair and a scraggly beard that was more the result of neglecting to shave than a conscious attempt to grow chin whiskers. The other two men were dark-headed. The woman — or girl — was a brunette with a dirty face, freckles, large blue eyes, and lissome arms, one of which was flung carelessly across the back of the rear seat. None of them appeared to be more than twenty years old, and Wilson guessed the girl to be in her teens.

"I rented the cabin for the summer," Wilson said, moving closer to the car so he wouldn't have to shout. "My name's Wilson Benton."

The girl appeared puzzled. "What for would you rent a place like this?" she asked in a grating soprano voice.

"I paint. I like it here."

"Paint what?" the driver asked. He rubbed a hand across a long nose that had been broken many times. His pale gray eyes were set too close together and regarded Wilson with indifferent curiosity.

"Pictures. Some of them for magazine illustrations."

"Oh, that kinda paintin'," the girl said.

"Ain't that somethin'?" the man with her in the back seat spoke up. His lank hair was hanging in his eyes. He had a

14

wide lantern jaw and was missing several front teeth. Wilson couldn't tell by the tone of his voice how he'd meant his remark.

The man on the front passenger's side, who would have been darkly handsome if he were clean and well dressed, grinned. "Don't mind 'em, Wilson," he said. "I'm Josh Edwards." He pointed to the driver. "Zach Wheelright. Them in the back is Bandy McCane and Maybelle Sue Dover."

"Lotsa pretty things around here to paint, all right," Maybelle said.

Bandy McCane gave a jut-jawed broken-toothed sneer and peered at Wilson from beneath his unshorn hair.

"Ol' Bandy'd be jealous if you was to pose for Wilson, Maybelle," the driver, Zach, remarked.

"Don' matter," Maybelle said to Wilson with a perfect smile, and took in the other occupants of the car with a circular wave of her arm. "These'ns are all gonna be gone into the Army afore the end of summer."

"How come you ain't in?" Bandy asked. "You look to be of age."

"I tried," Wilson said. Unaccountably, he felt himself blushing. The change of his color wasn't lost on Bandy McCane.

"How hard you try?" he asked derisively.

"Hard enough," Wilson said. "They told me I was Four-F."

"Lotsa reasons you can be Four-F," Zach observed skeptically.

"Glad I ain't a reject," Josh said in a solemn voice. "Comes a time to fight, an' this is it."

Wilson nodded. "I agree."

"I'd like to see your pictures sometime," Maybelle said, blatantly changing the subject.

15

"No time now," Zach shouted, jamming the old Ford into gear and gunning protesting life into the clattering engine.

"No call for painters in this man's war!" Bandy shouted over his shoulder at Wilson as the Ford's big wheels dug into the earth without slipping and the car shot forward. Maybelle lifted an arm in a languid farewell that Wilson barely saw through the dust as the car disappeared beyond the rise where the road gently curved.

Wilson walked back up onto the porch, listening to the measured hollow thunder of his boots on the warped planks as he strode to his canvas. The conversation with the four native Ozarkians had disturbed him more than it should have.

Two days later he returned after painting a landscape from high on a nearby bluff to find that the cabin had been broken into and many of his paintings had been slashed.

He stood staring at the disruption of the cabin's interior, unable to see clearly for a moment as an aching helpless rage flared deep in his stomach, then gradually receded to a painful smoldering. So personal seemed the attack, it was as if the torn canvas were an extension of his own flesh.

After cleaning up and salvaging what he could of his materials, Wilson drove into Colver to see the local sheriff.

"Who knowed you was at the cabin?" Sheriff Bayne Haynes asked. He was a large man with a vast stomach paunch, beady intelligent black eyes in a fleshy mottled face, and a walnut-gripped .45 Colt revolver holstered to his hip. He was gazing at Wilson amiably from where he sat turned in his swivel chair facing away from the long rolltop desk against the office's far wall. His lean deputy, Rawly Krebs, slouched nearby against a dusty switchboard.

Wilson hesitated, then told the sheriff about his conversation with Josh, Zach, Bandy, and Maybelle.

"I don't know definitely that it was them," he added.

"They's good boys, but they do tend to act up," Sheriff Haynes said absently.

"Thass a fact," Krebs added.

"Anything exceptin' your paintin's broke up?" the sheriff asked.

Wilson thought about that. "No," he said finally. "A few things were knocked to the floor, furniture turned over, but nothing really broken."

Haynes rose from his chair with the ease and seeming lightness of an ascending hot-air balloon. There were wide, almost black perspiration stains beneath the arms of his tan uniform shirt. "Down the road a short piece from your cabin," he said, "is a cutoff to Ezekiel Ferber's place. Now, Ferber's got himself a phone. You have any more trouble you run on down there, use that phone to call here, an' me and Rawly'll be up to your place faster'n you can shout rabbit."

Krebs looked at Wilson and nodded his narrow pockmarked head. "Thass a fact."

"All right, fine," Wilson said. There didn't seem much else that could be done.

"If'n it was who we figure, they had their fun an' ain't likely to come back. Thass the way they is, those three boys. Not mean — jus' too full a vinegar."

"As I said," Wilson emphasized, "I don't really know who it was. But I thought you should know that it happened."

Sheriff Haynes' bushy graying eyebrows rose and fell like writhing caterpillars. "Oh, you did the right thing, an' no doubt about it." Deputy Krebs nodded silent agreement.

17

Haynes licked his lips and squinted at Wilson. "You — uh — do anything to rile them boys? On accident, maybe?"

"I don't think so," Wilson said. And that was true. He hadn't done a thing. It wasn't his fault they were going into the Army and he was 4-F, or that Maybelle had seemed to take a shine to him. "I take it Maybelle is Bandy McCane's girlfriend," he said cautiously.

The sheriff raised his expansive chin and smiled faintly. "You might say she's the girlfriend of all of 'em, from time to time. Thass how it is sometimes here away from the city, Mr. Benton."

Wilson swallowed and nodded, imagining despite himself Maybelle's pale languid arms and luminous blue eyes. Sheriff Haynes was staring hard at him.

Wilson thanked the sheriff and walked toward the screen door to the street.

"Things'll sure be quieter when them boys is gone to the Army," the sheriff remarked behind him.

"Thass a fact," Deputy Krebs said.

From the sheriff's office, Wilson walked directly across the street to Holfer's Service Center and General Store, a small frame structure with two gas pumps in front and a flat-roofed addition that stocked groceries and hardware. He noticed that the sheriff's '38 Dodge was at Holfer's, being worked on by a lanky grease-stained young boy. The car was dusty-black with large gold replicas of a sheriff's badge emblazoned on its doors. When Wilson entered the store he saw Zach Wheelright slouching at the counter paying for a package of chewing tobacco.

Zach turned, spotted Wilson, and grinned guiltily as he scratched at his sparse blond beard. He unwrapped the tobacco and slowly bit off a large plug. Then, chewing laboriously behind his wide grin, he walked past Wilson and out

18

the door. Wilson saw that he had a slender broken paint-brush tucked behind his left ear.

For a moment Wilson wanted to return to the sheriff's office and inform Haynes of what he'd just seen. Then he decided against it. There was no point in further stirring up things if, as Haynes had predicted, the matter was over.

Wilson bought five dollars' worth of groceries to last him the week, loaded them in the trunk of the Chevy, and returned to the cabin.

That Friday, when he was working indoors near the cabin's north window, Wilson heard a scuffling sound on the front porch and felt his heart double-pump, then grow heavy with fear. He put down his brush and palette and walked softly to the door.

When he opened the door he found Maybelle standing on the porch alone.

"Tol' you I wanted to see your pictures," she said, smiling. She was wearing a low-cut gray blouse and a long skirt of material so thin that the outline of her compact body showed through. She was barefoot, and Wilson found himself involuntarily staring at the dusty neat squareness of her pale toes. "Ain't you gonna ask me in?" she said.

He raised his gaze to her eyes. *The girlfriend of all of 'em from time to time.* "Sure," he said brokenly. He gave her smile back to her, amplified. "Come on in."

She seemed to be genuinely enthralled by his work, giving awed girlish exclamations as she examined the pastel landscapes, crying that she recognized most of the views before her on the canvas. Wilson brought up the subject of the vandalism that had occurred two days before and Maybelle seemed horrified. But she didn't deny the probable identity of the culprits. "Zach, Josh, and Bandy, I 'spect," she said, shaking her head in disdain.

She offered then to show Wilson a spot he might want to paint, and they left the cabin. Maybelle led him up the hill on the other side of the road, then down along a path to a clearing dotted with wildflowers in the tall wind-stirred grass. It was an exceptionally pastoral spot, though too flat and indistinctive to paint. Wilson didn't tell Maybelle this. She teased him, moving up against him as if by accident as they walked, letting the backs of her fingers barely brush his hand.

"The view from between those big pines is sure pretty," she said, pointing with Michelangelesque grace toward a patch of cloud-marbled blue framed by green branches.

Wilson trudged up the slight rise to the high point between the pines, studied the unspectacular view, then turned to ask Maybelle where, specifically, she meant for him to look.

Maybelle was gone.

A hollowness in Wilson's stomach seemed to fill with something dark and bitter. He began to walk, then run back toward the cabin.

When Wilson flung open the door and saw the wreckage a sob expanded to form a lump in his throat, then erupted from him in a frustrated snarl. This time the damage was worse — almost every canvas slashed, furniture ripped open, food pulled from cupboards and smashed or scattered. But worst of all, Wilson knew that Maybelle had made a fool of him; she had used herself as a diversion while the three men returned to the empty cabin. On the wall near the sink was scrawled *4-F* in Wilson's yellow oils. The blood rushed to his face as he whirled, slammed the door, and stomped noisily from the buckled wood porch.

He got into the Chevy and started the engine. He would

drive down the road to Ezekiel Ferber's place, as the sheriff had suggested, and phone for the law.

Wilson had pulled out onto the narrow road and traveled fifty feet before he knew something was wrong. The car was bouncing violently, swerving and pulling to the right. He braked, turned off the engine, and got out.

The right rear tire was flat. Wilson kicked the misshapen rubber and pounded on the gray rounded slope of the car's fender. He would have to walk to Ferber's.

Then, bending down, he saw the wide slit in the tire's sidewall. It had been slashed.

But why only that tire? Could it be that his antagonists wanted him to think it was only an ordinary flat so he would walk to Ferber's? So they could return and do even more damage? Wreck anything they'd missed? Scrawl more messages? Perhaps even burn down the cabin?

Wilson opened the trunk of the car and got out the spare tire, the jack, and the X-shaped iron lug wrench. He could quickly change the tire, drive to Ferber's, and maybe phone the sheriff in time for him to get back up and catch the vandals in the act.

He jacked up the back of the car, loosened the lug nuts with the wrench, and fumbled with them, removing them the rest of the way by hand. Sweat was trickling down his face and tiny insects circled him, buzzing about his eyes and flitting at his mouth and nostrils. He wrestled the airless tire off the car and turned toward the spare.

Then he heard the unmistakable roar and clatter of Zach Wheelright's decrepit car approaching. He remained crouched behind the Chevy and peered over the fender to see traces of raised dust beyond the road's bend. The engine noise was loud; the car was almost upon him. They must have thought he had taken the path through the woods

21

to Ferber's on foot and the cabin was again deserted.

Then came the crash.

The surface of smooth metal before Wilson smashed into him as the Chevy was struck and bounced backward off the jack. There were startled cries, tinkling glass, and the hiss and trickling surrender of a broken radiator.

Wilson was on his hands and knees, fighting to catch his breath from the blow he'd received in the chest. Hazily he could see Zach, Bandy, Josh, and Maybelle tumble from the wrecked Ford. Zach sat down and held his head in both hands. Maybelle stood leaning dizzily against the side of the Chevy. Josh and Bandy were swaying, supporting each other. They had expected him to be gone, all right, Wilson realized. But they hadn't expected the crippled car to be jacked up in the middle of the road just beyond the bend.

"You wrecked my car!" Zach was saying, staring at Wilson from between splayed fingers vividly marked with blood. He cursed and struggled to his feet.

Josh and Bandy moved nearer to flank him, lending the threat of their presence to his words.

"*You* wrecked it!" Wilson managed to gasp.

"You come over here!" Zach screamed.

Wilson didn't move.

"Ain't you got ears?" Bandy asked. The initial shock of the accident had passed and although he was holding his injured left arm tight against his body, he was grinning. Josh still seemed woozy from his head striking the windshield. He was standing, swaying, with his fists on his hips.

Wilson sighed and began to rise.

"Not like that, you yellow coward scum!" Zach shouted. "Stay on your hands an' knees where you belong!"

Maybelle began to laugh.

Wilson stayed very still.

22

"We'll kill you if you don't," Josh said to Wilson. "Maybe we'll kill you if you do."

Wilson was paralyzed, breathing painfully as if each lungful of air were somehow thickened almost to a liquid consistency. Fear was a thing alive within him, pulling marionette strings despite his humiliation.

He began to crawl.

Maybelle laughed again. They were all laughing now except Zach, who was staring with a thin knowledgeable smile at Wilson.

Then Wilson's left hand was stung by one of the glass fragments from the shattered windshield and headlights. He paused.

"Keep comin'!" Zach warned.

Wilson's right hand came into contact with the lug wrench.

"You heard!" Bandy said, not laughing now. For emphasis he slapped his right hand hard against the loose fender of the Ford, causing the metal to twang and vibrate loudly.

Wilson didn't remember rising, but he had, still clutching the lug wrench. He surprised himself even more than the three men as he was suddenly before them, swinging the tire iron, hearing and feeling it smash the flesh and bone of Zach's skull. Arcs of bright blood glistened in the air. The injured Bandy tried to grab Wilson's arm. Wilson was too strong for that now — stronger than anyone had ever been. He brushed the clutching fingers aside, brought the wrench down behind Bandy's ear. Someone was clawing at Wilson's neck with sharp fingernails. Maybelle. He whirled, lashed out with the wrench that seemed weightless in his hand, then pursued Josh, who was trying to stagger around the rear of the Ford, and laid open his skull with one effortless swing. Then he returned to Bandy, who was sitting cross-

23

legged on the ground before Maybelle's bloody body. Bandy started to beg with his eyes and distorted mouth. The shadow of the raised lug wrench fell upon him like a cross. The shadow grew. The wrench descended.

It was Ezekiel Ferber who came across the scene and fled home to phone the law. Sheriff Haynes and Deputy Krebs arrived within half an hour in the sheriff's dusty black car with the gold insignia on the doors. The doors slammed in unison as Haynes and Krebs left the car to swagger toward where Wilson was sitting slumped on the Chevy's running board, the heavy lug wrench on the ground between his feet. The sheriff and his deputy paused.

Somewhere in a far dark part of Wilson's mind he could feel himself spinning, falling in intermittent, sweeping plunges toward an inevitable timelessness.

"Gawd, Gawd, Gawd," the sheriff was saying, "he killed 'em all." His face was white. "There weren't no reason whatsoever for this."

"Thass a fact," the deputy said in a soft, awed voice.

"Those are the facts," the prosecutor said.

"They're the plain facts," the jury foreman said.

"— Until you are dead," said the judge.

24

The Chess Players

The sky beyond the old man and the boy playing chess was dark and occasionally fractured by lightning. Against that backdrop, neither of them noticed the dust of the car approaching on the dirt road from the county highway.

Both the old man — who was younger than he at first appeared, with his white hair and beard — and the boy looked up when they heard the crunch of the tires and the soft thunking of rocks bouncing off the insides of the car's fenders. They remained seated beneath the branches of an elm, in the wooden kitchen chairs they'd dragged from the tiny farmhouse to place on either side of the small cedar table. On the table was a cheap chessboard and plastic pieces that were so light that from time to time the wind building up from the southwest tipped over the taller king, queen, or bishop. If the wind got much stronger, the pieces might blow from the board, but the old man and boy knew they wouldn't go far once they worked down in the coarse grass.

The boy, who was eight years old and named Andrew, looked at the old man, who was his grandfather. He was a thin, dark-haired boy with a narrow, symmetrical face and bright but sad blue eyes. The old man swiveled slightly in his chair to watch the car, and the boy's calm, intelligent gaze followed.

The grandfather, who was sixty-seven and whose name was Willis Sharp, watched the car brake to a halt next to the cottonwood tree near the barn. Beyond it, all around the farmhouse and barn, the cornfields spread for acres and acres so that only the water tower at Centerville, fifteen miles away, was visible from the house. Wavering in the heat, it looked like a drab gray lightbulb supported by a spindly framework. Andrew, who had quite an imagination, had once told Willis he'd dreamed the water tower was an alien spaceship that had landed so its occupants could learn chess.

The car was a dusty black Chrysler New Yorker with a rental decal on its front bumper. Both its front doors opened simultaneously, and the two men inside climbed out. One was short and broad, the other tall and broad. The shorter one had on faded Levi's and an armless red T-shirt. When the two men got closer, Willis saw that the T-shirt had one of those yellow smiley faces on it, only this one had a bullethole seeping blood in its forehead. The blood was the same red as the rest of the shirt.

"Whaddya know?" the short one said by way of greeting, when the two men were about ten feet from the old man and boy.

"Not much," Willis said.

"I don't doubt it," the tall one said in a voice that cut. He had pale eyes like diamond chips, thin, cruel features, and was beginning to go bald on top. The breeze whipped the long, sandy hair above his right ear out away from his head as he lifted a hand and smoothed it back with a look of irritation. "Kinda isolated out here in Dullsville, aren't you, old-timer?"

Willis thought he recognized his accent. "We like isolation."

"You didn't ask us what *we* know," the short one said with the same accent as his companion. He had greasy black hair slicked straight back, a coiled snake tattooed on one bulging bicep, and two glittering rings on each hand.

26

"You two don't need to be asked, being from New York."

The two glanced at each other, thrown off a bit by that.

The tall one grinned meanly, not sweating at all in the heat even in his dark suit, and said, "Wise guys, putting down the big city. Smart guys. Chess players." He aimed his predatory smile at Andrew, who was staring up at him without fear but with a trace of uneasiness. "You're Andrew," the tall man said, "and you, old man, you're his grandfather, Willis."

"Who are you?" Andrew asked.

Without hesitation the tall man said, "I'm Freddy Clark. My friend here's called Zinc."

Willis didn't like it that they'd given their names so readily.

"They used to call me Snake," Zinc said, "then some yardbird that couldn't talk right made it sound like Zinc and I was stuck with it. Prison's like that."

In the corner of his vision Willis saw Andrew stiffen.

"What we know that you didn't ask us about," Freddy said, "is that Andrew here is staying a month at the farm till school starts, like he's done the last two summers. You grow a little corn here, but you lease out most of this land to a big co-op. And except for Andrew's visits, you live all alone in that dump of a house since your wife died six years ago." Freddy and Zinc traded grins, proud of the fruits of their research. "Oh, and you weren't home five years ago on July fifteenth."

"That last I wouldn't know about," Willis said, wondering who these two were, but knowing they were the worst kind of trouble. When the trouble came, maybe there'd be some way to get Andrew clear of it.

"The important thing is, *we* know," Zinc said. He popped a stick of gum in his mouth, tossing the wrapper to

27

the breeze, and began chewing rapidly and grinning, now and then displaying the wad of gum on his tongue. He glanced around at the weathered old frame house, the leaning barn with only traces of red paint on it, the old green John Deere tractor sitting near the perfectly aligned rows of head-high cornstalks. "You about to plow or harvest with that thing?" Zinc asked, pointing at the tractor.

Freddy laughed at his friend's ignorance and winked. "You gotta forgive us, old man. We're city boys and don't know country ways."

"Yup, I could tell that right off."

Freddy cocked his head to the side and seemed to consider whether he'd been insulted. Apparently he decided not to take offense. "We came here to get something," he said.

"What I wish you'd get," Willis said, "is to the point." Not really so sure he wanted to hear the point, only that he wanted to know where he stood so he could formulate some kind of plan, even if it was a desperate one.

"Teaching the boy how to play chess?" Zinc asked.

"He doesn't need much teaching," Willis said. "He's always been the sort that thinks ahead."

"Runs in the family, I'll bet," Freddy said with a sneer.

"Sorta."

"Nothin' runs in my family but noses," Zinc said.

"Wanna play a game?" Andrew asked hopefully, as if perhaps a friendly game of chess would somehow set things straight with these intruders.

"No," Freddy said, "but chess is a good game. It teaches you to think, like your grandpa said. Making plans, that's what life's all about. Thinking ahead is what separates winners from losers."

"Right now," Willis said, "let's think back to when I wasn't home five years ago on July fifteenth."

28

"Okay," Freddy said. "That's when the money from the Hopkinstown Bank robbery was buried in your cornfield."

"You guys the bank robbers?" Andrew blurted out in awe.

"Not us," Zinc said. "That ain't our game."

"But we did get acquainted with certain people in a certain institution whose game it was," Freddy said. "And under a kind of pressure, they told us where they hid the Hopkinstown Bank money when they were on the run after the robbery. They're still in the institution, and will be for the next fifteen years, but here we are."

"We came for the money," Zinc said. "We been thinking and dreaming about it for a long time. We ain't gonna leave without it."

"Just in case somebody should happen to come by this godforsaken dump," Freddy said, "we're your nephews from the city, come for a visit. Got that, Uncle?"

"Sure."

"What about you, kid?"

"I've got it, sir — cousin."

Zinc stared at him curiously, flexing a bicep and scratching it simultaneously. "He got that right?" he asked Freddy.

"Once removed or something," Freddy said. "Directions to the money say it's buried fifty feet due north of a big tree, some hundred paces from the northeast corner of the house." He glared at Willis. "The thing is, I don't see any tree there. Nothing but corn."

"Lightning struck the tree four years ago and killed it, and I cut down what was left."

"A tree big as we were told, there must be a stump or something in there among that corn," Freddy said.

"No, I pulled the stump out with the tractor. That ground's been turned four times since then. I'd never be able to find exactly where that tree was now, even if I went looking for it."

"If we were in the big city," Zinc said, "I'd start doing things to the boy, and you'd find where that tree was in a hurry."

"In a New York minute," Freddy said. "But we're here in the heart of America where hard work's what people worship, so what's gonna happen is this, old man: You, Bobby Fischer there, and me and Zinc are gonna to some digging in the cornfield. We're gonna dig until we find the money."

"Hey! Looka the size of that fly!" Zinc yelled, and swatted at a huge black fly that had set down on his forearm. He watched the fly drone away, then stared at Willis in astonishment. "There one of them nuclear plants around here?"

"It's only a horsefly," Andrew said.

Zinc looked around. "I don't see no horses."

"They hang around cows and such," Freddy said. "I learned about them on a *National Geographic* special on TV."

"No cows around here, either," Zinc said.

"The wind carried it here from the next farm," Willis said, "where there's livestock."

"Long way," Freddy said.

"It mighta flapped its wings some," Zinc offered. "Or soared like an eagle."

"Well, us being city boys," Freddy said, "we've got no calluses, so you two'll do most of the digging. There shovels in that barn?"

"Sure," Willis said. "A pick, too." He didn't see how it would hurt to feign cooperation. Maybe the city cousins would let down their guard and make a mistake.

Freddy drew an automatic pistol from beneath his suitcoat. He left the coat unbuttoned and it flapped in the breeze, flashing a blue silk lining.

"Let's go dig," Willis said to Andrew, who was staring wide-eyed at the gun.

"What's gonna happen after we find the money?" Andrew asked.

Freddy motioned at the chessboard with the gun barrel. "Me and Zinc'll finish the game."

"Kid's a thinker, ain't he?" Zinc said, amused.

"Thinks *too* hard, though," Freddy said. "He's liable to have chronic headaches when he grows up." He winked at Zinc.

Andrew sidled over to Willis and gripped his hand. Willis felt something in his throat swell as they trudged toward the barn, with Freddy walking slightly ahead and to the side, half turned to face them so he could keep the gun leveled at Andrew. Zinc was walking behind them. Willis figured he had a gun, too. The only weapon Willis had was a twelve-gauge Ithaca shotgun locked away inside the house.

Willis squinted into the wind as he noticed several barn swallows wheeling above the open loft door. They tried to enter the barn but the wind had picked up to the point where they couldn't control themselves on the currents of air and they were whisked from sight.

"I got something in my eye!" Zinc shouted. "I hate this damned part of the country!"

The dark clouds had moved in over the farm now and seemed very low. Suddenly torrents of rain began to fall.

"What next?" Zinc yelled.

"Shut up!" Freddy shouted, using his free hand to turn up his collar.

"I'm getting friggin' soaked, Freddy!"

"Good! The rain'll make the ground softer so we can dig easier."

Then, just as suddenly, the rain stopped.

Hail began falling, not evenly like the rain, but erratically, so that it lay in heaps on the ground in golf-ball-size nuggets of ice.

Freddy had lowered his head, shielding his balding pate with his hand, all the while staring coldly at Willis over the barrel of the gun.

The hail stopped, and so did the wind.

"I never seen anything like that," Zinc said uneasily.

A pale, greenish light lay over everything, as if the dimmed sunlight was reflecting the green of the cornfields. The motionless air seemed thick enough to feel, like silk against flesh. There was no movement, no sound.

"Grampa!" Andrew cried, and pointed.

Willis saw a black funnel of swirling wind dip from the low clouds and sweep across the far edge of the cornfield. Dirt and cornstalks flew wildly as it touched down, skipped in a cloud of dust to the other side of the road, then back again. It was moving in their direction.

"What the hell's that?" Zinc screamed.

"Cyclone!" Freddy shouted.

"Tornado!" Willis corrected.

Zinc had shuffled around to face them, a silver revolver dangling at his side in his right hand. His thick features were knotted in confusion. "Whadda we do?"

"Let's get in the barn!" Freddy yelled. Fear raised his voice an octave and glittered in his eyes.

"That'd be suicide," Willis said.

The wind was with them again, pressing hard against them so they had to lean into it. As they watched, the tractor began to roll, then gained speed as if someone were driving it, and disappeared into the high corn. The big Chrysler the two men arrived in was broadside to the wind and began to rock violently on its soft suspension.

"There's a storm shelter there by the house," Willis said, holding Andrew tight to him, "but it's only big enough for two!"

Andrew looked up at him, realizing what was going to happen. He began to scream.

Zinc bolted and ran for the raised, square wooden door set in concrete six inches above the ground. He flipped open the door and leaped inside, the door slamming behind him in the wind.

Andrew's screams were like the wail of an emergency siren.

"Stay where you are!" Freddy yelled, waving the gun at them.

"You can't leave us out here!" Willis pleaded.

"Just like a good ol' boy to give shelter to his city cousins!" Freddy said, grinning like death in his terror as he held the gun on them and backed to the wooden door.

"For God's sake, man! We'll be blown into the next state!"

"He better not have locked this thing!" Freddy said with sudden panic, as he tugged the door up and open and flung himself inside out of the wind.

Immediately Willis scooped up Andrew, who'd become silent, and sprinted for the house.

Inside, he opened a window to equalize pressure in case the tornado hit, then ran to the door to the fruit cellar, opened it, and scrambled down into the small, musty space, shoving Andrew ahead of him.

The tornado ripped and roared above them, threatening to reach down with a finger of whirling destruction and pry them from their meager shelter.

They stayed there, huddled together, until the angry

howl of the tornado had given way to silence.

When they emerged from the cellar and ventured back outside, Willis saw that the tornado had cut a wide swath across the south end of the cornfield, following almost exactly the same course as the one that had struck a few years ago. Usually when tornados blew through, they stayed on the other side of the highway; something about rising air from the river a mile to the west. Quite a few shingles had been blown off the house roof, and one of the barn doors was open and hanging crookedly on its remaining hinge. If the tractor was okay, that was the extent of the damage.

"What are we gonna do now, Grampa?" Andrew asked. He no longer seemed frightened.

"Phone lines'll be down because of the tornado," Willis said, "so we can't call. Guess the thing to do is get the truck outa the barn and drive into town and fetch the sheriff, if he's not too busy. Then we'll drive back here, get what's left of them two fellas outa the well, and try to find enough of the chess set so we can finish our game."

Andrew said, "I think I remember where all the pieces were."

Explosive Cargo

It don't matter a whit to me. Nothing does. I wasn't supposed to be hauling that load. The schedule had me bobtailing my Kenworth tractor back to Saint Louis instead of pulling 60,000 pounds in a new trailer on a special run to Philadelphia. It's all the same to me. The trucking company knows it and that's why they gave me the unscheduled run. Because I don't live by any schedule or set of rules. They say Ruddy Kane don't give a damn if the sun drifts away like a red balloon, that he don't care for anything or anybody, including himself. They're pure right.

A big flatbed hauling steel pipe in the opposite direction on the divided highway had told me over the CB that it was clear of bears over his shoulder all the way to Allenville, so I was cutting a fat path, holding the big Kenworth well over the legal limit and damn near pushing the pesky four-wheelers into the slow lane where they belonged so I could pass. You get no argument out of anyone you outweigh by over thirty tons.

Just past the Route Nineteen cloverleaf I saw the hitch-hiker, standing well up on a grade that I had to gear down to climb. He was a square-shouldered guy with a blondish beard, wearing a long-sleeved old army fatigue jacket despite the eighty-plus heat. One of his feet was propped up on a beat-looking black suitcase painted red at the corners. As I passed, he braced himself against the coming backwash of the big truck and made a sweeping motion with his thumb, already looking past me for the next vehicle. The company's got a rule against picking up hitchhikers. I pulled two quick blasts out of the air horn and let the grade help me slow so I could steer onto the shoulder and wait.

He had almost a half a mile to run with the old suitcase, and I sat watching him in the right-hand mirror. A string of four-wheelers swished by me on the left and headed like bright-colored darts toward the crest of the rise. The big diesel under the hood rumbled like it wanted to give chase.

The hitchhiker was breathing hard when he reached the truck. Even over the rumble of the diesel I could hear him panting as he opened the passenger-side door and hoisted his suitcase up onto the floor. The cab's seat was higher than he'd thought, and I reached over and grabbed him by the wrist to help him in. He seemed to resent that as he pulled the door shut with a slam and settled back in the upholstery. I dropped the Kenworth into low range and steered back onto the highway, working through the gears as I took the rest of the grade.

"Ruddy Kane," I said by way of introduction. "Where you headed?"

"Far as you're goin' in this direction."

He hadn't given me his name. That should have clued me. Up close he was a scruffy-looking little guy with a twice-broke nose and a U-shaped scar on his forehead. Too bad he couldn't grow that beard over the rest of his face.

"I'll be turnin' north at Seventy-seven," I told him.

"My name's Brogan," he said, as if he'd thought it over. I nodded like Brogan was everybody's name. "I'm headin' east to get a job."

"What do you do?"

"Most anything."

What he was best at was being vague. I caught a faint mildewed odor from his wrinkled fatigue jacket and faded denim Levis, and I recognized what that scent might mean. I'd slept outside on the ground before.

The hell with it. None of my business.

"You had supper yet?" I asked Brogan.

He looked sharply at me and shook his head no.

"Place up there around the next curve I usually stop at," I told him. "Dale's Speed Grill. They serve top hamburgers fast and so are the waitresses."

Brogan said nothing, dug his hands into the baggy pockets of his jacket.

We took the curve and I saw the big neon hamburger on the roof of Dale's, bright red and green in the fast-fading light. The restaurant was small and kind of dumpy-looking, but it was neat and clean inside, and almost everyone who traveled this highway regularly made it their meal stop if they were in the area.

I slowed the Kenworth, waited for a station wagon to pass, and edged into the right lane. There were half a dozen road rigs parked in Dale's big graveled lot, and a Highway Patrol car nosed up against the side of the low building.

Brogan's hands came out of his jacket pockets. The right one held a revolver. I couldn't say I was surprised.

"Keep right on drivin'," Brogan said.

I hit the accelerator and glanced at him as I shifted gears. "To where?"

"Wherever I tell you."

He pressed the barrel of the gun into my ribs to show me he was sincere. I saw Dale's bright neon hamburger fall away and disappear in the right outside mirror.

"The law on you?" I asked.

Brogan looked at me from beneath the curved scar on his forehead. You could've chilled beer with his eyes. "You don't need to know nothin' except how to drive this hunk of iron."

37

I made high range and considered. "And when you don't need me for that anymore, you don't need me at all."

He held the gun out where it would attract my eyes. "You scared, Mr. Driver?"

"Some." I concentrated on my driving with half my mind while the other half wondered just who this mildewed little desperado thought he was.

"Stick to the speed limit!" he ordered, purposely working the pistol barrel on my ribs to produce pain. I edged back to within the law.

"Somethin' you oughta know," I told him. "I'm haulin' explosives. Quick-dry cement and blasting powder for a big engineering project in Pennsylvania."

Brogan shrugged. "If it wasn't safe, you wouldn't be haulin' it."

"It's safe as long as I'm on smooth highway. Otherwise it could blow a fifty-foot crater in the ground. I thought you should know that in case you got plans to take this rig anywhere it's not supposed to go."

Brogan's grin was yellow in the glare of oncoming headlights, crooked in contrast to his pale level eyes. "I'll tell you when it's time for you to know my plans. This thing got plenty of fuel?"

"I topped the tanks just before I picked you up," I told him. "That should add to the explosion if anything goes wrong."

He ignored me, still grinning, and settled back in his seat with the gun still pointed at me.

We drove for almost an hour that way, without talking. When we reached the Route Twenty-two intersection I veered gently right and downshifted for a steep grade. Brogan didn't move beside me. He might have been sleeping, sitting the way he was with the back of his head against the upholstery. I got the impression maybe he wanted me to think he might be asleep so I'd try to get tricky.

Now that the sun was down the evening was cool, so I cut the air conditioner and rolled down a window. That caused Brogan to stir, nothing more.

The Highway Patrol weigh station was ahead on the right. As we approached I saw that the barrier arm was up and the station was open. There were two rigs waiting to drive onto the scale, where a trooper we called Rock Face Evans would be waiting to record their axle weights to make sure they weren't beyond the legal limits. I didn't slack speed as I went past.

We'd gone another four miles before I heard the siren.

Brogan sat up straight, swiveled his head. He couldn't see behind us from where he sat, but I could see the flashing red lights in my rearview mirror.

"State Patrol," I said. "Want me to stop?"

The gun barrel raked down my ribs. "I want you to drive," Brogan snarled, "like you never drove before!" He was some pumpkin.

I worked the gears and took us up to seventy. Wind screamed around the mirrors and diesel stacks and Brogan looked a little alarmed. I checked the mirror and saw that we were being pursued by two cars now. They were half a mile back and closing.

"No way to outrun 'em," I said. The sirens continued to wail behind us over the sound of the wind. I took us up to eighty. Brogan began to squirm in his seat.

"If you don't want to get caught," I told him, "there's only one thing to do."

I yanked on the wheel and we were off the pavement, bouncing across the wide grass median toward the other two lanes of the divided highway.

"Get us back on the road!" Brogan shouted. "The explosives!" He jabbed with the gun.

The truck hit a grassy rise, jounced to the side, wind and sirens still screaming at us. There were some small trees along the center of the median. Brogan's eyes were as wide as his gaping mouth as we mowed down the trees, picking up speed. Dust and a few leaves swirled inside the cab. "They can't follow us!" I yelled as the truck bounced back onto cement and we roared easy in the westbound lane with the right wheels on the shoulder. I took us up over ninety. The diesel howled.

"Gawdalmighty!" Brogan screamed.

Oncoming headlights flashed past us at a combined speed of a hundred and fifty. Brogan was staring straight ahead, sitting so stiffly pigeons might have lit on him. I looked over at him and spit on his gun hand, holding the wheel firm as the side of the truck shot sparks as we scraped the concrete rail of an overpass.

We both saw the roadblock ahead, two cars with flashing lights, parked to block the highway, distant small figures running in the shadowed red glare. On either side of the highway at that point the ground sloped up at close to a forty-five degree angle.

"We can go around 'em!" I called over the wind and the roar of the diesel.

Brogan was shaking now, the gun forgotten. I laughed at him. The world's Brogans don't like being laughed at, but who does?

"It's a roadblock!" he screamed. "You're crazy!"

"Let's crash it!"

His eyes were wide and straining, his mouth working so that his beard bobbled up and down as if his teeth were chattering. Maybe they were.

"Don't worry about flippin' on that hill!" I shouted.

"We'll turn over! Stop this thing!"

I paid no attention to him and swept to the side of the v'd Highway Patrol cars. We heard shots.

"Please!" Brogan screamed.

I stamped on the accelerator. The trailer was whipping behind us and I wrestled the wheel as we jolted and tilted to the left so far that Brogan's limp body slammed against me, then back to the right so he flew to the other side of the cab and slumped against the door.

I braked the rig to a slow, hissing stop.

They were coming on foot and by car behind me. I sat and watched them in the mirror. The passenger-side door was yanked open and Brogan would have fallen out if two troopers hadn't caught him and lowered him to the ground. One of them eased the revolver from his hand.

My door was pulled open. More guns.

"Hey, crazy man!" Rock Face yelled at me. "What in the hell was this all about?"

"He had a gun on me," I said, climbing down on rubbery legs, "made me drive him where he wanted to go."

"This is Dennison!" one of the troopers said as a handcuffed and staggering Brogan was led around the side of the truck. "He's wanted for three drug murders in Saint Louis!"

I stared. "He told me his name was Brogan. I picked him up hitchhiking."

"You should have known better," Rock Face said.

"I should have," I agreed.

Rock Face squinted at Brogan-Dennison from under the wide brim of his trooper's hat. "What did you do to him?"

"I told him I was hauling explosives. Guess it wore on his nerves. And all I've got is a load of foam insulation."

41

Rock Face shook his head, then chuckled.

I chuckled along with him. Then he laughed aloud and I laughed.

More patrol cars arrived. The questions and answers began.

They didn't hold me long, and soon I was back on the road, feeling the numbing heat of the wind through the rolled-down window. When I looked at my watch I saw that I wasn't too far off schedule.

There was a steep grade ahead and I built up speed so the weight I was hauling wouldn't slow me too much as the truck climbed. Cement and blasting powder was what I was hauling, not foam insulation. But I couldn't tell that to Rock Face.

I was overweight on both axles. I couldn't have stopped for that scale.

Games for Adults

It was seven P.M., and a fine, cool drizzle was settling outside the cozy Twelfth Avenue apartment building when the Darsts' telephone rang. Bill Darst got up from where he'd been half reclining on the sofa reading the paper and moved to answer it. His wife Della had been in the kitchenette preparing supper and he beat her to the phone in the hall by three steps. A medium-sized, pretty brunette, she smiled at her husband and stood gracefully with a serving fork in her hand, waiting to see if the call was for her.

Apparently it wasn't, but she stood listening anyway.

Bill watched her at a slightly sideways angle as he talked. "Oh, yes, sure I do. Yes," he said. ". . . Well, sort of short notice, but I'll see." He held the receiver away from his face and spoke to Della.

"Is supper so far along you can't hold it up? We have an invitation for this evening from the Tinkys."

"The what?"

"He's on the phone," Bill said impatiently. "Quick, yes or no." He smiled knowingly, aware that she hated to cook and seldom turned down an opportunity to escape the chore.

"Sure," she said, shrugging. "Why not?"

As Bill accepted the invitation and hung up, he watched her walk back into the kitchen, untying the apron strings from around her slender waist. They had been married only two years, and he still sometimes experienced that feeling of possessive wonderment at what he considered his incomprehensible and undeserving luck.

"They'll pick us up here in about twenty minutes," he called after Della. "Said the directions were too complicated to understand over the phone."

"Fine." Her voice came from the bedroom now, where she was changing clothes.

Della appeared shortly, wearing the form-fitting but modest green dress that he liked on her. "Now, just where are we going?" she asked. "Who on earth are the Tinkys?"

Bill grinned at her. "Cal and Emma Tinky," he said. "Remember, we met them in that lounge on Fourteenth Street when we went there to escape the rain last week."

Recognition widened her eyes. "The toy manufacturer and his wife! I'd forgotten about them completely."

"Well, they didn't forget about us. Cal Tinky said something at the bar about inviting us for dinner and games some night, and I guess he meant it. I don't see any harm in us taking him up on a free meal."

"Games?" Della asked, raising an artistically penciled eyebrow.

"Tinky's the president and owner of Master Games, Incorporated," Bill reminded her, "and they're not toy manufacturers. They make games, mostly for adults. You know, three-dimensional checkers, word games, party games. They're the ones who make crossword roulette."

"We played that once," Della said, "at the Grahams'."

"Right," Bill said. "Anyway, the Tinkys live outside of town and Cal Tinky happened to be in this neighborhood, so he invited us out to his place."

"I hope his wife knows about it."

"He said she does." Bill picked up the paper again and began idly going over the football scores that he'd read before, but he didn't really concentrate on them. He thought back on the evening he and Della had met the

Tinkys. Both couples had gone into the tiny lounge to escape the sudden deluge, and they had naturally fallen into an easy conversation that had lasted as long as the rain, well over an hour. Cal Tinky was a large-boned beefy man with a ruddy complexion and a wide, toothy smile. His wife, Emma, was a stout woman in her early forties. While friendly, she seemed to be rather withdrawn at times, the line of her mouth arcing downward beneath the suggestion of a fine mustache.

Only fifteen minutes had passed since the phone call when the doorbell rang and Bill went to answer it.

Cal Tinky stood in the hall, wearing an amiable grin and a tweed sportcoat and red tie that brought out the floridness of his complexion. "You folks ready? Emma's waiting down in the car."

"Sure," Bill said. "Come on in a minute and we can go."

"Evening, Mrs. Darst," Tinky said as he stepped inside.

Della said hello and they chatted while Bill went into the bedroom and put on a coat and tie. He could hear Della's laughter and Tinky's booming, enthusiastic voice as he stood before the mirror and ran a brush over his thick dark hair. He noted his regular-featured, commonplace appearance marred by a slightly large, slightly crooked nose and again counted his good fortune for having Della.

"We'll just take my car," Tinky said as Bill crossed the living room and got the coats from the hall closet. "You're apt to lose me in the fog, and it's not so far I can't drive you back later on."

"You don't have to go to all that trouble, Mr. Tinky," Della said, backing into the raincoat that Bill held for her.

"No trouble," Tinky said reassuringly. "And call me Cal — never did like that name Tinky."

Bill put on his topcoat, and they left and took the elevator to the lobby, then crossed the street to where Emma Tinky was waiting in a rain-glistening gray sedan.

The ride to the Tinkys' home took almost an hour through the misting, foggy night. They wound for miles on a series of smooth blacktop roads surrounded by woods, listening to the steady muffled rhythm of the sweeping wiper blades. Cal Tinky kept up an easy conversation of good-natured little stories as he drove, while Emma sat silently, gazing out the side window at the cold rain.

"I hope you won't go to too much trouble," Della said from the rear seat.

Bill watched Emma Tinky start from her silent thoughts and smile. "Oh, no, I put a roast in the oven before we came into the city. It's cooking now."

The big car took another turn, this time onto a steep gravel road. Bill caught a glimpse through the trees of the distant city lights far below them. He hadn't realized they'd driven so far into the hills.

"I don't suppose you have much in the way of neighbors," he said, "living way up here."

"You're right there, Bill," Cal Tinky said. "Nearest is over two miles. Folks up here value their privacy. You know how it is when you work hard half your life and manage to become moderately wealthy — always somebody wanting to take it away from you. Up here we're not pestered by people like that."

By the looks of the Tinkys' home they were more than moderately wealthy. As the car turned into the long driveway bordered by woods, Bill gazed through the rain-streaked windshield at a huge house that seemed in the dark to be built something like a horizontal wheel. Its rounded brick walls curved away into the night in perfect symmetry on either side of the ornate lighted entrance. Off to the left of the car Bill saw a small beach house beside a swimming pool.

"Like it?" Cal Tinky asked. "I can tell you it cost more than a pretty penny, but we sure enjoy it, Emma and I."

"What I can see of it looks great," Bill said.

"You shouldn't brag," Emma said to her husband.

"Just giving them the facts," Tinky said heartily as he neared the house and a basement garage door opened automatically.

For just a moment the sound of the car's engine was loud and echoing in the spacious garage, then Cal Tinky turned the key and they sat in silence. Bill saw a small red foreign convertible parked near some stacks of large cartons.

"No fun sitting here," Cal Tinky said. "Let's go upstairs."

They got out of the car and the Tinkys led them up some stairs to a large utility room of some sort. After passing through that room they entered a large room containing some chairs, a sofa, and a grand piano.

"Come on in here," Cal Tinky said, "into our recreation room."

Bill thought the recreation room was fantastic. It was a spacious room, about thirty feet square, with a red-and-white checkerboard tiled floor and walls hung with large decorative dominoes and ornate numerals. At strategic spots on the gleaming tile, four-foot-tall wood chessmen stood on some of the large red squares. Several tables were situated about the room, with various games spread out on them — chess, dominoes, and several complex games that were manufactured by Master Games, Incorporated. A smoldering fire glowed in the fireplace, over which hung a huge dart board.

"Let's sit down," Cal Tinky invited. Dinner'll be ready soon."

Bill removed his coat and crossed an area rug designed to resemble the six-dotted plane of a huge die. We sat down next to Cal Tinky on a sofa embroidered with tic-tac-toe symbols.

"Is there anything I can do to help?" Della asked Emma Tinky as the heavyset woman took her coat.

"No, no," Emma said, "you are a guest."

Bill watched Emma remove her own bulky coat and saw that she was wearing slacks and a black sweater covered with a heavy corduroy vest. There was something that suggested hidden physical power in her walk as she left the recreation room to hang up the coats and prepare dinner.

Della sat opposite Bill and Cal on a chair that matched the sofa. "Quite a decorating job."

Cal Tinky beamed. "Thanks. Designed most of it ourselves. After we eat we can make use of it."

"A house this big," Bill said, "do you have any servants?"

Cal Tinky stood and walked to an L-shaped bar in a corner. "No," he said, "we mostly take care of it all ourselves, fifteen rooms. Had servants, but they stole on us. Now we have someone come in from the city twice a week to clean. Course, most of the rooms we don't even use." He reached for a top-brand bottle of Scotch and held it up. "Good enough?"

Bill nodded.

"Make mine with water," Della said.

Cal Tinky mixed the drinks expertly. When he'd given the Darsts their glasses he settled down on the couch and took a long sip of his straight Scotch.

Emma Tinky came back into the room then, picked up the drink that her husband had left for her on the bar, and

48

sat in a chair near the sofa.

"You certainly must be fond of games," Bill said, looking around him again in something like awe at the recreation room.

Cal Tinky smiled. "Games are our life. Life is a game."

"I agree with that last part," Bill said, raising the excellent Scotch to his lips.

"There are winners and losers," Emma said, smiling at Della.

They sat for a moment in that awkwardness of silence that sometimes descends on people who don't really know one another. Bill heard a faint clicking that he'd noticed in the car earlier. He saw that Emma was holding in her left hand one of those twisted metal two-part puzzles that separate and lock together only a certain way. With surprisingly nimble fingers she was absently separating and rejoining the two pieces expertly.

"Winners and losers," Della said to fill the void. "I suppose that's true."

"The basis of life," Cal Tinky said. "Have you folks ever stopped to think that our whole lives are spent trying to figure out bigger and better ways to amuse ourselves, bigger and better challenges? From the time we are infants we want to play the 'grown-up' games."

Bill didn't say anything. It was something about which he had never thought much.

"And business!" Cal Tinky laughed his booming laugh. "Why, business is nothing but a game!"

Now Bill laughed. "You appear to be a winner at that game." He motioned with his hand to take in the surroundings.

Emma joined in the laughter. She had a high, piercing laugh, long and lilting with a touch of . . . Of what? "Yes," she said then in a suddenly solemn voice, though a smile still played about her lips. "Material possessions are some of the prizes."

"Enough talk of games." Cal Tinky said. "I'm hungry."

Emma put the twisted pieces of shining metal into her vest pocket. "We can eat any time," she said, "unless you'd like another drink."

"No," Bill said, "not unless the food's so bad you don't want me to taste it."

Again came her high, lilting laugh, backgrounded by her husband's booming laughter.

At least she has a sense of humor, Bill thought, as they all rose and went into the large and well-furnished dining room.

The meal was simple but delicious; a well-done roast served with potatoes and carrots, a gelatin dessert with coffee, topped by an excellent brandy.

Throughout the meal they had kept up a running conversation, usually led by Cal Tinky, on the importance and celestial nature of games in general. Emma would join in now and then with a shrewd comment, a high and piercing laugh, and once, over the lime gelatin, Bill had seen her staring at Della with a strange intensity. Then she had looked away, spooning the quivering dessert into her mouth, and Bill heard again the soft, metallic, clicking sound.

After the brandy Cal Tinky suggested they go back into the recreation room for some drinks and relaxation. For a short time the Tinkys stayed in the dining room as Cal helped Emma put away some perishables, and Bill and Della were alone.

Della nudged Bill playfully in the ribs and moved close to him. "These people are weird," she whispered.

Bill grinned down at her. "Just a little eccentric, darling. Maybe we'd be, too, if we had their money."

"I hope we find out someday," Della said with a giggle. She quickly hushed as the Tinkys came into the room.

Cal Tinky was carrying a fresh bottle of Scotch. "The first order is more drinks," he proclaimed in his loud voice.

He mixed the drinks at the bar and served them, then he looked around at the many games and entertainment devices. "Anything for your amusement," he said with his wide grin.

Bill smiled and shrugged his shoulders. "You're the game expert, Cal."

Cal Tinky looked thoughtful and rubbed his square jaw.

"Make it something simple, if you will," Della said. "I don't feel very clever tonight."

"How about Bank Vault?" Cal asked. "It's a simple game, but it's fun for four people."

He walked to a shelf and took down the game. Bill and Della followed him to a round shaggy rug, where he opened the box and spread out the gameboard. Emma spread four cushions for them to sit on.

When they were seated with fresh drinks, Cal Tinky proceeded to explain the rules.

It was an easy game to learn, uncomplicated, based like so many games on the advance of your marker according to the number you rolled on a pair of dice. The board was marked in a concentric series of squares, divided into boxes, some of which had lettering inside them: "Advance six squares," "Go back two," "Return to home area." Occasionally there were shortcuts marked on the board where you had your choice of direction while advancing. Each player had a small wooden marker of a different color, and if the number he rolled happened to land his block on the same square as an opponent, the opponent had to return to the home area and start over. Whoever reached the bank vault first was the winner.

They rolled the dice to determine in what order they'd play, then settled down on the soft cushions to enjoy themselves.

Cal and Emma Tinky played seriously and with complete absorption. Cal would roll his number and move his red block solemnly while his eyes measured the distance his opponents were behind him. Emma would move her yellow block in short firm steps, counting the number of squares as she moved it.

The game lasted through two drinks. Bill had rolled consecutive high numbers, and his green block was ahead until near the end of the game. Then he had landed on a "Go back ten" square and Cal had overtaken him to win. Emma was second, only three squares ahead of Bill, and Della's blue block brought up the rear after an unfortunate "Return to home area" roll.

"Say, I have another game similar to this only a little more interesting," Cal said, picking up the board. "Let's try it."

Bill reached to help him put the game away and found that his fingers missed the block he'd tried to pick up by half an inch. He decided to go easier on the Scotch.

Cal returned with the new game and spread it out on the soft rug to explain it to them. It was almost exactly like the first game. This time the board was laid out in a circle divided into compartments. The compartments were marked as rooms and the idea was to get back first to the room in which you started. This time the obstacles and detours were a little more numerous.

"Does your company manufacture this game?" Bill asked.

"Not yet," Cal Tinky said with his expansive grin, "but we're thinking about it. It's not the sort of game with mass appeal."

They rolled the dice in the same order. Bill rolled a twelve and moved well out ahead, but on his second roll he came up with a seven, landing him in the dining room, where the lettered message instructed him to skip his next turn for a snack. Della moved out ahead of him then, landing in the den. Emma rolled a three but landed in the utility room, where she was instructed to advance ten squares. This brought her yellow block only two squares behind Della's and she emitted her high, strange laughter. Cal rolled snake eyes, allowing him a free roll, and he came up with a twelve. His red block landed on the den, and he placed it directly atop Della's blue block.

"Does that mean I go back to the entrance hall?" Della asked, smiling like a sport but feeling disappointed.

"In a manner of speaking," Cal Tinky said. He drew from beneath his sport jacket a large revolver and shot Della.

The slam of the large-caliber bullet smashing into her chest sounded almost before the shot. Della flopped backward, still smiling, her legs still crossed. A soft sigh escaped her body and her eyes rolled back.

"Della . . . " Bill whispered her name once, staring at her, wanting to help her, knowing she was dead, finally and forever. A joke, a mistake, a horrible, unbelievable mistake! He turned toward the Tinkys. Cal Tinky was smiling. They were both smiling.

Words welled up in Bill's throat that would not escape — anger that paralyzed him. He stood unsteadily, the room whirling at first, and began to move toward Cal Tinky. The long revolver raised and the hammer clicked back into place. Bill stood trembling, grief-stricken, enraged and afraid. Cal Tinky held the revolver and his smile steady as the fear grew, cold and pulsating, deep in the pit of Bill's stomach. The floor seemed to tilt and Bill screamed, a hoarse sobbing scream. He turned awkwardly and ran in panic from the room, from death.

He stumbled through the dining room, struggling to keep his balance. At the edge of his mind he was aware that Cal had put something in the drinks, something that had destroyed his perception, sapped his strength, and he tried to fight it off as he ran to a window. The window was small and high, and as he flung aside the curtains he saw that it was covered with a steel grill. With a moan, he ran awkwardly into the next room, to the next window. It, too, was barred. All the rooms that had windows were inescapable, and all the outside doors were locked. He ran, pounding against thick barred windows that wouldn't break or open, flinging himself against doors that wouldn't give, until finally, exhausted and broken, he found himself in the kitchen and dragged his heaving body into a small alcove lined with shelves of canned goods, where he tried to hide, to think, to think . . .

In the recreation room Cal Tinky looked at his wife over the gameboard. "I think he's had enough time," he said. "It never takes them more than a few minutes to run to cover."

Emma Tinky nodded and picked up the dice. With a quick expert motion of her hand she rolled a nine.

Cal rolled a six. "Your shot," he said.

Emma rolled the dice again, a seven. She leaned over the board and, counting under her breath, moved her yellow block forward in short tapping jerks.

"The kitchen," she said. "Damn! They never hide in the kitchen."

54

"No need to get upset," Cal Tinky said. "You'll probably get another roll."

Emma drew a long revolver exactly like her husband's from beneath her corduroy vest and stood. Stepping over Della, she walked from the recreation room toward the kitchen. Her husband picked up the game and followed, careful to hold the board absolutely level so that the dice and the colored blocks wouldn't be disturbed.

The sound of the shot that came from the kitchen a few minutes later wasn't very loud, like the hard slap of an open hand on a solid tabletop — but Emma Tinky's high, long laugh might have been heard throughout the house.

Say this about Bernice — she believed in getting things done, and so she did them.

Her husband Eldon, on the other hand, was more than something of a procrastinator. It was his philosophy that problems, like clouds, if simply ignored long enough would often drift away. And while Bernice wasn't exactly careless with money, she wouldn't hesitate to spend what had to be spent. Eldon, to the contrary, was notoriously tight-fisted.

Another of Bernice's traits was curiosity, or nosiness, as Eldon thought of it. Not that she was overly interested in other people's concerns. She would enter the affairs of acquaintances slowly but inevitably, gradually permeating their situations as water wends its way into too-porous cement. There was no defense against her. Eldon, however, was aloof, self-contained, even secretive at times in the jealous protection of his privacy. Eldon was tall, sharp-featured and almost completely bald; Bernice was a short, round-featured woman, attractive for her forty-five years, and with a huge mop of naturally curly chestnut hair.

After fifteen years of marriage, Eldon and Bernice Koins were living examples of the adage that opposites attract, but only initially.

"Eldon," she said to him one morning before breakfast, "it's already so hot in here I could fry your eggs right on your plate. *When* are you going to have the air conditioner repaired?"

The air conditioner unit for the house had stopped working in mid-July, and week after week Eldon had debated whether or not they could afford to have it repaired at that time. They had sweltered through many an argument about the air conditioner, and now here it was August.

"It'll be fixed soon," Eldon told her, thinking that September and cooler weather was right around the corner. "The Jantzens down the street don't even have an air conditioner."

"The Jantzens are also in Canada," Bernice said, setting his plate of bacon and eggs before him.

"Maybe my raise will be on my next pay check," Eldon said, nibbling a piece of bacon and ignoring Canada. "I'm bound to get a raise. The company gives everyone a raise after five years."

Eldon was a representative of Loomis Tranquilizer Company, and he traveled almost continuously, which was fortunate for the preservation of his marriage. He was due to leave that very day on a flight to New York and would be gone six days.

"I'm getting tired of being cooped up in this steam bath while you're in some air-conditioned hotel room," Bernice said, flouncing across the kitchen and seating herself opposite Eldon. "I'm liable to just draw some money from the savings account and call an air conditioner repairman while you're gone."

Eldon didn't change expression. He knew she wouldn't dare do that.

"That money's in the savings account for a particular reason," he said firmly, adding cream to his coffee. "I told you we might get the air conditioner fixed next week."

"Always next week or next this or next that," Bernice complained, spooning sugar into her black coffee. "The only way I can get anything fixed around this house is save

57

up enough money myself from my household allowance to pay for it."

"So save enough to buy a new compressor for the air conditioner," Eldon said derisively. He dabbed at his lips with his folded napkin and stood from his unfinished breakfast, irritated and completely without appetite. "I have to go now if I'm going to catch my plane. I'll be at the *Langton* if you want to call me."

Bernice stared up at him coldly, with her round blue eyes. "Your reservation says the *Reardon Hotel*."

Eldon's thin lips drew even thinner and a gray vein throbbed near his temple. "You've been in my attaché case, haven't you?"

"And why not?" Bernice said indignantly. "I am your wife. I needed a pen in a hurry and thought you might have one in there. You did, clipped on that little notebook with all those people's names and addresses in it. Is that Mr. Calder the same man we knew in Buffalo?"

"No," Eldon said evenly, "he's not."

Bernice started to say something else, but Eldon turned and walked abruptly from the kitchen. He would file for divorce against Bernice, he told himself for the hundredth time. Then he began to ponder the various consequences, especially the alimony payments he would have to begin making.

The main trouble with living with Bernice was that Eldon's privacy, one of the things he valued most, had diminished to the point where it was almost nonexistent. Intolerable. He had even thought — very fleetingly of course — of murdering Bernice, arranging a fatal "accident". But for all the methods he considered Eldon lacked the courage even if he could summon up the decisiveness.

He was in the living room, by the door, with his luggage and his attaché case.

"I'm going," he said loudly. He thought he should say something.

"Go," came the voice from the kitchen. "I'll call the *Reardon* later to make sure you got there."

Intolerable. Eldon hesitated on the porch, trying to decide if he should slam the door. He concluded that would only give Bernice the satisfaction of knowing she had angered him, and he closed the door softly and turned away to the heat of the rising morning sun.

Perhaps it was the quest for privacy that caused Eldon to construct the room in the basement. He had an inexact layman's ability at carpentry, but he planned ahead thoughtfully and was painstakingly careful.

The room wasn't very large, about ten by ten, occupying one corner of the basement. Eldon purchased the material and worked on it most of his vacation then in the evenings after work. During the various stages of construction, Bernice would come down the basement stairs, look about and try to draw him into conversation so she could find out exactly why he was building the room. Did he plan to use it for storage, an office, a den? But Eldon studiously ignored all questions concerning the room, casually drowning out some of them with buzz of saw or crash of hammer.

Once he had the studwork up the rest went quickly. Eldon certainly hadn't skimped on the materials. The studs were broad and close together, the panelling fairly expensive, thick and deeply grained birch. The floor was made up of squares of gray asbestos tile with swirling designs in them. There was a solid wooden door, thick and soundproof. For ventilation Eldon had cut into the ductwork and installed a small register near the double-layered wallboard ceiling.

When he was finished he closed the door to his room and told Bernice to stay out of it.

Eldon didn't leave town for over a week after the room was finished, then he was called on to make a four day jaunt through the midwest. He left as usual with his beat up luggage and his black leather attaché case, and he surprised Bernice slightly by telling her the hotels he'd be staying at so she could call him.

The first day of Eldon's absence Bernice merely walked down the basement stairs and stood for a long time scrutinizing the closed large wooden door to the room. The second day she tried the knob, found that it turned. She pressed her ear hard against the cool wood of the door, heard nothing, then went back upstairs. On the third day she had a late breakfast, walked down the basement stairs, stood before the room's door for a moment, turned the knob, drew several deep breaths, and shoved the door open.

The room was empty.

Absolutely empty, spotlessly clean and empty. Bernice backed out, shut the door and walked slowly up the stairs.

Eldon was back as scheduled, but was due to leave again in three days and would be gone almost two weeks. He acted perfectly normal, didn't mention the room or even seem to go near it. The night before he was to leave Bernice cooked his favorite veal and potato dinner and tried to draw him out.

"Incidentally," she said absently as she passed him the butter, "what are you planning to use it for?"

"It. What do you mean?"

"The room you built," Bernice said casually. "You know, in the basement."

Eldon said something unintelligible around a mouthful of veal.

"Did you say den, dear?"

"Tender," Eldon corrected as he took a sip of tea. "I said

60

the veal is exceedingly tender."

"Thank you."

"What I meant," Eldon said, "was that it probably is an unnecessarily expensive cut."

"But the room —"

"There is no need to change the subject," Eldon said, clashing serving spoon on plate as he took another huge helping of mashed potatoes.

Eldon left early the next morning for the airport, holding to his silence.

It was two mornings later before Bernice again made her way down the basement stairs to stand before the room. This time she found the door partway open. Decisively, she pushed it open wider and stepped inside.

Still empty. Bernice left the room and went slowly back upstairs.

She poured herself a second glass of tomato juice and sat thoughtfully at the kitchen table. Something! He had to have built the room for something! She sipped the juice slowly, staring out the window at high unmoving clouds.

When Bernice was finished with her tomato juice she went back downstairs, entered the room and began to examine the sturdy panelling carefully for some kind of concealed compartment or trick door. She was lightly tapping the north wall with her knuckles when the telephone rang faintly from above.

The caller was a man who understood that she and her husband owned their own home and wanted to sell her some storm windows. Bernice refused him, hung up and came back to the basement. She reentered the room and absently closed the door behind her.

When Eldon returned from his business trip late the next week, he walked through the front door, stood listening, then called his wife's name three times, each louder than the last. When there was no answer he began to walk slowly, almost aimlessly, from one room to the next. At last he went to the basement.

He stood before the door to the room, his ear pressed to the wood, as Bernice had once stood. After a few minutes his hand went to the knob, twisted slowly, more slowly. He was perspiring and breathing rapidly as he pushed inward.

Eldon looked first at the long scratches on the paneled walls, the inside of the door, even the ceiling. The vibrant silence hummed in his ears as he forced himself to look at what had been only a shapeless form on the edge of his vision.

Bernice lay curled on her side near the center of the floor, arms crossed, mutilated, claw-like hands grasping her forearms. Her right cheek was pressed flat to the smooth tile floor and her blue eyes were open and calm, as if equating the near horizon.

Kneeling beside her, staring at her with that curiosity reserved for the dead, Eldon wondered how she had died. Not suffocation, for he'd vented the room. Hunger perhaps. Thirst? Fright? The empty calm in her eyes was belied by the grotesquely leering tautness of her mouth.

Where before Eldon couldn't bring himself to look at Bernice, now he couldn't stop looking at her as he rehearsed in his mind the story he'd tell the police.

My God, it was one of those freak accidents. She must have just happened to walk in to look around and . . . The room was going to be my office. I never intended to lock the door so when I hung it I never even noticed what side the lock was on. I never even knew the knob had one of those locks that held the outside knob firm while the inside one turned. Only this time the outside was the inside. One of those freak accidents . . .

Eldon was satisfied he could appear sufficiently grief-stricken for the next week or so. Still staring at Bernice, he straightened, and for a split second the distant snap and low hum that he heard meant nothing to him. Then there was a subtle movement of air, a low swishing sound ending in a soft click, and Eldon was standing in total darkness, the vision of Bernice's lifeless face still before him, a lingering image in his startled eyes.

The air conditioner! She'd had the air conditioner repaired and the pull of air as it came on had closed the door! His mind refused to believe it, but his heart leapt.

Cautiously Eldon's trembling fingers groped through darkness and tested the doorknob. It wouldn't turn. The door was locked.

A hoarse cry broke from Eldon and he flung himself against the door, staggered back from the impact and his heel dug into something soft, tripping him to sit spread-legged on the cold tile floor. He drew back and with low, rhythmic sobs crept to a wall, crawled pressing cat-like against it as he explored the thick baseboard with futile searching fingers. Finally he came to the inevitable corner and sat whimpering, wedging himself firmly, violently, into the unyielding angle of the solid walls, and began his wait.

The room was very dark, and soon it became very cold, and but for Eldon's desperate whimpering it was almost completely quiet.

It wasn't so much the prospect of his own imminent death like Bernice's that drove Eldon to dig his aching heels into the floor, fighting to press ever backward into the corner. It was the madly irrational yet terrifyingly persistent illusion that, as the final darkness closed and the door latch had clicked, she had smiled at him.

"You are *not* leaving this house tonight except to go with me to the Hartmans'!" Henrietta Bartamer said to her husband. "They have a new hot tub in their back yard, and Janet and Phil want us to help them christen it. And we *will!*"

Bartamer knew enough not to argue when Henrietta spoke in italics. He had intended to work late tonight, but now he wouldn't. He would instead sit nude in a wooden hot tub beneath a clear California mountain sky and trade mundane remarks with the Hartmans. Henrietta's friends.

He did so, and found the next morning that something in the water had given him a rash.

At breakfast he studied Henrietta. She was her usual blonde classically pretty self. She was thirty-five now but could easily pass for a tall lithe twenty-five. It was a pity she had such a grizzly-bear personality.

Bartamer, in contrast, was short, dark, and somewhat weasely looking. He kissed his Nordic beauty of a wife goodbye and left, carrying his briefcase. He had done some paperwork late last night after Henrietta was asleep.

Bartamer fumed as he drove his red Ferrari up the mountain road just outside Carmel. Life seemed always to be a trap. Bartamer was an acknowledged genius in biochemistry, but a genius with decidedly unconventional ideas. Ten years ago he had lost his position at Northwestern University and found that word had gotten around as to his supposed eccentricities. No other position worth considering was offered. So he had married Henrietta, the young widow of Norris Feeber of Feeber Fidelity Trust. Despite Henrietta's great wealth and considerable beauty, she had been somewhat in the same boat as Bartamer. So foul and aggressive was her disposition that no one else would have her.

Bartamer used his bride's money to purchase an isolated house in the mountains. Then he had gone about building and equipping a more isolated mountaintop laboratory where he could carry on his research undisturbed. He was even incorporated, under the innocuous name of Research West Development. Money no longer was a problem, but Henrietta was.

She had become almost impossible to coexist with, Bartamer thought, as he used his coded signal control to open the high iron gate at the laboratory entrance. He drove through, glancing in his rearview mirror to see the gate swing closed and lock behind him.

The laboratory was housed in a low brick building invisible from below. There were several high narrow windows on each side of the glass front door, and very expensive and sophisticated heating and cooling equipment on the roof. Bartamer noted with satisfaction that his assistant Melfore's gray sedan was parked in its slot.

Melfore was already at work when Bartamer entered the lab. He was a youngish man with large, intense dark eyes. Melfore had been a juvenile delinquent before discovering that he had an exceptional brain. Bartamer had met him at Northwestern, where he had been impressed by the young man's inquisitiveness and willingness to explore any hypothesis. Melfore had seemed intelligent and opportunistic, but not the type that would steal university laboratory equipment, then physically assault the dean when confronted with the crime. But a jury had decided that Melfore *was* that type, and a judge had handed down a five-year sentence. When he was paroled after two years, Bartamer had looked him up and employed him. And for the past seven years Melfore had made an ideal assistant.

It was cloning that Bartamer was working on, that consumed him. And his experiments were gradually showing him the avenue to success. He already had succeeded with some of the higher primates, and when his techniques were perfected he would be ready to show, and then to snub, the rest of the scientific community. That was important to Bartamer. That was why he stayed with Henrietta.

Melfore smiled at Bartamer. "There have been no significant changes other than the usual."

"The usual?"

"Chimp Two is in every way identical to Chimp One, except that already Chimp Two is showing overall better health, strength, and aggressiveness. The aging process accelerated and then leveled off as anticipated, and the intelligence and comp-tech transference of the brain's programs and responses has been repeated."

What Melfore was saying, in short, was that the chimpanzee that had been cloned now had an exact duplicate that was in all respects the dominant of the two.

Bartamer looked at Chimp Two. Chimp Two glared back at him from behind the wire of its cage. Chimp Two was mean and getting meaner. That was a problem for which Bartamer was sure he already had the solution. After a delicate and unfortunately risky adjustment of the clone's chemical balance, Chimp Two would be as docile and compliant as a newborn kitten. But first Bartamer had in mind another experiment. He placed Chimps One and Two in the same cage.

A week later, after Chimp Two had killed Chimp One

and then been reduced by chemical modification to an amiable pet, Bartamer was sure he had the answer to his problems with Henrietta.

In human nature it is to an extent true that opposites attract. By the same token it is no secret what familiarity breeds. Bartamer knew that another Henrietta, slightly larger, slightly healthier and stronger, increasingly aggressive, would not be able to tolerate the original Henrietta for long. And after Henrietta One had been dispatched, Bartamer would see that Henrietta Two was altered to become as mild-mannered and agreeable as any woman could be. All that was needed was a microscopic tissue sample from Henrietta, which was easy enough to obtain. The beauty of the scheme was that if, by some remote chance, the authorities did discover that Henrietta One had been murdered, Bartamer technically would be innocent of the crime. He had to hand it to himself.

Six months later Bartamer brought Henrietta Two home from the lab. Henrietta One was mildly astonished, even a bit complimented, that her husband should create another her. But of course she was too pea-brained to realize the significance of Bartamer's accomplishment.

"We can have her do the housework around here," Henrietta One said. "It will free me to go into town more often."

Henrietta Two, glowing with health and strength, heard that and glared. Bartamer recognized that glare.

At first things seemed to go smoothly. Henrietta Two became the maid that the Bartamers' chosen isolation had prevented them from employing. She followed Henrietta One's orders literally and thoroughly, even moving furniture and appliances with seeming ease to clean behind them.

The sprawling ten-room house that previously was always in disarray now was almost a showplace of neatness and cleanliness. Henrietta One was obviously enjoying her new environment and leisure. She took to going for long drives or sunning herself most of the day by the pool, while Henrietta Two toiled.

Occasionally Bartamer would see his wife's blue sportscar on the road to the laboratory. Melfore told him that Henrietta One had visited the lab several times, asking questions, showing an interest she'd never shown before. But they were not intelligent questions.

With increasing frequency now, Bartamer would over-hear Henriettas One and Two arguing. Then one afternoon Henrietta One approached him on the patio.

"I think you should take it back to the lab."

"It?" Bartamer asked.

"The — other me. I mean, it — she — is becoming too much of a problem. She objects to everything I do, and when it comes to any difference of opinion she's more and more stubborn. Then there's the way I sometimes catch her looking at me."

"Looking at you? How?" Bartamer asked.

Henrietta One shivered. "I don't know how to explain it, but there's something in her eyes — as if she's not human."

"Well, strictly speaking —"

"I don't want to *hear!*" Henrietta One interrupted. "Take her back *tomorrow!* That's settled!" And she flounced away.

Bartamer happened to glance toward the patio doors and saw Henrietta Two staring after her prototype.

That very evening he found the body of Henrietta One in the den, stretched backward over the stereo console. Her neck had been broken.

Bartamer removed her left shoe and examined the sole of the bare foot to make sure it wasn't marked with the tiny star he'd tattooed on Henrietta Two. He smiled and replaced the shoe.

Henrietta Two had murdered. She was learned enough to know that her freedom depended on Bartamer not reporting her. And after he'd used her to help dispose of Henrietta One's body, she would be given treatment to remove her aggressive tendencies. To the outside world, she would be Henrietta One, and life would go on as before — only much more agreeably.

After summoning Henrietta Two over the intercom, Bartamer mixed himself a drink and sat waiting on the sofa. Henrietta Two arrived almost immediately.

But she wasn't alone.

Melfore was with her. Melfore was grinning the same grin he'd displayed after assaulting the dean. And Henrietta Two was smiling a carnivorous smile. Neither of them bothered to glance at the remains of Henrietta One.

"I'm afraid Henrietta Two and I have struck a bargain," Melfore said.

Bartamer stood up from the sofa, feeling the cold weight of fear drop through him.

"Melfore has a brilliant scientific career ahead of him," Henrietta Two said fervently.

"I think I can guarantee that," a third voice said, and Bartamer Two stepped into the room.

He was slightly taller than Bartamer One, slightly more muscular and virile. His face was not so weasely, though his eyes glittered like those of a wolverine. He was holding a revolver.

"Imagine," Melfore was saying, "just try to imagine the future —"

"Pull the trigger," Henrietta Two instructed, and Bartamer Two did.

Bartamer One felt a powerful jolt. A fiery pain erupted in his chest and its heat began to spread. He was on the carpet. The room was whirling, fading.

"Shoot him again," he heard Henrietta Two say calmly. "We ought to make doubly sure he's dead."

"I'll second that," Melfore said.

Bartamer Two made it unanimous.

Fair Shake

They were in the commissioner's office at headquarters. Snodman, B.S. in liberal arts, number one in his police academy class, ex-debating team captain and regional chess champion, adjusted his black horn-rimmed glasses with his little finger and peered down at the slip of paper the commissioner had handed him:

> I know everything about my marks
> At least I know enough
> To catch them always unawares
> They're never up to Snuff

"Crude," Snodman said. "What does it mean, sir?"

"I've seen them before," Commissioner Moriarty said. "They're the work of a man the underworld calls 'The Snuffer'."

"A professional assassin, sir?" Snodman asked, looking at Moriarty through emotionless blue eyes. It had always intrigued Snodman, the fact that a man named Moriarty would be decreed by fate to be a police commissioner and look so like the fictitious Sherlock Holmes would have looked, with lean hawk nose, shrewd gray eyes, even smoking a pipe the stem of which was at least slightly curved.

"Possibly the greatest hired killer the police have ever run up against," the commissioner said. "Rumor has it that he works for the syndicate no more than once a year and receives at least fifty thousand dollars a job. I personally know

71

of six jobs he's definitely completed in various cities."

Snodman, who smoked a pipe himself, placed the stem between his thin lips and reached for his tobacco pouch. "How can you be so sure they were all the work of this . . . Snuffer, sir? *Modus operandi?*"

The commissioner smiled. "It is his M.O. that he is proud of. It varies with every job. In Chicago, concerning the sports fixing racket, it was an exploding basketball; two years ago Hans Greiber, the passport forger, was found drowned in one of those little German cars filled with water; and surely you remember when Joe Besini, who was going to turn state's evidence against the syndicate, was found smothered by a hot pizza."

"Gruesome," Snodman said.

"Anchovies, too." Commissioner Moriarty shook his head reminiscently. "The fact is that in each of these cases the victim knew he was marked for death and had police protection. In each of these cases The Snuffer warned the victim with one of these little poems. A highly developed sense of fair play, if you ask me."

"Yes," Snodman agreed, shifting position in the leather office chair so that his trousers wouldn't become too wrinkled. He was one of the best dressed detectives on the force, and he was proudly aware of it. "I suppose every attempt has been made to trace him through the poems," he said.

The commissioner nodded. "As you can see, they're in hand printed ink on cheap stationery. The paper is too common to mean anything and Handwriting Analysis can't make anything out of the simple printing except that it's the work of a careful, precise individual, which I could have told you."

Snodman wrinkled his still youthful brow. "But why on earth does he send the poems? Doesn't he realize they merely increase his chances of being caught?"

The commissioner leaned over his desk. "Fair play, Snodman. The psychologists say that he's so clever and supremely confident that his conscience compels him to give his victims warning. They say that The Snuffer wants to preserve his anonymity yet boast about his work, so he writes poems. Some of them are quite good."

Snodman, who fancied himself something of an expert on literature, wanted to disagree with his superior but thought better of it. Besides, he was curious as to why the commissioner was filling him in on this subject, so he sat patiently and waited for his boss to get to the point.

"The point is," Moriarty said, biting on his curved stem pipe, "that a man named Ralph Capastrani has agreed to testify next month before a Senate Subcommittee hearing on organized crime. We thought it was a hush-hush thing, but kept Capastrani under protection anyway. Then, this morning, I received this poem in the mail."

"Does Capastrani know anything about it, sir?"

"No. We don't want him to die of worry before the hearings. We're taking every precaution to keep The Snuffer from earning another fortune from the syndicate. Capastrani is under guard in a room at the Paxton Hotel, just two blocks from here. We moved him in this morning." The commissioner paused for effect and pressed his fingertips down onto the glass desk top. "Starting in ten minutes, your job will be to guard him."

"I'm honored you have the confidence in me, sir," Snodman said, actually rather insulted that the commissioner should think he would have a hard time outwitting the composer of these jingling trivialities.

Commissioner Moriarty smiled his Holmes-like smile. "You are one of the most highly educated men on the force,

Snodman, and in the few years you've been with us you've proven yourself to be an efficient and hardworking policeman. Few men of your caliber choose policework as a profession, and your dedication is unquestioned. I can think of no man on the force who would have a better chance of outwitting The Snuffer."

Snodman took this deluge of compliments with aplomb.

The commissioner picked up a silver letter opener and neatly opened one of many letters on his desk. "Capastrani is in room twenty-four on the third floor," he said by way of dismissal. "I'll be over later myself to check on things."

Snodman rose casually and took his leave.

Suite 24 was small and sparsely but tastefully furnished. Shades had been pulled over the third floor, ledgeless windows; heating and air conditioning ducts had been blocked and the comfort was being inadequately supplied by a rented window air conditioner; food was brought up three times a day by a room service waiter who was duly searched before being admitted. Outside the door to the hall stood an armed patrolman; outside the door to the bedroom sat Snodman; inside the bedroom lay Capastrani, sleeping peacefully. Suite 24 was invulnerable.

Obviously Capastrani, a squat, hairy individual, had faith in his police department, for almost all of his time was occupied by sleeping and eating; but then, besides listening to the monotonous watery hum of the air conditioner, there really wasn't much else to do in suite 24.

Snodman's mind dwelt on how much the syndicate would pay to have Capastrani killed. It dwelt on Commissioner Moriarty and his thorough knowledge of The Snuffer. The commissioner had even consulted a police psychologist. Snodman had seen the gleam in the commissioner's eyes as he'd discussed the cunning assassin, and he

74

was sure that Moriarty had dedicated himself to foiling or even capturing The Snuffer. A policeman's dream, Snodman said to himself, smiling.

The long day went by without event. The patrolman outside the door had changed when the three o'clock shift came on. Capastrani had emerged from his room only to eat a late breakfast and lunch, which he'd wolfed down before returning to stretch full length and fully clothed on the bed. Snodman had read a travel magazine three times. He yawned and looked at his watch: five o'clock.

At five forty-five he was speaking frantically into the telephone to Commissioner Moriarty. "You'd better come over here right away with a lab man, sir. I think somebody tried to poison Capastrani!"

Within five minutes the door to suite 24 flew open. Snodman's police revolver was out of its shoulder holster in a flash, but he relaxed as he saw it was the commissioner and a lab man. They looked in surprise at Snodman's revolver as Wilson, the uniformed patrolman guarding the hall, closed the door behind them.

"It's all right," Commissioner Moriarty said. "We should have knocked."

Snodman slipped the revolver into his suitcoat pocket. "Have a look at this," he said, pointing to the tray of food that room service had brought up for Capastrani's supper. To the lab man he said, "I think there's arsenic on the steak."

"I'm glad you called me personally," Commissioner Moriarty said. "You did the right thing."

Snodman smiled. "I knew you had a special interest in the case," he said. "I thought you'd want to come right over."

The commissioner nodded soberly. "That's why I chose

a hotel only two blocks from headquarters."

The three of them leaned over the tray of food. "You can't see it now," Snodman said, "but there were traces of white powder on the underside of the steak when it was brought up. Most of it's dissolved in the juices now."

The commissioner picked up the plate and sniffed. "What made you suspicious?" he asked, replacing the plate.

Snodman shrugged. "A hunch. And I thought there was a peculiar odor about the steak."

"Check it out," the commissioner told the lab man. Then he drew Snodman over to the sofa to talk with him.

"Capastrani know about this?" Moriarty asked.

Snodman shook his head. "He's still asleep. I was going to wake him when supper came."

"Hmm," the commissioner said. "I don't understand how anybody could have slipped arsenic into that food. I toured the kitchen this morning and checked out the help myself. They're all trustworthy, long-time employees."

"Maybe somebody was bought," Snodman suggested. "The Snuffer would be able to afford it."

"Good point," the commissioner said. "Does Capastrani eat steak every night?"

"It's a standing order with room service. That's just the sort of habit The Snuffer would take advantage of. You said he studied his future victims carefully before each job."

"I didn't say that," the commissioner said. "He did — in his poem."

The lab man, a studious looking young fellow, walked over to them. "There's arsenic on the steak," he said. "I checked the salt, pepper, ketchup, coffee, even the cream for the coffee. Everything on the tray besides the steak is okay." Then he held out the slip of paper in his right hand. "This was stuck to the bottom of the steak plate, sir."

The commissioner took it, unfolding it slowly as Snodman watched closely. They read:

I am quite sure my little trick
Nicely stilled your Pigeon's song
'Cause a little bit of arsenic
Never hurt a soul — for long

The commissioner crumpled the poem and put it in his pocket. Then he turned to the lab man. "You can go now," he said. "On the way out tell the kitchen to send up another steak, and this time you stand right there while it's cooking."

"Right," the lab man said, and walked briskly and efficiently out of the room to implement his orders.

"We won't tell Capastrani about this," the commissioner said to Snodman. "He doesn't even know The Snuffer is after him. There's no point in rattling the state's star witness."

"Yes, sir," Snodman said.

The commissioner stretched his lean body. "You've been cooped up in here all day," he said to Snodman. "Why don't you go out for a while and get a bite to eat and some fresh air. The patrolman's outside the door, and I'll stay here myself and keep an eye on things until you return."

"Thank you, sir," Snodman said with appreciation. "To tell you the truth, I was about to ask that little favor myself. I could sure use some fresh air and a change of scenery." He walked to the door and paused. "Is there anything I can bring you, sir?"

"No, no thank you." The commissioner seemed almost eager for Snodman to leave. "Take an hour if you want, Snodman."

"Why, thank you, sir." He stepped into the hall and softly

77

shut the door behind him.

Just after Snodman had left, room service arrived at the door with Capastrani's new steak. The commissioner let them in, examined the steak, made sure the patrolman in the hall was alert, then went into the bedroom to awaken Capastrani.

As he first emerged from sleep the squat little man was shocked to see the commissioner. Then he blinked his eyes a few times and recognized him. Without a word, he looked at his watch and rose from the mattress to leave the bedroom and eat supper.

With a smug little smile, the commissioner sat on the sofa and watched as Capastrani settled himself before the tray. Apparently the little man had been sound asleep and was completely unaware of the recent occurrence. Capastrani sprinkled salt and pepper liberally on his steak and buttered a roll. Then he unscrewed the cap on the ketchup bottle and tipped it. As was not unusual, nothing came out. He shook the bottle a few times, gently, then shook it harder. He was holding it upside down looking at it curiously, when the force of its explosion blew out the entire third floor west wall.

As the ominous sound of the explosion reached police headquarters two blocks away, Snodman leaned back in his desk chair in his tiny office and smiled. He drew the genuine ketchup bottle from his shoulder holster and placed it in his bottom desk drawer. Then he picked up the slip of paper on which was the poem he'd just compulsively jotted down, tore it into tiny pieces and let the pieces flutter down into his wastebasket. For all his cleverness, the one thing he couldn't do was write poetry. Still, bad as they were, even in his lifetime his little jingles might yet achieve a certain degree of fame.

Heat

The city had been an oven for seventeen days and nights. During that time the temperature hadn't dropped below ninety, and the old brick buildings that housed most of the poor had heated up and stayed hot. Many of the elderly had been evacuated to cooling centers set up by the city. Others had refused to leave their homes because their pets needed care or because they feared that when they returned they'd find their few possessions stolen. Portable fans were donated to some of the disadvantaged in the poorer sections of town, but they only created blast furnaces if all the windows were closed — and cooped up in their tiny apartments, afraid of who might enter if they left a window open at night, many of the ill and infirm virtually baked to death. Ambulances were overworked, and obtained only after long waits. Deal and Hastings had used the patrol car to rush an old woman to the hospital two nights ago and found her dead from heatstroke when they arrived.

Thirty-two deaths had been attributed to the heat in the past two weeks. Unless the weather pattern broke, there would be more.

Patrolman Buddy Deal was walking into the precinct garage after evening muster when he stopped suddenly and gaped. His cigar almost dropped from his mouth, tilting forward at a precarious angle and spilling gray ash onto his uniform shirt to join the taco-sauce stain that hadn't come out in the wash. There was his partner, Dave Hastings — at least he thought it was Hastings — with his rump extending

79

from the back seat of the parked patrol car, moving a hand back now and then to drop wadded cigar- and gum-wrappers and various debris into a metal waste can. A steady humming sound was wafting from the back of the car.

"We haven't even left the precinct house yet," Deal said, flicking more cigar ash dangerously close to one of Hastings' gleaming black shoes. "Isn't it a little early to be cleaning out the car?"

Hastings backed out of the car, straightened, and smoothed back his razor-styled hair. "I'm getting rid of the mess you made last night," he said. "Those slobs on the day shift refuse to clean up after you — they just toss everything to the back of the car."

Deal grunted. Whatever the day shift did was okay with him. "What's that in your hand?" he asked.

Hastings glanced down. "It's a portable vacuum cleaner. I'm keeping it in the car as long as we ride together."

Deal grunted again, spilled more ash. "You and your gadgets," he mumbled and climbed in behind the steering wheel. He saw with dismay that Hastings had emptied the ashtray. Deal had left a wrapped-up, half-chewed piece of gum buried under the ashes where the day shift wouldn't find it. And *The Sporting News* was gone from above the sun visor. Trust Hastings to remove the little amenities that made a car a home. Deal might be more than a little on the irresponsible and sloppy side, but Hastings could drive a saint to sin with his rigid conformity and compulsive neatness. The other cops were calling Hastings E.T., for Extra Tidy.

If all that weren't bad enough, Hastings would replace things he removed from the car with useless gadgets like extra ammunition clips, a see-through tinted visor to en-

80

hance night vision, even a portable steam iron to remove wrinkles from his uniform in case he was unexpectedly summoned to Headquarters. Now, as he got into the car to sit beside Deal, he snapped the little vacuum cleaner that looked like a mechanical anteater into a bracket he'd mounted beneath the dashboard. Next he removed a leather pouch from the glove compartment and placed it beside him on the seat.

"What's that thing?" Deal asked.

"Camera," Hastings explained. He removed a 35-millimeter camera from the pouch to show Deal. "It's equipped with a wide-angle lens. I read in *Police Digest* about this officer out west who used a camera and wide-angle lens to keep a photographic record of his beat."

"Photographic record why?" Deal asked, irritated.

"At night, after work, he'd study the photos of the streets. That way he could note day-to-day differences — unfamiliar cars in the area, apartments with shades that were never raised, anything suspicious. When he studied the photos with a magnifying glass one night, he spotted a wanted drug dealer in the neighborhood and effected his arrest. And this camera has an attachment that records the time of each photograph, so changes in the neighborhood can even be noted on an hour-to-hour basis."

"Aren't you forgetting we're working nights?" Deal asked.

Hastings smiled his handsome, infuriatingly smug smile. He tapped the side of the camera with his forefinger. "Extra fast, light-sensitive film," he explained. "And a lens that will photograph in dim light. Also, I've made arrangements with a film processor —"

"Spare me the technicalities," Deal interrupted. He started the engine, loosened his belt, switched on the inadequate air conditioner, and settled back in the seat. It was going to be a long, hot shift.

"Let's get a fix on what Arnie Brubaker is up to tonight," Hastings suggested, referring to a professional burglar he and Deal had been assigned to keep under loose observation.

"Let's get something cold to drink," Deal said, and drove from the precinct garage with a squeal of hot tires and called the car into service.

Snick, whir. Snick, whir. The camera's shutter was tripped and the film advanced automatically over and over again. Hastings was nearer than he suspected to being shot with Deal's service revolver.

"Will you quit takin' pictures!" Deal said, Orange Delight spilling onto his pants to join the cavalcade of stains.

"One more shot," Hastings pleaded, with his recruitment-poster grin. "This is a high-crime neighborhood. I've used up almost an entire roll of film here. I figure two rolls a shift will —"

"Time to check on our pal Brubaker," Deal said, braking as he yanked the wheel to the left. The car dipped into a violent U-turn and headed south on North Twelfth Street. Hastings began to hum what sounded like a military march as he fidgeted with his camera.

Deal parked across the street from Brubaker's apartment. Most of the building was dark, but there was a light showing in Brubaker's window. "Think he's home?" Hastings asked.

"It's too hot to worry about it," Deal answered. "Let's sit here a while and see if we can spot him coming or going, or crossing our line of sight in the window. We might as well be here as cruising around — it's so hot most of the criminals are taking a break."

82

"They're waiting for the streets to cool," Hastings said. "We're not the only ones who've been working nights the past few weeks."

Deal didn't laugh. Hastings wasn't joking. Nighttime wasn't cool, but the temperature usually did fall to below a hundred degrees. A lot of daytime activities had been relegated to the night. He kept the engine running. The air conditioner was on high but the car was still stifling. He could feel the heat radiating from the rolled-up windows. He shifted his 240 pounds and fired up one of his abominable cheap cigars that made Hastings sick.

"Edward Eight," the dispatcher's metallic voice crackled from the radio. "Code Seventeen at six fifty-four Allister."

"Us," Deal said, and barked acknowledgment into the microphone before the call to investigate a domestic disturbance could be repeated.

"Just a minute," Hastings said, gripping Deal's shoulder. "Look." He pointed to Brubaker's window.

A man's shadow passed the window, then passed again in the opposite direction, as if pacing.

"Okay," Deal said, "so we know he's home." He put the car in gear.

"Keep the car still for a few more seconds," Hastings said. He raised his camera, held it steady, and waited for the shadowy figure to cross behind the window again. *Snick, whir.* "Got him!"

Deal stamped down on the accelerator, then switched on the siren and the rooftop cherry light.

Beside him, Hastings loaded another roll of film into the camera and cranked down his window to let some of the cigar smoke out of the car.

The domestic disturbance turned out to be a squabble

between neighbors over a dog that had leaped a fence and snatched a steak from a spilled bag of groceries. By the time Deal and Hastings arrived, the husbands, wives, and children were exhausted from screaming at each other in the heat. Under the baleful eyes of neighbors on lighted porches and behind windows, the matter was soon resolved without the necessity of arresting anyone. The dog lost interest in the steak and trotted away, glancing back placidly over its shoulder.

"Why don't you get a shot of that dog?" Deal asked Hastings.

By the end of the shift both men were tired. There was no way not to be affected by the simmering weather. When Deal handed over the patrol-car keys to the day shift, Sergeant Lowry, who was assigned to the car, grinned and pointed as Hastings was walking away. "What's that your partner's carrying?"

"Vacuum cleaner and a camera," Deal replied unsmilingly. He had been sapped of his sense of humor.

"Eggers wants to see you and Hastings," Lowry added, lowering himself into Edward Eight.

Deal caught up with Hastings and they went together to Captain Eggers' office.

In the anteroom Eggers used for interrogation sat Arnie Brubaker. Eggers and Sergeant Hall were with him.

Eggers was a truck of a man gone to fat, but not so much fat that muscle didn't still show on his wide frame. He had a florid pug face that gave the impression he might bite. The white-haired, elderly Sergeant Hall was standing against one wall, looking more apprehensive than Brubaker.

Eggers was bending over Brubaker, who was sitting comfortably in a wooden chair with his legs crossed. When the captain saw Deal and Hastings enter, he stood up straight and glared down at Brubaker with contempt. Brubaker smiled. He had a disarming smile. He was a dapper, amiable-looking man whose specialty was preying on senior citizens.

"We have a bad situation," Eggers told Deal and Hastings. "An eighty-year-old invalid named Edna Croft was found unconscious in her apartment on North Twelfth about three hours ago."

"I remember the squeal," Deal said. "It came down just after we went out of service to drive to a burglary-alarm call over on Freemont, Charles Eight took the North Twelfth call."

"We'd been driving up and down North Twelfth much of the night," Hastings said. "I used a lot of film there. It's a particularly crime ridden environment, as you know, the result of population displacement and urban decay."

"Yeah," Eggers said, cocking his head to the side and squinting at Hastings as if to fix him in his mind. "A neighbor who works nights dropped in to check on Edna Croft and make sure she was awake to take some prescription medicine, found her comatose, and called us. The temperature in the apartment was a hundred and three."

Deal could picture the buildings on North Twelfth, old brick two-story structures with flat tar roofs. He winced as he thought of the old woman languishing in the sweatbox of an apartment.

Eggers continued. "Sometime during the night, the neighbor says, Edna Croft's portable TV was stolen from her apartment."

"Maybe the neighbor took it," Brubaker suggested.

"Shut up, Mr. Brubaker," Eggers said, meaning all but the "mister." Brubaker was about to say more, then thought better of it. "We all know Mr. Brubaker's M.O.," Eggers

85

went on. "We're familiar with how he allegedly makes his living by burglarizing the homes of the very old. Good business that, because even if he's caught his lawyer manages to stall the case until the victim either expires or can be accused of senility. Either way, the victim can't effectively testify against Mr. Brubaker."

"If I'm not being charged," Brubaker said patiently, "I think I'll wander on home."

Eggers rested a broad hand on his shoulder, and Brubaker sat still and sighed. What was the law, an instrument for harassment? "I'd phone my lawyer," he said, "only I don't believe we'll reach that point. Because we all know I don't deserve this heat. But I'm getting tired of seeing a cop car outside my apartment every time I look out the window."

Eggers ignored him and drew Deal and Hastings into the main office. He closed the door on the interrogation room. "You guys were supposed to keep an eye on Brubaker. Was he home last night?"

"He was there at eleven thirty-two, sir," Hastings said. "We checked his place of residence several times through the night and there was always a light on, but the eleven thirty-two time is the only one we can confirm on the basis of physical sighting."

Eggers stared at Hastings.

"Verification by way of a photograph, sir," Hastings added.

"What?"

"He means he took Brubaker's picture when he walked past his window," Deal explained.

Eggers looked perplexed. "Why did you do that?"

"He's an incurable shutterbug," Deal cut in, before Hastings could launch into an endless explanation.

"That would help provide an alibi for Brubaker," Eggers said bleakly, and even Hastings knew enough to keep quiet.

"How long can we hold Brubaker?" Deal asked.

"About five more minutes," Eggers said. "Which is when I expect a report from Identification."

Even before he'd finished speaking, the desk phone buzzed. Eggers picked up the receiver, punched the blinking line button, and as he listened his face glowed and became almost handsome.

"That was I.D.," he said, replacing the receiver. "Brubaker made a mistake. There was a fingerprint on the window frame of Edna Croft's apartment, and it belongs to him. That's enough to get a search warrant for his apartment." He charged into the interrogation room.

Brubaker was standing up, tucking in his shirt.

"Sit back down," Eggers commanded. He informed Brubaker that he was under arrest and began reading him his rights.

Brubaker sat tolerantly until Eggers was finished. He was a pro. He realized he must have dropped a print. "I was in that lady's apartment about a week ago," he said, "to ask if she needed any odd jobs done. She gave me a portable television to fix for her. It's in my apartment now."

"We'll see what she says about that," Eggers told him, "as soon as she regains consciousness."

Brubaker shrugged with exaggerated nonchalance and grinned. "I think I'll make that call to my lawyer."

Sergeant Hall escorted Brubaker to the front desk, where he would be booked and allowed his phone call.

As Deal and Hastings were about to leave Eggers' office, the phone buzzed again. This time Eggers' face changed for the worse as he listened. He aged a decade in the time the receiver went from his ear back to its cradle.

"Edna Croft died ten minutes ago," he said glumly. "Another heatstroke victim." He slammed a meaty fist into his palm. "Now there's no one to refute Brubaker's story, no one to testify against him. There's no way to get a conviction when the victim is dead. Legally, it's almost impossible to prove that a crime has even taken place."

"When are you going to release Brubaker?" Deal asked.

"Now," Eggers snapped. "I have to."

When Deal joined Hastings the next evening after muster, Hastings had already vacuumed the patrol car and was standing beside it waiting for him. Deal was tired. The business with Brubaker had disturbed him and he hadn't been able to sleep this morning. He'd spent most of the day downing popcorn and beer and watching a ball game on television. Hastings looked as if he'd spent the entire day getting a facial and having his uniform pressed.

"Let's get going," he said as Deal approached. "We've been given the pleasure of arresting Arnie Brubaker."

Deal's eyebrows arched in disbelief. "Says who?"

"Captain Eggers. I talked to him this afternoon at his home."

"You went to Eggers' house when he was off duty and weren't thrown out?" Deal stared incredulously as Hastings nodded.

"We don't have much time," Hastings said, climbing in behind the steering wheel. "The news media have already received anonymous phone calls instructing them what time to be at the precinct house."

"Anonymous phone calls?" Deal said. "How would you know that?"

Hastings started the car and they drove from the garage. "I'll explain it all in good time," he said.

* * * * *

They interrupted Brubaker's late-night snack, which Brubaker angrily pointed out to them as they entered his apartment. Deal gazed at the half eaten burned pizza on the formica table and didn't see why Brubaker minded being interrupted.

"I thought this burglary charge was all settled," Brubaker said, glancing at a portable TV on the floor in a corner.

"I talked to a social worker who delivered a portable fan to Edna Croft last night," Hastings said. "Edna Croft was a complete invalid. The social worker put her to bed, then stayed to visit with her, watching the *Tonight Show* on the television set you said the deceased gave you last week to repair for her."

Brubaker's pale eyes reflected an uneasy moment, then hardened. "Finish what you came to say. The anchovies on my pizza are getting cold."

"At twelve-twenty A.M. I took a photograph that included Edna Croft's apartment building. She lived in a one-room efficiency. It has only one window. In the photograph, which I had enlarged, that window is open, and you can even see a corner of the portable fan sitting inside it — all exactly the way the social worker says she left things around twelve-thirty. Which means that you had to steal that TV and leave your fingerprint *after* that time, and before Edna Croft was found unconscious."

Brubaker sneered. "So you can place me in the apartment last night. Haven't you heard?" he said. "The old lady died. It's kinda difficult for the prosecutor to make a case when there's no victim around to press charges or testify."

"Murder victims never press charges or testify," Hastings pointed out.

"Murder?" A puzzled wildness entered Brubaker's eyes.

89

Deal moved between him and the door.

"Edna Croft died of heatstroke," Hastings said. "My photograph shows her window the way the social worker says she left it — open. When Edna Croft was discovered unconscious in that oven of a room, her window was closed. She couldn't have gotten out of bed to close it even if she'd wanted to. You closed it behind you on your way out, which resulted in her death. Causing a death during the commission of a felony is second-degree murder. And that's what I'm placing you under arrest for — murder." He began informing Brubaker of his rights, reciting from memory.

Brubaker bolted for the open window to the fire escape. Deal hit him behind the knees with a shoulder in a perfect flying tackle. Brubaker grunted and dropped hard, his upper body slamming against the window sill. Deal dragged him back to the center of the room and handcuffed him just as Hastings was finishing his recitation.

It was a neatly tied package, Deal thought, lifting Brubaker to his feet. Hastings' photograph and statement would substantiate the social worker's testimony and the stolen television set would be the kind of hard physical evidence a jury couldn't ignore. And it was all possible because Hastings had compared his photograph with the report stating that Edna Croft's window was closed when she was discovered dying.

With the television set loaded into the trunk of the patrol car, Deal drove them back to the precinct house. As they pulled into the garage with their prisoner, he noticed several TV-news vans parked nearby. He let Hastings lead the subdued Brubaker toward the stairs to the booking area where the press would be congregated, then as they were almost to the steps he called Hastings' name and both men turned.

"Hold that pose," Deal said, aiming Hastings' camera at

90

policeman and prisoner. *Snick, whir.* "*One* of you is gonna like this picture!"

Hastings smiled handsomely even though he knew there was no film in the camera. Just to get in the practice.

Life Sentence

Marvin Millow lay quietly, feeling the somehow unfamiliar rhythm surge through his body. For a moment, just a fraction of a second, he'd thought he was dead, but now with logical disappointment and instinctive joy he realized the operation had been a success. It didn't surprise him, but still he'd hoped for death.

Millow was remembering vaguely now as he came out of the anesthetic that had blanked his mental processes for the past five days. He'd been eating dinner and watching the telescreen in his cell (some ridiculous ad about the new turbine cars) and suddenly the pain had shot through his chest. Then had come the clatter of his food tray on the cement floor, the hurried footsteps of the guards, the long, smooth ride on the motorized stretcher down the cell-lined halls as the other prisoners looked out with only mild interest. Their faces, Millow remembered, had been almost featureless, only pink blurs of expression behind the dizzying vertical gleaming bars rushing past.

Millow remembered his body being shifted around, an inhalator being fitted over his mouth and nose, the weakening struggle he'd put up, and now . . . now here he was, propped up slightly in his bed with his eyes open.

"How do you feel?" Dr. Steinmetz asked, and they both knew it really didn't matter, not even from a clinical standpoint. Millow was alive.

"I didn't make it," Millow croaked in a distant, sad voice.

"You should be glad to be alive," Dr. Steinmetz said. He

was a plump, shiningly clean man with dark framed glasses over very intelligent eyes. "You should be thankful for the excellent medical attention you receive."

"Why," the slow, faltering voice asked from the bed, "so I can go back to my cell now and do the same things I've done for sixty-three years?"

Dr. Steinmetz was turning on his best bedside manner. "You got life imprisonment with no eligibility for parole," he said. "There was a time, under archaic law, when you would have been sentenced to death. You did kill a man."

"I did," Marvin Millow said wearily. "I did kill a man."

Dr. Steinmetz smiled down at him as if he'd achieved some minor victory.

"It was my heart this time, wasn't it?" Millow asked.

"Yes, but it's all right now."

"You've given me a plastic heart?"

Dr. Steinmetz nodded. "The newest synthetic. There's no danger at all of the body rejecting it."

Millow closed his eyes. Why should there be any danger from this, after what he'd been through over the years? First had come the leukemia, when he was in his sixties, and they had completely replaced his blood with a fluoral carbon emulsion that served him just as well or better. Then had come the liver transplant, the artificial kidney, the abortive suicide attempt that had required only a few stitches, and six years ago the artificial lung. Despite all this, Millow was, in his own way, healthier now than he'd been in his twenties. Of course he *looked* ninety-six years old. It was the responsibility of the state to maintain his health, but the taxpayers didn't pay for cosmetic surgery.

"Are you all right?" Dr. Steinmetz asked, but he wasn't really curious. He too had unshakeable faith in modern medicine.

Millow didn't bother to open his eyes. His chest ached deeply with each breath and his body throbbed, but he was "'all right."

"Will they ever let me die, Doctor?"

"None of us is immortal," Steinmetz said. "On the outside you would have been dead twenty years ago. But here you're the state's responsibility." He was silent for a long moment. "You know, Marvin, you don't really *want* to die. None of us do."

"It seems that it should be my prerogative," Millow said with old bitterness.

"It should be," Steinmetz agreed. "And the man you killed should have had the same prerogative."

Millow opened his eyes and stared at the spotless white ceiling as the doctor left the small room and closed the door behind him.

The man he'd killed. But that had been so long ago. So very long ago. Was he now the same Marvin Millow who had carefully plotted and carried out the murder of his wife's lover? Could he ever have felt that strongly about anything, have had that much will? Could he ever have loved a woman as he must have loved Marian?

Millow remembered the Marian of his youth as if she'd been a character in a book he'd read years ago, or a cast member in a movie he'd seen at some time on the telescreen. That Marian didn't seem quite real to him now, didn't seem as if she ever had been real. Neither did Creighton, the man he'd killed. For that matter, had there ever been a tall, proud, dark-haired Marvin Millow who had breathed love so deeply he had killed for it? Of course there had been. But not anymore. Those fires had died now, and the ashes had long since blown away.

Marian had divorced him after the trial, and for over fifty

years Millow hadn't seen her or heard from her. Then one day seven years ago, with terrifying suddenness, she had visited him. She had looked so much older that Millow hardly recognized her. So much older! Her blonde hair had turned a lusterless gray, her full lips had become thin and sunken, her once graceful figure was now thick and stocky. It could be that she finally came to see him because in a strange way she was indebted to him. He had loved her enough to kill for her. And yet there might have been something else, something he could never fathom.

Every Sunday then, for the next three years, Marian came and sat and talked to him through the clear plexiglass shield. And then one Sunday she didn't come, and he heard that she'd died. That was all he heard, but he managed to clip her obituary from the newspaper, and he still had it, curled and yellowed, among his personal effects.

How was it he still missed Marian, not the young Marian who was only a dream, but the Marian who had come to visit him faithfully every Sunday afternoon for those three years? A man who was dead in everything but body should miss no one.

The accelerated healing pain in Millow's chest was growing. Strangely, as if the pain had been anticipated, a young intern entered and injected him with a sedative.

Days passed in dizzying cycles of wakefulness and sleep. Then one morning when Millow awoke Dr. Steinmetz was there, his eyes smiling behind the dark glass frames.

"You're progressing nicely, Marvin."

Millow said nothing. The pain was still in his chest, though not as bad, and he felt slightly nauseous most of the time.

"You should be well enough to have visitors soon,"

Steinmetz said, studying some X-rays he had in a yellow folder.

"Tell the warden he can see me anytime," Millow said, and immediately he was sorry he'd said it, for he saw that it gave Steinmetz some small satisfaction to see that the patient was recovering his sense of humor.

Millow drew a deep breath and focused his gaze on the doctor. "I almost died this time, didn't I?"

Dr. Steinmetz nodded. "It was rather close — until we got you to the operating room."

"I wish you had let me die," Millow said. "Just living is no reason to want to live. A man has to have *something,* some hope or interest in the future."

"You may be right," Steinmetz agreed, surprising Millow with his frank reply.

Millow let his head sink back into the soft white pillows. He only knew he didn't want to spend even one more endless night back in his cell, pacing on stiff, unwilling ninety-six-year-old legs, while the thing inside him paced.

"I'll check with you the beginning of next week," Dr. Steinmetz said, pinching the yellow folder closed and smiling.

"I'll be here," Millow said as the donor left and the door locked automatically behind him.

The room was as small and bland as Millow's cell, and like his cell there was no escape from it except death. But they were careful to eliminate even that avenue to freedom. Every item and furnishing in the rooms and cells of the prison were dull, soft and harmless as possible. If only one of the nurses or an intern would forget and leave a sharp instrument behind! A scissors, a glass bottle he could break! Anything! Millow sighed. He probably wouldn't even have time to bleed to death. They'd check him on the closed circuit viewscanner and pump more of the cursed artificial blood in him to prolong his artificial life.

As he'd promised, Dr. Steinmetz came to see Millow at the beginning of the week. The doctor looked unusually cheerful, even for him.

"How's the unwilling patient today?"

"Feeling better, damn you!"

Steinmetz laughed. "Yes, you must be improving, though naturally there's still some pain. You were on the operating table a long time."

"It still hurts," Millow said, "but not as much."

"You'll be on your feet shortly," Steinmetz said, "and as brooding and unhappy as ever."

"That's comforting."

A buzzer sounded, one long, one short. Dr. Steinmetz, his features set in an absent smile, looked up. "That's for me," he said to himself as much as to Millow. "I'll be back shortly." He turned and left the room.

But the door! He hadn't shut the door quite hard enough to latch it, and there was a slender strip of darkness where Millow could see out into the dim hall.

And instantly Millow knew what he would do. He would step out into the hall, and he would run, as fast as he could, away from this dread room, away from their life saving, life prolonging drugs. And when he felt that he must stop, he'd run harder, until something in his ancient, half natural body gave. Millow's lined face broke into a grin as he climbed painfully from the bed. Death by running.

He tested his legs carefully. Yes, there was enough strength in them, just enough. Millow moved to the door and peered through the crack out into the hall. There was no one, no one in sight. A pang of exultation shot through his body and he was out, out into the hall and running.

At first nothing happened, and Millow's strength surprised him. He felt rather ridiculous as he ran unnoticed, like some white flanneled, geriatric track star, his bare feet plopping regularly on the tile floor. Then the pain came, hot and sharp, and Millow groaned despite himself. He could imagine stitches popping, tissue tearing, and he made his legs strain harder to propel him forward. The hall ended, and he turned down the corridor lined with cells, and he was aware of those blank, pale faces staring out at him as he passed. The corridor was silent but for the sound of his footfalls and his labored breathing. The pain invaded his body again and stayed longer, causing Millow's breath to catch, his legs to buckle. He was on the cool tile floor without realizing he'd fallen, and he struggled to his feet and began to run again. He made only a few steps before the pain sapped the will from his mind and he collapsed, rolling slowly onto his back. This time he couldn't rise.

Millow lay there, feeling the pain come and go, for only a minute before he was aware of rushing, echoing footsteps drawing nearer. Leather soles and heels scuffing on the smooth tile. Dr. Steinmetz and two young interns were suddenly standing over him.

Steinmetz's face was angry and appraising as he bent over Millow and examined him. "Get a stretcher," he said calmly to one of the interns, who turned and ran.

Sighing deeply, Steinmetz stood, and the intern knelt and placed something soft beneath Millow's head.

"It's too late," Millow said in triumph, and he tasted blood in his mouth.

Steinmetz's face didn't change. He turned away for a moment, then turned again and knelt. Millow felt the bite of a hypodermic needle.

"Can we get him to the operating room in time?" the

young intern asked. "He's failing fast."

Failing fast. . . . The words were like a benediction.

There was a vast and growing darkness in Millow.

Darkness, gradually giving way to a burning red.

At first Millow thought he was dead, then with logical disappointment and instinctive joy he realized he was alive. He opened his eyes.

Dr. Steinmetz glanced up from whatever he was studying in the yellow folder and smiled down at Millow. "How's the unwilling patient today?"

Millow let his head sink deeper into the soft pillows. Dr. Steinmetz, the tiny white room he was in, the prison, all seemed to shrink until it was as if he were looking at them from a great distance. Then they disappeared altogether, and he was aware only of the throbbing that ran through his body, the inexorable beat, beat, beat of his artificial heart.

On Judgment Day

It's on this bleak Dublin morning that they're about to hang O'Hara. We go far back, do O'Hara and I, to the time when I was a youth of fourteen on my father's retreat and fishing resort on the wild North Coast.

It was then that O'Hara was the most wanted of the organization terrorists in Ireland, fresh from shooting the kneecaps off a treasonous pub owner in Londonderry. On the run, was O'Hara, and the English had never so much as caught a glimpse or obtained a description of who they were seeking. They chased a rumor here, a false lead there, and shadow was all they caught.

I remember when first I laid eyes on O'Hara. When I stumbled one bright afternoon into my father's office, straight from a hapless day's fishing, there was a giant red-headed man registering at the desk. He had on a short-sleeved shirt that revealed powerful forearms, and it was easy to imagine a ship or an eagle tattooed beneath the material stretched tight over his massive chest. There was the very smack of adventure in the way he talked and carried himself.

With the redheaded man, nearly hidden behind his bulk, was someone who, once caught in my eye, held me fascinated in my youth. *Kate* turned out to be her name. She was in her early twenties but seemed nearer my own age, so small and fine was she. The thing about her was in her crystal-brilliant green eyes and her gold hair that fell to her bone-narrow shoulders. When she saw me staring at her, she smiled tolerantly and mortally wounded me.

"Carry Mr. and Mrs. Muldoon's bags to their cabin, Johnny lad," said my father.

Gladly, I obeyed, hoisting a large case and a flowered valise.

"I'll just take this one, Johnny," said the redheaded Muldoon, and picked up a medium-sized leather suitcase as if it were empty, and followed me down the wooden steps and along the path to the secluded cabin on the edge of the green woods overlooking the green sea.

"Boats are free for those renting a cabin, and can be found down at the pier," I said to Muldoon in the cabin, looking all the while at Kate, who in some embarrassment looked away.

"Your father told me, lad," said the redheaded giant, and handed me down a pound note.

Over the next week, my enchantment with Kate didn't escape the notice of my parents, though my father said not a word. It was my mother who one day warned me, "You quit gaping at Mrs. Muldoon lest her husband throw you like a dart."

I didn't answer her but with a nod. I hadn't suspected I was so obvious.

It was that very night that I heard the arguing coming from the Muldoon cabin, angry voices I couldn't quite understand.

The next morning, Kate seemed beaten down, and there was a redness about her fine eyes.

"Is everything all right?" I impulsively asked her in a soft whisper, as I untied their fishing skiff from the pier.

She glanced at me, surprised, and nodded. I stood on the dock and watched the redheaded Muldoon steer the tiny boat out into a sea broken by the reef but still choppy and capped with foam.

For the first time, I experienced a strong protective instinct toward a woman, and I realized that while the Muldoons were out fishing, their cabin stood empty. Perhaps, if I looked, I might find some evidence of the red-headed giant mistreating his companion, or even holding her captive of sorts, and could bring about her rescue and gratitude. So it was that I, love-stricken fool, let myself into their cabin through a rear window.

I was disappointed to find nothing in the least unusual, except for a pretty pink dress that Kate would have no use for here. I ran the soft silk of it along my cheek and let it drop back into place on its hanger in the cedar closet. The thought of Kate in the dress was a sharp ache in me.

When I was about to leave, feeling ashamed, was when I spotted the corner of the leather suitcase, the one the red-headed man had insisted on carrying, beneath the bed. I dragged it out, unbuckled its thick straps, and opened it.

In the quiet, hot stillness of the cabin, I almost fell in a faint.

Inside the suitcase was a weapon I later learned was an Israeli Uzi submachine gun, as well as a pistol, and some substance in a wooden box that turned out to be plastique explosives. And there were newspaper clippings about the shooting of the pub owner in Londonderry the week before.

I drew in my breath, remembering then that O'Hara was rumored to like young girls and to bring them with him on his travels. "Sainted mother!" I said, actually crossing myself even as I closed the suitcase and placed it back under the bed exactly as I'd found it.

There was nothing for it but to tell my father. Not a political man, he. There was nothing for him to do but to telephone the law.

"You stay well clear of that cabin," he said to me, his face

102

ashen as he hung up the phone. "The English are sending a force for that man, and he won't go along peaceably, you can be sure."

I nodded, walked onto the back porch, and watched the sun inch down to the horizon. Excitement fueled my pounding heart. And something else.

I couldn't help it. I leaped from the porch and cut through the darkening woods to the Muldoon cabin. Through the window I looked, and saw them sitting at the tiny kitchenette table eating a light supper.

So I crept around to where their small Hillman sedan sat parked. Staying low, I opened the car's door, depressed the clutch with my hand, and slipped the shift lever into neutral. Then I shoved the car so that it rolled down the slight grade, off the dirt road, to rest against a tree. I swallowed then and knocked on the cabin door.

"Your car has rolled off, sir," I said, when the redheaded Muldoon himself answered my knock.

He craned his thick neck to look, then cursed. "Thank you, lad," he said, and walked toward the car, shutting the cabin door behind him.

Well, I couldn't just walk in, so I went back around to the rear of the cabin to where I'd peered in the window. Kate was still at the table, sipping tea from a cracked blue cup.

"Kate!" I whispered hoarsely, not having to speak loudly because the window was partially raised. Her head jerked around, long hair swinging in a graceful arc. At first she was shocked, then she smiled and walked over as I beckoned.

"They're coming for Muldoon!" I said.

Her green eyes widened, luminous in the failing light. "What?"

"The English are coming for this Muldoon you're with!"

103

I knew he wasn't her husband; he couldn't be! "He's O'Hara, the terrorist!"

She grinned and said, "Bosh to you, young Johnny."

"It's true, I swear! Look in the suitcase he keeps beneath the bed! Then get away before the shooting starts!" I could hear the hum of the Hillman's motor as Muldoon backed the car up the hill toward the cabin.

As I watched, Kate quickly dragged out the suitcase and looked at its militant contents. Her face grew frightened and sad.

"Out now, while you have the chance!" I pleaded.

She gazed at me with a curious kind of new respect I still hold dear, then she nodded and climbed out the window.

It wasn't ten minutes later that the English arrived to find the redheaded man on the cabin porch, looking for Kate. Smart and quick, he was. No sooner had they shouted a warning than he broke for one of their own vehicles sitting with its engine idling, ducking bullets as he ran.

Ten years ago it all happened. And now, finally, we've run O'Hara to ground and the dread hanging day is here.

I can picture O'Hara on the scaffold now, her crystal green eyes yet clear and defiant, her blond hair taken by the wind like a flaxen banner.

But no, that's a poetic misconception of my own devising. It's hoods the condemned wear when they're hanged; black hoods.

It had never occurred to me, so long ago, that O'Hara would be using a man for cover and diversion. For it was the same young woman — O'Hara herself — often reported in the company of whatever poor devil she was traveling with at the time. Like the hapless Muldoon, gunned down years ago, a victim of British bullets. O'Hara's guile, and my innocent heart.

Was it knowing Kate O'Hara that prompted my own life to change course so that I joined the organization as an undercover agent for the British? Was it a young boy not able to glimpse the steel and the killer's resolve within her?

It's true I can't forget her words to me before she melted into the woods behind the cabin, or the cool, light press of her lips on my own.

"God bless you, young Johnny Bender," she fervently whispered, "for helping a naive and foolish girl gone astray to return to family, safety and sanity!" So saying, she disappeared into darkness and time.

And never since have I trusted anyone.

Death by the Numbers

I saw in the morning paper that the chief of police said that if the present crime rate continued, within the next three years one out of every five citizens could expect to be a victim. I couldn't get concerned.

My breakfast toast had burned slightly and the charred scent lingered, rather pleasantly, throughout my well-furnished tenth floor condominium apartment. I walked into the modern, deep-carpeted living room with my third cup of strong black coffee. Yesterday had been my fifty-eighth birthday, and as I passed the mirror-tiled wall I glanced at my sallow but still handsome face. I laughed at my vanity.

The doorbell chimed curtly, as if to call time to my foolishness.

When I opened the door I was looking at a medium-height, broad shouldered man in his early thirties. I knew the type. He was wearing dark slacks and a checked sport coat with an elaborately knotted tie. He had thick black hair, strong dark eyes, strong white teeth and a high-voltage smile. He was high-voltage.

"Mr. Clark Stone?" he asked.

I said that I was.

His hand flicked out to give me a standard business card. When I glanced down at the card in that studiously poker-faced manner people use to glance at business cards, I saw that it was engraved with the words *Guarantee Insurance*.

"I'm Dan Bent," the man said, shaking my hand with

106

firm intimacy. "You told me on the phone yesterday that ten o'clock would be all right."

I remembered then that I had told him that yesterday, when my mind had been occupied with more important matters.

Bent pushed past me, still smiling, into the living room.

I shut the door and turned to face him as he sat down on the low-slung sofa and snapped open his leather attaché case in a businesslike manner.

"I don't need any more insurance, Mr. Bent."

Bent had heard those words before. "You do," he said. "You just don't know it yet."

He was cheerfully determined. I decided maybe the simplest thing to do was to hear him out, then send him on his way. His healthy white smile widened as I sat in a chair opposite him. Outside the tall window I could see three or four distant gulls circling.

"What do you think of statistics, Mr. Clark?" Bent asked.

"I don't like them. They're the closest thing to astrology."

Bent's face glowed with the newly acquired morsel of wisdom found in that analogy. "I never thought of it quite that way, but statistics do have a way of foretelling our fate. And you're . . . let's see, fifty-eight yesterday — right?"

I said that was right.

"Get ready to die, Mr. Clark."

It was a sales gambit designed to startle, and it worked.

"Not in the near future, perhaps," Bent added. "But when you do go, what will you leave behind?"

"It doesn't matter," I said. "I haven't any relatives, any favorite charities." I considered offering Bent a cup of coffee, then decided that would only prolong his visit.

"Oh, we know how alone you are, sir. We also know your net worth. And we know how when you were with Gem-

Stone Jewelers as an active partner, jewelry of . . . questionable origin was made accessible to potential buyers."

I stood up, propelled out of my chair by surprise and anger. Bent was smiling a challenge to me now, letting me know he could easily handle whatever my reaction might be. He was probably right. I smiled, too.

"Our research department is as thorough as any," he said.

"Just what does Guarantee insure, Mr. Bent?"

"Why, we deal in life insurance. We insure that nothing fatal is likely to happen to you in the near future. At least not at Guarantee's hands."

I laughed. The shakedown was out in the open. "And if I don't buy the policy?"

"Then we insure that something will happen."

"So you're an extortionist and Guarantee is a phony company."

"Not at all," Bent said with an injured air. "We mainly sell legitimate life insurance policies. Call it a front, if you will. But if you go to the police and repeat what I've told you, the company and I are able to deny this part of the conversation and still account for our existence and my visit here. And as I said, Mr. Clark, we're very much aware of your background."

I sat staring at Bent, envying him. He was a man playing with his deck, someone else's money and all the chips.

"How much are the premiums?" I asked.

Bent studied something inside his open attaché case. "Five thousand a year, half payable every six months. Not unreasonable, Mr. Clark."

"Guarantee must have a number of clients," I said, "to be able to be so reasonable."

Bent glanced up from the open case and nodded

brightly. "Oh, more than you can imagine. It's all done by computer, both the legal and illegal ends of our business. Statistically, we were bound to get to you sooner or later, Mr. Clark. If projected over a long enough period, statistics are one of the few sure things in this world. Death, taxes and statistics."

"You're quite a believer in statistics, aren't you."

Bent nodded, displaying his wide white smile. "Because we lease our computer and its memory bank to certain parties, we have access to the facts surrounding a great many illegal transactions everywhere in the country.

"This hard information, when crossed with reliable personal information, invariably links names to transactions. The computer is then fed more information concerning the bearers of those names, furnished by our research department, and it prints out prospective clients on a selective basis."

He cocked his head, his smile gaining candlepower. "And here I am."

"Sounds efficient," I had to admit. "Now let me understand the proposition. The policy costs me five thousand dollars a year, half payable every six months. And if I *don't* buy the policy, who knows what could happen to me tomorrow?"

Bent nodded again. I expected him to say "Guarantee knows," but he didn't. Statistically, I was sure that few of his carefully researched "clients" refused to buy the policy.

I ran my palms over my thighs to my knees and sighed, flicked at my pants leg creases. "How about a cup of coffee?" I asked.

"Thank you," Bent said. "Then we can settle the particulars, when and where to send the money, that sort of thing . . ."

He was all business, that one.

109

I went into the kitchen and rattled things around for a while.

When I returned, Bent was leaning forward on the low sofa, leafing through some papers in his attaché case.

"Instant okay?" I asked.

"Fine," he said.

I walked up behind him and plunged my longest butter knife exactly between his shoulder blades at an angle to the heart.

He sat up straight, turned and stared wide-eyed at me for that appalling breach of etiquette. His eyes asked me why, then they asked nothing and he slumped sideways on the sofa and started a gradual slide to the floor. The couch and carpet were ruined.

By the time you get this tape cassette at Police Headquarters I'll be . . . well, you'll find out where soon enough.

You see, Bent was right about statistics, but wrong in assuming they'd never catch up with him or Guarantee Insurance. Eventually the company was bound to approach someone like me, and the story could and would get out. I hadn't much choice, really.

I'd just been released from the hospital the day before, on my birthday. There was nothing more they could do, and with my medication I wasn't in any great pain. The doctors told me about the sort of cancer I had, how I could expect to live only a few more weeks, maybe not even that long.

What they were saying, when you boil away all the medical jargon, was that my number was up.

A Handgun for Protection

I had to have her. Lani Sundale was her name, and for the past three Saturday nights I'd sat at the corner of the bar in the Lost Beach Lounge and listened to her talk to her friends — another girl, a blonde — and a tall, husky guy with graying hair and bushy eyebrows. Once there was an older woman with a lot of jewelry who acted like she was the gray haired guy's wife. They'd sit and drink and gab to each other about nothing in particular, and I'd sit working on my bourbon and water, watching her reflection in the back bar mirror.

It wasn't until the second Saturday night, when she got a telephone call, that I learned her name, but even before that I was — well, let's say committed.

Lani was a dark haired, medium-height, liquid motion girl, shapely and a little heavier than was the style, like a woman should be. But with her face she didn't need her body. She really got to me right off: high cheekbones, upturned nose, and slightly parted, pouty little red lips, as if she'd just been slapped. Then she had those big dark eyes that kind of looked deep into a guy and asked questions. And from time to time she'd look up at me in the mirror and smile like it just might mean something.

The fourth Saturday night she came in alone.

I swiveled on my bar stool with practiced casualness to face her booth. "Where's your friends?"

She shrugged and smiled. "Other things to do." Past her outside the window, I could see the blank night sky and the huge Pacific rolling darkly on the beach.

111

"No stars tonight," I said. "You're the shiningest thing around."

"You're trying to tell me it's going to rain," she said, still with the smile. It was a kind of crooked, wicked little smile that looked perfect on her. "I drink whiskey sours."

I ordered her one, myself a bourbon and water, and sat down across from her in the soft vinyl booth. Two guys down the bar looked at me briefly with naked envy.

"Your name's Lani," I told her. She didn't seem surprised that I knew. "I'm Dennis Conners."

The bartender brought our drinks on a tray and Lani raised her glass, "To new acquaintances."

Three drinks later we left together.

It was about four when Lani drove me back to the Lounge parking lot to pick up my car. Hard as it was for me to see much in the dark, I knew we were in an expensive section of coast real estate where a lot of wealthy people had plush beach houses, like the beach house I'd just visited with Lani.

She drove her black convertible fast, not bothering to stop and put up the top against the sparse, cold raindrops that stung our faces. What I liked most about her then was that she didn't bother with the ashamed act, and when we reached the parking lot and the car had stopped, she leaned over, and gave me a kiss with that tilted little grin.

"See you again?" she said as I got out of the car.

"We'll most likely run across one another," I said with a smile, slamming the heavy door.

I could hear her laughter over the roar and screech of tires as the big convertible backed and turned onto the empty highway. I walked back to my car slowly.

During the next two weeks we were together at the beach house half a dozen times. The place spelled money, all right.

Not real big but definitely plush, stone fireplace, deep carpeting, rough sawn beams, modern kitchen, expensive and comfortable furniture. There was no place the two of us would rather have been, the way it felt with the heavy drapes drawn and a low fire throwing out its twisted, moving shadows. And the way we could hear that wild ocean curl up moaning on the beach, over and over again. It was a night like that, late, when she started talking about her husband.

"Howard's crippled," she said. "An automobile accident. He'll never get out of his wheelchair." She looked up at me as if she'd just explained something.

"How long ago?" I asked.

"Two years. It was his own fault. Drunk at ninety miles an hour. He can't complain."

"I've been drunk at ninety miles an hour myself."

"Oh, so have I." The shrug and tilted smile. "We all take our chances."

I wondered how much her husband knew about her. How much I knew about her. From time to time I'd marvelled at how skillfully she could cover up the bruises on her face and neck with makeup. She was all that mattered to me now, and it made me ache with a strange compassion for her husband, thinking how it would be watching her from a wheelchair.

"Let's get going," she said, standing and slipping into her suede high heeled shoes. "The fire's getting low."

I yanked her back by the elbow. Then I walked over and put another log on the fire.

Where I lived, at a motel in North Beach, was quite a comedown from the beach house love nest. During the long days of dwindling heat and afternoon showers I'd lie on my bed, sipping bourbon over ice and thinking about Lani and myself. I'm no kind of fool, and I knew what was happening didn't exactly tally. With her money and looks Lani could have had her choice of big husky young ones, her kind. I never kidded myself; I was over thirty-five, blond hair getting a little thin and once-athletic body now sporting a slight drinker's paunch. Not a bad looking guy, but not the pick of the litter. And my not-so-lucrative occupation of water skiing instructor during the vacation season would hardly have attracted Lani. I already owed her over five hundred dollars she never expected to get back.

Maybe any guy in my situation would have wondered how he'd got so lucky. I didn't know or really care. I only knew I had what I wanted most. And even during the day I could close my eyes and lean back in my bed five miles from sea and hear the tortured surf of the rolling night ocean.

"He has more money than he could burn," Lani said to me one night at the beach house.

"Howard?"

She nodded and ran her fingernails through the hair on my chest.

"You're his wife," I told her. "Half of all he owns is yours and vice versa."

"You're something I own that isn't half his, Dennis. We own each other. I feel more married to you than to Howard."

"Divorce him," I said. "You'd get your half."

She pulled her head away from me for a moment and looked incredulous.

"Are you kidding? The court wouldn't look too kindly on a woman leaving a cripple. And Howard's really ruthless. His lawyers might bring out something from my past."

"Or present."

She tried to bite my arm and I pulled her back by the

114

hair. I knew what she'd been talking toward and I didn't care. I didn't care about anything but her. She was twisting her head all around, laughing, as I slapped her and shoved her away. She was still laughing when she said it.

"Dennis, there's only one —"

I interrupted her. "I'll kill him for you," I said.

We were both serious then. She sat up and we stared at each other. The twin reflections of the fire were tiny star-points of red light in her dark eyes. I reached for her.

The beach house was where we discussed the thing in detail, weighing one plan after another. We always met there and nowhere else. I'd conceal my old sedan in the shadows behind a jagged stand of rock and walk down through the grass and cool sand to the door off the wooden sun deck. She'd be waiting for me.

"Listen," she said to me one night when the sea wind was howling in gusts around the sturdy house, "why don't we use this on him?" She opened her purse and drew out a small, snub-nosed .32 caliber revolver.

I took it from her and turned it over in my hand. A compact, ugly weapon with an unusual eight shot cylinder, the purity of its flawless white pearl grips made the rest of it seem all the uglier.

"Whose?" I asked.

Lani closed her purse and tossed it onto the sofa from where she sat on an oversized cushion. "Howard gave it to me just after we were married, for protection."

"Then it can be traced to you."

She shook her head impatiently. "He bought it for me in Europe, when he was on a business trip in a communist block country. Brought it back illegally, really. I looked into this thing, Dennis. I know the police can identify the type and make of weapon used from the bullet, only this make gun won't even be known to them. All they'll be able to say for sure is it was a .32 caliber."

I looked at her admiringly and slipped the revolver into my pants pocket. "You do your homework like a good girl. How many people know you own this thing?"

"Quite a few people were there when Howard gave it to me three years ago, but only a few people have seen it since. I doubt if anybody even knows what caliber it is. I know I can pretend I don't."

She was watching me closely as I thoughtfully rubbed the back of my hand across my mouth. "What happens if the police ask you to produce the gun? Nothing to prevent them from matching it with the murder bullet then."

Lani laughed. "In three years I lost it! Let them search for it if they want. It'll be at the bottom of the ocean where you threw it." She was grinning secretively, her dark hair hanging loose over one ear and the makeup under one eye smudged.

"Why not let me in on your entire plan?" I said. "The whole thing would come off better."

"I didn't mean to take over or anything. I just want it to be safe for you, baby, for both of us. So we can enjoy afterward together."

I wondered then if afterward would be like before.

"I know this gun is safe," Lani went on. "No matter where you got another one the police might eventually trace it. But with this one they can't."

"Is it registered or anything?"

"No, Howard just gave it to me."

"But the people who saw him give it to you, couldn't they identify it?"

"Not if they never saw it again." She took a sip of the expensive blended whiskey she was drinking from the bottle and looked up smiling at me with her head tilted back and kind of resting on one shoulder. "I think I've got an idea you'll like," she said. Her lips were parted wide, still glistening wet from the whiskey.

That's how three nights later I found myself dressed only in swimming trunks and deck shoes, seated uncomfortably in the hard, barnacle-clad wooden structure of the underside of the long pier that jutted out into the sea from Howard Sundale's private beach. To the right, beyond the rise of sand, I could see the lights of his sprawling hacienda style house as I kept shifting my weight and feeling the spray from the surf lick at my ankles. I'd always considered myself small time, maybe, not the toughest but smart, and here I was killing for a woman. There'd been plenty of passed up opportunities to kill for money. I knew it wasn't Lani's money at all; I'd have wanted her rich or poor.

I unconsciously glanced at my wrist for the engraved watch I'd been careful not to wear, and I cursed softly as the white foaming breakers surged out their rolling lives beneath me. It *had* to be ten o'clock!

Lani had guaranteed me that Belson, her husband's chauffeur and handyman, would bring Howard for his nightly stroll out onto the long pier at ten o'clock.

"Belson always wheels him there," she'd said. "It's habit with them. Only this time I'll call Belson back to the house for a moment and he'll leave Howard there alone — for you."

The idea then was simple and effective. I was to climb up from my hiding place, shoot Howard, strip him of ring, watch and wallet, then swim back along the shoreline to near where my car was hidden and drive for North Beach Bridge, where I'd throw the murder gun into deep water.

At first I'd been for just rolling Howard wheelchair and

all into the ocean. But Lani had assured me it was better to make it look like murder and robbery for the very expensive ring he was known to wear. Less chance of a mistake that way, she'd argued, than if we tried to get tricky and outwit the police by faking an accident. And Howard's upper body was exceptionally strong. Even without the use of his legs he'd be able to stay afloat and make his way to shore.

So at last we'd agreed on the revolver.

I looked up from my place in the shadows. Something was passing between me and the house lights. Two forms were moving through the night toward the pier: Howard Sundale hunched in his wheelchair, and Belson, a tall, slender man leaning forward, propelling the chair with straight arms and short but smooth steps.

As they drew nearer I saw that the lower part of Howard's body was covered by a blanket, and Belson, an elderly man with unruly curly hair, was wearing a light windbreaker and a servant's look of polite blankness. They turned onto the pier and passed over me, and I crouched listening to the wheelchair's rubber tires' choppy rhythm over the rough planks.

A minute later I heard Lani's voice, clear, urgent. "Belson! Belson, will you come to the house for a minute? It's important!"

Belson said something to Howard I couldn't understand. Then I heard his hurried, measured footsteps pass over me and away. Then quiet. I drew the revolver from its waterproof plastic bag.

Howard Sundale was sitting motionless, staring seaward, and the sound of the rushing surf was enough to cover my noise as I climbed up onto the pier, checked to make sure Belson was gone, then walked softly in my canvas deck shoes toward the wheelchair.

"Mr. Sundale?"

He was startled as I moved around to stand in front of him. "Who are you?"

Howard Sundale was not what I'd expected. He was a lean faced, broad shouldered, virile looking man in his forties, keen blue eyes beneath wind-ruffled sandy hair. I understood now why Lani hadn't wanted me to risk pushing him into the sea. He appeared momentarily surprised, then wary when I brought the gun around from behind me and aimed it at him. His eyes darted for a moment in the direction of the distant house lights.

"For Lani, I suppose," he said. Fear made his voice too high.

I nodded. "You should try to understand."

He smiled a knowing, hopeless little frightened smile as I aimed for his heart and pulled the trigger twice.

Quickly I slipped off his diamond ring and wristwatch, amazed at the coolness of his still hands. Then I reached around for his wallet, couldn't find it, discovered it was in his side pocket. I put it all in the plastic bag with the revolver, sealed the bag shut, then slipped off the pier into the water. As I lowered myself I found I was laughing at the way Howard was sitting motionless and dead in the moonlight, still looking out to sea as if there was something there that had caught his attention. Then the cold water sobered me.

I followed the case in the papers. Murder and robbery, the police were saying. An expensive wristwatch, his wallet and a diamond ring valued at over five thousand dollars the victim was known always to wear were missing. At first Belson, the elderly chauffeur, was suspected. He claimed, of all things, that he'd been having an affair with his employer's wife and was with her at the time of the shooting.

That must have brought a laugh from the law, especially with the way Lani looked and the act she was putting on. Finally the old guy was cleared and released anyway.

The month Lani and I let pass after the funeral was the longest thirty days of my life. On the night we'd agreed to meet, I reached the beach house first, let myself in and waited before the struggling, growing fire that I'd built.

She was fifteen minutes late, smiling when she came in. We kissed and it was good to hold her again. I squeezed the nape of her neck, pulled her head back and kissed her hard.

"Wait . . . Wait!" she gasped. "Let's have a drink first." There was a fleck of blood on her trembling lower lip.

I watched her walk into the kitchen to mix our drinks.

When she returned the smile returned with her. "I told you it would work, Dennis."

"You told me," I said, accepting my drink.

She saw the pearl handled revolver then, where I'd laid it on the coffee table. Quickly she walked to it, picked it up and examined it. There was surprise in her eyes, in the down-turned, pouting mouth. "What happened?"

"I forgot to throw it into the sea, took it home with me by mistake and didn't realize it until this afternoon."

She put the gun down. "You're kidding?"

"No, I was mixed up that night. Not thinking straight. Your husband was the first man I ever killed."

She stood for a moment, pondering what I'd said. After a while she took a sip of her drink, put it down and came to me.

"Did the police question you about the gun?" I asked her.

"Uh-hm. I told them it was lost."

"I'll get rid of it tonight on my way home."

"Tomorrow morning," Lani corrected me as her arms

120

snaked around my shoulders. "And we'll meet here again tomorrow night . . . and the night after that and after that . . ."

Despite her words her enthusiasm seemed to be slipping. That didn't matter to me.

Lani was the first one at the beach house the next evening. It was a windy, moon-bright night, only a few dark clouds racing above the yellow dappled sea at right-angles to the surf, as she opened the door to my knock and let me in. Her first words were what I expected.

"Did you get rid of the gun?"

"No." I watched her eyes darken and narrow slightly.

"No? . . ."

"I'm keeping it," I said, "for protection."

"What do you mean, Dennis?" The anger crackled in her voice.

I only smiled. "I mean I have the revolver, and I've left a letter to be opened in the event of my death telling a lawyer where it's hidden."

Lani turned, walked from me with her head bowed then wheeled to face me "Explain it! It doesn't scare me and I know it should."

"It should," I said, crossing the room and seating myself on the sofa with my legs outstretched. "I wiped the gun clean of prints when I brought it here, then lifted it by a pencil in the barrel when I left here after you last night. Your fingerprints are on it now, nice and clear."

She cocked her head at me, gave me a confused, crooked half-smile. "So what — it's my gun. My prints would naturally be on it."

"But yours are the *only* prints on it," I said. "No one could have shot Howard without erasing or overlapping them. Meaning that you had to have handled the weapon

121

after the murder — or during. If that gun ever happened to find its way to the police . . ."

Her eyebrows raised.

"I could tell them I found it," she said with a try for spunk, "and then it was stolen from me."

"They wouldn't believe you. And it isn't likely that anyone would take the gun without smudging or overlapping your prints. What the law would do is run a ballistics test on it, determine it was the murder weapon then arrest you. What's your alibi?"

"Belson —"

"You'd be contradicting your own story. And I doubt if Belson would come to your defense now. No one would believe either of you anyway. Then there's that past you mentioned."

I grinned, watching the fallen, trapped expression on her pouting face. A bitter, resigned look widened her dark eyes. When I rose, still grinning, and moved toward her she backed away.

"You're crazy!" Fear broke her voice and she raised her hands palms out before her. "Crazy!"

"It's been said," I told her as calmly as I could.

I made love to her then, while the moon-struck ocean roared its approval.

Afterward she lay beside me, completely meek.

"We were going to be together anyway, darling, always," she whispered, lightly trailing her long fingernails over me. Her fingernails were lacquered pale pink, and I saw that two of them were broken. "It doesn't matter about the revolver. I don't blame you. Not for anything."

She'd do anything to recover the gun, to recover her freedom.

"I'm glad," I said, holding her tight against me, feeling

the blood-rush pounding in her heart.

"It doesn't matter," she repeated softly, "doesn't matter."

That's when I knew the really deadly game was just beginning.

Prospectus on Death

Roger Tabber sat quietly behind the wide desk in his private office, listening to the muted sounds of the traffic streaming below him on Seventh Avenue. He was visible really from three angles, for the plush office was furnished with several huge mirrors stretching from floor to ceiling, to give the impression of space. It was the nature of Tabber's business that he spent much time confined to his office, and he wanted to spend that time in an unstifled atmosphere conducive to decision-making. The three Roger Tabbers were men of about fifty, beginning to gray, with handsome, aggressive faces becoming slightly padded with the excess flesh of middle age. They lifted their right arms simultaneously and picked up the telephone receiver.

"Louis?" Tabber said into the telephone. "Give me a quote on Laytun Oil."

"I see," Tabber said after a pause. He drummed his fingers on the smooth desk top, letting the man on the other end of the line wait. "Buy me five hundred shares," he said then. "I'll talk to you later, Louis."

Tabber hung up the phone and gazed around him at the many handsomely framed charts hanging on the walls, at the wide table in the office corner covered with more charts and graphs, financial reports, figure sheets on great corporations and small alike. With his pencil, with his ascending and descending lines and sheet after sheet of figures, Roger Tabber was able to keep his finger on the pulse of the stock market. As an independent speculator and investor he had to in order to stay in business.

Tabber was intimately familiar with the countless graphs around him, and he believed in them. If all the pertinent facts were known, almost anything could be reduced to a graph, could be analyzed, plotted, and, more importantly, predicted, at least to the degree that Roger Tabber had made a profitable business out of it.

When he'd returned from Haiti last year he had started the business, working out of his apartment, but soon the reams of graphs and assorted information, the tools of his trade, became too numerous. He was making plenty of money, so he rented this office on Seventh Avenue, had it lavishly decorated and had two telephones installed. Here, alone in his office with his charts and telephones, he was building his fortune.

Tabber gave a little start behind his desk at the knock on his door. It was most unusual for anyone to be calling on him at the office. He straightened his tie and called for the visitor to enter.

A tall, dark-complected man stepped into the office and closed the door behind him. He was broad-shouldered and muscular, though the trim cut of his dark-blue business suit made him appear almost slender. With a wide smile on his pleasant face, he glanced around him at the imposing graphs hanging upon the walls before advancing on the desk.

"Mr. Tabber," he said, extending his right hand, "I am Siano . . . of the Leasia family."

Tabber's heart leaped as he shook hands. Well, there was nothing this man could do about it now, even if he were fully aware of what had really happened.

"Yes," Tabber said, "I know of the family from my stay in Haiti. And I have heard of you."

"I'm honored, sir," Siano said in his velvet, high-pitched voice. It was a cultured voice, grammatically precise, and Tabber could almost see the verbal punctuation in the air. "I have been a long time away from the island. It surprises me that you have heard of me."

"I heard you mentioned in a conversation about your father," Tabber said. "Your father, you know, is rumored to be a . . . What is it?"

"A hungan," Siano said pleasantly, "and it is good, sir, that you know I am of his family."

Again Tabber felt an irregularity in his heartbeat. He remembered now — native superstition. A hungan, or shaman as he'd heard them called, was a voodoo witch doctor. There was always talk of such nonsense when he was on the island; it had developed into quite a gimmick for the tourist trade. And this was Siano, one of the sons of the Leasia clan, well-traveled and educated in Europe — on some kind of foundation grant, no doubt.

"Well," Tabber said, "what is it that brings you to New York?"

"I will be here for some time," Siano said, "staying at the Hilshire, and I thought I would talk with you about the Sweet Kane Sugar Company."

"But . . ." Tabber shrugged, ". . . it no longer exists."

"I am aware," Siano said in a sad voice behind his smile. "Bankruptcy, liquidation — it was cruel."

"Cruel?" Tabber shook his head. "It was unavoidable."

Siano's smiling dark eyes met Tabber's directly. "You, sir, as the manager, should know better. After an entire tribe of people had migrated from their homes, after they had been promised wages to live on, you got them to help you strip the land and then liquidated the company, paying them no wages, leaving them to poverty and hunger."

Tabber pressed the flat of his hand on the desk. "But there simply *was* no money! Don't you understand?"

"I understand, sir, the mechanics of business," Siano said. "I know that the profits of Sweet Kane Sugar went to the parent company that owned most of the stock, that all assets went in various ways to the parent company so that when liquidation occurred there was nothing for the people. I am not inexperienced in the world of finance, sir."

Tabber drew a gold fountain pen from his pocket and began toying with it. "Well," he said, staring at the pen, "it does no good to talk about it how."

"That's true," Siano said, "but I must tell you that my people will not tolerate what happened. I, too, have called the Loa, I am also a hungan, and I have been sent to New York to see that death visits you."

Tabber's body stiffened in sudden shock. "And how do you propose to do that?" he asked in a tight voice.

"You needn't fear death by the hand of man," Siano said in his pleasant, smooth voice, "but death will come to you; death is on the way to you."

Tabber felt himself getting angry. "What the hell do you intend to do, stick pins in a doll or something? I don't believe in your malarkey any more than I believe in leprechauns, and I'm surprised an educated man like yourself does. You must know that voodoo works by the power of suggestion; the intended victim must believe in it or it's worthless. And I assure you I don't believe in it!"

"I am aware," Siano said calmly.

"I am aware, too," Tabber said angrily. "Now get the hell out."

He watched Siano smile and get up slowly. Tabber felt the hardness of his walnut desk top for reassurance. Around him were the wall charts, the square-cornered filing cabinets, the accouterments of commerce, of civilization, while below him he could hear the Seventh Avenue traffic passing below his window in an endless stream of reassuring noise and gleaming metal. This was New York, not Haiti. Was this savage in an expensive business suit out of his mind?

Siano turned and walked gracefully to the door. Tabber expected him to turn back and say something before leaving but he didn't.

Tabber sat motionless for a while, looking at the blank panel of the closed door. Then the heavy quiet of the office was broken by the jangle of one of the telephones on the desk. It was Louis, calling to tell Tabber that he had been able to buy Laytun Oil at 24 1/4.

Within a week Tabber had forgotten about Siano's visit, and there was no reason for him to remember it when he received the piece of mail from Snowden Investment Research advising him to consider buying Belfor Electronics. The letter, an ordinary form letter, was like hundreds of others that Tabber received each year. He was always deluged by mail from private research firms, hoping to get him to subscribe to their weekly or monthly newsletter at bargain rates; and like Snowden Investment Research, they often supplied sample tips to lure customers. Tabber tossed the letter onto a pile with the rest of his correspondence and promptly put it out of his mind.

Three days later he noticed that Belfor Electronics had risen almost three points, from 30 5/8 to 33 1/2. He began to watch it more carefully.

That same day another letter arrived from Snowden Investment Research, advising him again to buy Belfor Electronics. Tabber folded the letter and placed it in one of his desk drawers.

Belfor remained around 33 for the next week, then

128

Tabber received another letter telling him that, due to certain information they couldn't divulge, Belfor's stock was due for a sudden upsurge.

Tabber stared at the letter for a long time. Then he picked up the telephone and called his broker to inquire about Belfor Electronics and to ask for a prospectus.

Louis knew nothing about the stock that might suggest it would rise. Belfor was a fairly large company that made radio parts and showed a steady increase in earnings each year, though last quarter they had taken something of a beating due to the expense of opening a new plant.

The next day the prospectus on Belfor Electronics came in the mail, along with another letter from Snowden urging again the purchase of shares in the company. This time the letter was accompanied by a set of graphs showing the expected curve of Belfor's sales and profits into 1972. Tabber compared the graphs with the information on the prospectus and found that up to the last quarter they tallied exactly. Apparently Snowden Investment Research had done some accurate homework. But would their upward sweeping curve into the future be correct?

Belfor seemed to be a solid company at least, so after studying the prospectus Tabber picked up the phone and bought a hundred shares, just for a feeler.

Within a few clays Belfor Electronics stock was up to 38 1/4. Another letter and set of graphs arrived from Snowden Research, telling Tabber that Belfor was still a smart buy despite the rise, that the stock was destined to move higher very shortly. Tabber talked to Louis, who told him that there were rumors about Belfor now, about possible takeovers, mergers, government contracts, but only rumors. Tabber studied his charts from Snowden carefully, called Louis back and bought 500 shares.

Profit-taking drove Belfor stock down to 34, then it began to climb steadily on heavy volume. The news broke in the papers that Belfor Electronics had been awarded a fat government contract to make components for the space project, and by the end of the month the stock had soared to 47 3/8.

A letter came from Snowden Research, advising Tabber to hold all his Belfor stock, and this time, along with the letter and graphs, came a curious thing.

It was a carefully composed actuary chart from one of the biggest insurance companies in the country, showing the decreased life expectancy of people with a history of heart trouble at various ages. There was no explanation, only the chart. Perhaps it had been placed in the envelope by mistake — but Tabber had a history of heart trouble.

When the next letter from Snowden arrived, Tabber got a momentary jolt. Along with the usual information was a chart listing the unfavorable life-expectancy statistics for people who had suffered exactly the same type of heart attack that Tabber had suffered three years before. Smoking decreased the number of years these people had to live; being overweight cut more years from their lives; working in professions that tried the nerves was unfavorable; married ex-heart patients tended to live longer than those unmarried; rural patients outlived urban dwellers. As Tabber's eyes studied the deadly statistics he realized that all of these things, *all* of them applied to him.

It was then that he remembered Siano's visit and a flash of indignation and anger shot through him. Of course Tabber's heart attack hadn't been a secret, and Siano would have the money and resources to research him quite thoroughly. Imagine trying something like this! He lifted the telephone to call Siano at the Hilshire and vent his anger, then he thought better of it and replaced the receiver in its cradle. Why give the man the satisfaction of knowing he'd gotten his intended victim angry? Tabber cursed himself for becoming upset over such superstitious harassment and crumpled the information from Snowden and tossed it into the wastebasket. He noted as he did so, however, that Snowden still advised holding Belfor Electronics.

The next week, out of curiosity, Tabber inquired into Snowden Investment Research's address in Brooklyn and found it to be the address of a mortuary. That, he thought, was a nice touch.

That same afternoon another letter arrived from the fictitious Snowden Research, telling Tabber to sell Belfor Electronics. The letter stated that despite the government contract another unfavorable earnings report would drive the price of the stock down. There was another graph enclosed with the letter, a graph that made Tabber's breathing quicken and his right hand move unconsciously to his chest. At the top of the lined paper was the heading: Life And Projected Life Expectancy Of Roger Tabber. A thick black line started at the left side of the graph in a column marked Oct. 3rd, 1920, the date of Tabber's birth, rose through adolescence into adulthood, remained steady, curved downward into middle age, then dipped sharply at the date of his heart attack. Then the line went into a gradual decline, turned gray at today's date, extended to the end of the month and finally stopped completely.

Tabber reached for the telephone again to call Siano, but he paused, the receiver pressed to his ear, and instead called Louis and sold half his shares of Belfor Electronics stock.

A week later Belfor did issue a very unfavorable earnings report, and their stock plummeted. Tabber sold the rest of his shares at 43 and still made a nice profit. Letters from

131

Snowden were arriving almost daily now, accompanied by graphs and information sheets that predicted Tabber's demise. Tabber was becoming nervous, irritated at the slightest things, but the last thing he would do, the most unwise thing he could do, would be to call Siano and ask him to quit. He could call the police, of course, but what would they be able to prove? They would think that he, Tabber, was the superstitious fool.

It was the day the elevator was out of commission that it happened. Tabber had to climb the six flights of stairs to his office, but he took the steps slowly and carefully. His heart had been beating quickly and irregularly of late anyway, and after the operation his doctor had told him not to exert himself. Nevertheless, when he closed his office door behind him he was breathing quickly, too quickly. From the corner of his eye he saw the top of an envelope from Snowden Research sticking out of the wastebasket. *Did his heart skip a beat?* A waver of fear went through Tabber as he leaned on the door. Of course his heart *might* have skipped a beat! That was normal, he was out of breath, it had skipped a beat before.

Tabber drew a deep, steadying breath and began to cross the office toward his desk, and his heart did skip a beat, it *did!* His hand moved to his chest, wrinkling his white shirt front beneath his tie. Now his heart seemed to be beating irregularly, spasmodically!

Siano! Could it be possible? Was he actually able with his statistics and graphs to suggest to Tabber the moment of his death? Of course not! . . . But he had been right about Belfor Electronics stock, and Belfor Electronics stock had gone down!

Then Tabber felt the pain. It was a quick, subtle pain that might have been all in his mind, or might not have been. He felt his heart leap beneath his clutching fingers and fear shot up in him like a flame. Clumsily, he stretched out his left hand and supported himself on the desk, waiting for the next pain. It came, searing through his chest like fire, moving up and out, cutting off his breath, turning his arm to molten lead! Gasping, his face mottled and distorted, Tabber struggled around the desk to the telephones and dialed the first person he could think of. "Louis . . . !"

It was a massive heart attack, but not a fatal one. Afterward, though the doctors claimed Tabber was in critical condition and too ill to have visitors, they finally acquiesced to his demands to see his "old friend" Siano.

Tabber watched him come through the door to the tiny hospital room, somehow walking silently over the tile floor. Siano was immaculately groomed, as before, wearing a tailored dark suit and with the suggestion of a smile on his dark face. "They told me you wished to see me," he said pleasantly.

Tabber waited for the nurse to leave before answering, then he looked up at Siano. Siano had lost, Tabber told himself. Tabber had had his heart attack, but he was still living.

"You've caused this," he said to Siano in a hoarse voice. "You have caused me to be an invalid for the rest of my life if I'm wheeled out of here alive."

Siano smiled down at him. "You are the one who caused it, sir."

Tabber felt the anger stir in him, but he had promised himself that he'd stay calm. After all, it was just possible he'd have had his heart attack if Siano had never entered his life. That was the thing he really wanted to believe. He was not a superstitious man, but there was something he still didn't understand.

"I called you here to ask you one question," Tabber said, "and I want you to promise to tell me the truth."

Siano considered for a moment before answering. "I will give you that promise."

Tabber raised his head slightly from his pillow. "How did you know that Belfor Electronics stock would go up?"

Again Siano smiled down at Tabber, and his dark eyes seemed to grow deeper and darker. "I am on the board of directors, sir." He turned then, still smiling, and strode silently from the room.

From that day on Tabber struggled desperately to recover, but his heart had been severely damaged, irreparably damaged, and the chart at the foot of his bed showed a steady decline until death.

Understanding Electricity

Glistening with chrome and tinted glass, the headquarters of the Powacky Valley Light and Power Company soared needle-like fifty stories heavenward, as if taunting the lightning. In the building's top floor were the spacious ultramodern offices of the company's top executives, and in a tasteful outer office sat the moderately attractive, though impeccably groomed, Miss Knickelsworth. She smiled with her impeccably white teeth, lighting up her whole mouth if not her face and unchanging wide brown eyes, and said, "Mr. Appleton from out of town is already in the conference room, Mr. Bolt."

B. Bainbridge Bolt, president of Powacky Valley Light and Power, revealed his own capped dentures, nodded, and strode briskly past her and through a tall doorway. He was the "human dynamo"-type executive in image and action, and was proud to think of himself as such.

Behind Bolt, Elleson of Pubic Relations entered the office with a PR smile for Miss Knickelsworth as he strode through the tall doorway.

Five minutes later young Ivers, regional vice president and renowned hard charger, went into the conference room. The smile he flashed on Miss Knickelsworth was his bachelor's best, but she responded with the blank expression that had earned her the company title of "Miss Resistor" two years running.

Grossner of Advertising followed Ivers in, then old Stabler of Customer Relations, who was something of a fixture with the company. The tall doors were silently closed on the

135

outer office wherein sat Miss Knickelsworth, and after orderly hellos and introductions the immaculately attired, somehow similar men all sat down at a long tinted-glass conference table with gleaming chrome legs and trim. The table matched the glass-and-metallic decor of the large room. Everyone had his accustomed place at the long table but for Appleton from out of town, who remained where he'd been sitting at ease in his chrome-armed chair at the opposite end of the table from B. Bainbridge Bolt, who cleared his throat and drew a slip of paper from his attaché case.

With a nod to Appleton from out of town, Bolt said, "There is some business to be discussed before we get on to Mr. Appleton's investigation of yesterday's five o'clock power failure . . . if Mr. Appleton agrees."

"Surely," Appleton said, nodding ever so slightly his handsome head of flawlessly combed graying hair.

"We have something of a public relations problem," Bolt went on, "concerning our last raise in the rates for electricity. Let me read you this note that arrived in the morning mail."

He placed gold-rimmed reading glasses on the narrow bridge of his nose and glanced commandingly at each man. The note read:

Gentlemen:
  I was shocked by your letter stating that my monthly bill was ten days past due. At your current rates, I'm afraid that you find me a little short. However, I do believe ten days is rather a brief period of neglect and that it does not behoove a company of your stature to conduct yourself in such a negative manner. In farewell, I regretfully must fuse and refuse to send your requested remittance, and as another futile outlet

for my frustration I have wired my congressman direct.

> *Tired of plugging away,*
> *A. C. McCord*

Bolt lowered the slip of paper, sat back, and sipped on a glass of juice from the silver tray Miss Knickelsworth had left on the table.

After a pause, Stabler of Customer Relations said, "The work of a madman in its phrasing, but other than that it seems the usual sort of letter we receive."

"There's one other difference," Bolt said dramatically. "This is a suicide note."

"That should solve part of our problem right there," young Ivers said. "Especially since this McCord was obviously unbalanced when he wrote such a letter."

"How did he commit suicide?" Stabler asked.

"He wrote and mailed this note yesterday," Bolt said, resting his large clean palms on the metal table trim. "He left a carbon copy in his home; then, during our Karl and Karla Killowatt commercial before the five o'clock news yesterday afternoon, he pulled his radio into the water in his bathtub with him."

Grossner of Advertising looked concerned.

Bolt sat unnaturally still, as if waiting for something.

"Wait a minute!" young Ivers said. "Is this McCord —"

"Still alive." Bolt finished the sentence without a question mark.

"Of course!" Elleson said. "The power failure at five yesterday! It must have coincided with his pulling the radio into the tub with him."

"Almost," Bolt said. "McCord was found stunned, in a state of shock, but still alive. He'd also left a message for a reporter friend, explaining what he was going to do, and his

137

story was written up in the papers for tonight's late edition."

"But the man's obviously a maniac," Ivers said.

"Remember," Grossner cautioned, "our last rate increase was legal but not what an uneducated public would call ethical."

"They were notified of the public hearings," Ivers said, referring to the public notices in the newspapers that Elleson and Grossner had cleverly worded for maximum confusion.

"There were the necessary three people at the meeting," Elleson said. "The vote constituted a majority."

"No one is arguing the legality of the last increase," Bolt said sharply, to stop that area of discussion. "That and the subject of this meeting are poles apart. What we have here is a problem in maintaining some rapport with the public, and I've taken some steps to insulate us from any critical comment."

"If the story will be printed showing us in an unfavorable light," Ivers said, "it seems that the cat is already out of the bag."

"What I have done," B. Bainbridge Bolt said, "is change the nature of the cat."

Elleson the PR man nodded approvingly, though he resented not being consulted on the matter. Appleton from out of town chuckled softly.

"We have taken space in both daily newspapers to remark on the silver-lining-in-every-cloud aspect of a power failure saving a life." Bolt paused.

"There's a switch," Ivers said brightly.

"Excellent," Elleson said admiringly, but he wondered if it was.

"Agreed," Grossner said, "but won't it also draw further attention to the incident?"

138

"To continue," Bolt cut them off reprovingly, having successfully sprung one of his little conversational traps, "we will then explain how Powacky Valley Light and Power is generously paying for the would-be suicide victim's complete recovery."

"Great!" Grossner said. "Really sock it to 'em!"

"I believe we will have gone full circuit," Bolt said smugly, "transformed a lemon into lemonade."

Everyone laughed as always at the familiar lemon analogy.

"But how do we know he *will* recover?" Ivers asked. "People who unsuccessfully attempt suicide usually try again."

Bolt shrugged. "Doesn't matter. The whole thing will be out of the public's collective mind in a week or so. This McCord ought to stay alive that long. Right now he's confined in the psychiatric ward at State Hospital at our expense, undergoing electrotherapy treatment."

"Can you be sure of that?" Appleton from out of town said.

"Of course," B. Bainbridge Bolt said.

Appleton smiled indulgently. "I mean, what if he escaped? What if he somehow made his way here, to Powacky Valley Headquarters?"

"I get it," Grossner said. "He could do something drastic — generate some tremendous adverse publicity."

"Not only drastic," Appleton said, "but fantastically daring and grand."

Bolt squinted at Appleton. Several throats were cleared.

"Security isn't very tight here," Appleton said. "An imaginative man could find out things, make his way to the top."

Bolt leaned forward in his chair and cocked his head. "You're not —"

"Correct," Appleton from out of town said. "A. C. McCord, at your service."

Ivers' eyes widened. "But . . . where's Appleton?"

"Tangled up in some high-voltage lines, actually," McCord said, placing a small black box on the table. He smiled. "I took the liberty of attaching some wires to the table and chairs," he said, "so together you can all experience with me, one of your many customers, the unpleasant sensation of being overcharged," and he pressed a button on the box.

"Watt now?" Miss Knickelsworth asked herself in the outer office, as her electric typewriter suddenly went dead.

The Man in the Morgue

It was a big house, with enough gables, dormers, and cupolas to resemble a maniac's chessboard. I smoothly braked and curbed my beige Volkswagen Beetle in the semicircular driveway, conscious of the car's faded paint and character-forming dents in contrast to the symmetrically bricked and shrubbed entranceway to the house. The engine turned over a few times after I'd killed the ignition.

I half expected a butler to answer my ring. Instead, a large cop in a sweat-stained blue uniform opened the door and stared at me. He was about fifty with shrewd gray eyes, a shaggy gray moustache that turned town at the corners, a bulging stomach that dictated he shop in the big men's department.

"Mr. Aloysius Nudger to see Mrs. Emily Stein," I told him.

"If you had a hat and a coat," he said, "I could take them for you and hang them up." He stepped back so I could enter. "She's expecting you, Nudger. I'm Chief Gladstone, Marlville Police."

I followed him down a tile-floored hall into a large room furnished in dainty French provincial. The carpet was the same deep pearl color as the grip of the revolver in Gladstone's leather hip holster, and ceiling-to-floor powder-blue drapes were opened to admit soft light through white sheer curtains. The walls were papered in light gold patterned in darker gold fleurs-de-lis. It struck me as the sort of place where it might be difficult to read the menu.

Emily Stein rose from a fragile-looking sofa and smiled a strained smile at me. She was more beautiful now than twenty years ago when her name was Emily Colter and she was still single and chasing a modeling career. I couldn't understand how she'd failed to catch that career. She was tall and slender but curvaceous, and she had angular faintly oriental cheekbones and oversized compassionate blue eyes. I'd been in love with her once, back in Plainton, Missouri. But that was over twenty years ago, and she'd considered us only good friends even then. She had phoned me at my office yesterday and said she'd found herself in trouble, would I drive out and talk with her about it. I said yes, what were friends for?

"Thank you for coming, Alo," she said, simply. There were circles of worry beneath her large eyes. "This is Chief Fred Gladstone of the Marlville Police Department."

I nodded and we all sat down politely, Gladstone and I on silkily upholstered, breakable-looking matching chairs that were too well bred to creak.

"Chief Gladstone agreed it might be a good idea to call you in on this," Emily said, "when I told him we were old friends and you're a private detective in the city."

When I glanced over at Gladstone's gone-to-fat craggy features, my impression was that he hadn't had much choice.

"Larry's been kidnapped," Emily said.

I waited while she paused for what they call in drama circles "a beat." Emily had always been stagy in an appealing way. Larry Stein was the man she married five years ago, a wealthy importer of leather goods, dark-haired, handsome, in his thirties. I'd been at the wedding.

"Or do you use the term 'kidnapped' for a grown man?" Emily asked.

"You do," I told her. "When was Larry kidnapped?"

"Yesterday at three P.M., by the statue of Admiral Farragut in the park."

"Was there a ransom demand?"

"Even before the kidnapping," Gladstone cut in.

"Three days ago," Emily said, "Larry got a letter in the mail here at home. It was to the point and unsigned. If he didn't deliver five thousand dollars to the sender at three yesterday afternoon near the Farragut statue, I would be killed."

Gladstone stood up from his chair, moved to a secretary near the window, and handed me a white envelope. "It's already been checked for prints," he said. "Nothing there. Postmarked locally, widely sold cheap typing paper, typed on a Royal electric portable."

The folded note inside the envelope was as Emily had described — short, direct, neat, and grammatically correct. I asked her, "Did Larry follow these instructions?"

Emily nodded. "And he told me to call you if anything happened to him. He thinks a lot of you professionally."

I found it odd that he'd think of me at all, since I'd only met him twice. But then I'm sure he knew, in that instinctive way husbands have, that I greatly admired Emily.

"Larry knew something wasn't right about it, even as a straight extortion demand," Emily went on. "He said the amount of money they demanded was too small and what they really might want was an opportunity to grab him with enough money on him for them to be able to hold out while they waited for a huge ransom."

"It turns out Larry was right," Gladstone said. "Emily got this in this morning's mail." He handed me another envelope, identical to the first — same paper, same typing — but this time with a demand for $100,000. Otherwise dead

143

Larry. The kidnappers ended the note by assuring Emily they'd stay in touch.

I looked at the postmark. Yesterday's date, time 11:00 A.M., local.

"Right," Gladstone said, following my thoughts. "Mailed before Larry was snatched. So it was planned, not spontaneous."

"How about the F.B.I.?" I said.

Emily shook her head no, her lips a firm, thin line.

"She refused," Gladstone told me. "She wants you instead."

I sat back in my chair, digesting what I'd learned. It gave me a stomach ache. Extortion, kidnapping, threatened murder, a ransom demand from someone or some group that seemed to know what moves to make. I didn't have the nerves for my profession. Automatically, I reached into my shirt pocket, peeled back some tinfoil, and popped a thin white antacid tablet into my mouth.

"Call the F.B.I., Emily," I said. "The odds are better that way."

"Larry told me not to do that. He said it would be a sure way to get him killed. The F.B.I. has a file on him. In the sixties he was what you might call a student radical — nothing serious, but his photograph was taken with the wrong people and he was in the wrong spot when a building burned down. It's all behind him, but they might not believe that."

From student radical to Larry the capitalist.

"What now?" Emily asked in a lost voice.

"We wait for instructions and take it from there. It wouldn't be a bad idea to get a recorder on the phone in case they decide to stop using the mail."

"That's been taken care of," Gladstone said.

144

"Can you get the hundred thousand?" I asked Emily.

"I can." No hesitation.

"Do you have any idea who might be doing this? Sometimes a kidnapping is a personal matter."

"No one I can think of." Outside a jay started a shrill chatter on the patio. The strident notes seemed to set Emily more on edge. "Larry never told me much about his business; he knows people I don't know. But he was — is — the type who never made enemies."

"Except for the F.B.I.," I said, rising from my fragile chair. The sheer curtains were parted slightly, and beyond the brick patio I could see a tilled garden about twelve by nine feet, lined with cabbage, lettuce, and staked tomato plants. Near the center of the garden were two rows of young tomato vines that would mature toward the end of summer and keep the Steins in tomatoes all season long. The garden was neglected now and needed weeding. Still, it was a garden. I smiled. Plainton, Missouri. A part of Emily would always remain a country girl.

"Maybe somebody ought to stay here with you nights," Gladstone said.

"No," Emily said, "I'll be fine. The house is equipped with dead bolt locks and has a burglar-alarm system. And I have Bruno."

I raised my eyebrows. "Bruno?"

Emily got up and walked to the door at the other end of the room. When she opened the door, a huge black and tan German shepherd ambled in and sat, his white teeth glinting against his black lips and lolling pink tongue. Bruno was a factor.

Before I left, I gave Emily and Gladstone each one of my printed cards with my home and office phone numbers. I told Emily to try to keep occupied and worry as little as possible. Hollow advice but my best under the circumstances.

The Volkswagen's oil-starved engine beat like a busy machine shop as I drove past Marlville's exclusive shopping area of boutiques, service stations bordered by artificial green grass and shrubbery that would fool you at a thousand feet, and a red-brick and yellow-plastic McDonald's harboring half a dozen scraggly teenagers with nothing better to do on a sunny June day in swank suburbia.

I turned onto the cloverleaf and headed east toward the city, glad to be away from all that manicured spaciousness.

From a phone booth on Davis Avenue, I checked with my answering service. No one had called, and I didn't feel like returning to my desolate office to reread my mail.

My apartment was also a lonely place, but the loneliness was in me, wherever I went. I phoned a colleague at police headquarters who had an F.B.I. connection and promised to get me information on Larry Stein in a hurry and call back. Then I took a quick shower, leaving the bathroom door open so I could hear the phone.

It rang while I was toweling myself dry.

Larry Stein had been a member of a short-lived left-wing student organization called LIFT, Leftist Insurgents For Tomorrow. He had attended some demonstrations that turned violent and had been photographed near the R.O.T.C. building at Washington University when it burned down. He was never formally charged with arson, and someone else eventually was convicted of the crime. This was in 1966. Who cared now? Probably no one.

I cooked up some hamburger steaks and stewed tomatoes and sat down with it and a glass of beer to watch a ball game on television.

At a few minutes after five, the jangle of the phone woke me from a sound sleep in front of the TV.

"Nudger?"

"I think."

"Chief Gladstone. I got a call from the city police. Larry Stein is at the morgue."

I could think of nothing to say. I wasn't sure myself how I was taking the news.

"Refuse collectors found his body this afternoon in a big cardboard box behind a restaurant. He was shot to death. How about going down and making the I.D.?"

"Does Emily know?"

"Not yet."

"I'll tell her," I said. "I'll let you know when I get done at the morgue."

I replaced the receiver and stood for a moment, despising myself. I knew that hidden in my compassion for Emily was a secret joyous voice reminding me that she was a widow now, she was free.

But when I got to the morgue and old Eagan slid Drawer #16 out on its metal casters, I found that I wasn't looking at Larry Stein. This man had been close to Stein's height and weight, and his hair was dark brown if not black, but his face was broader than Stein's, and slightly pockmarked.

Whoever he was, he'd been shot five times in the chest.

When I phoned police headquarters and told them it wasn't Stein, they told me to come down. I took an antacid tablet and went.

Lieutenant Jack Keough, an old friend from when I was on the force, talked to me. He's a few years older than I am, with candid brown eyes and an often-broken nose that wasn't Roman to begin with. His office is so barren and battered that even after the morgue it was depressing.

"We sent the prints to Washington," Keough said, "so we should know soon who we've got chilled." Then he dumped the contents of a large brown envelope onto his desk. He didn't have to tell me it was what was found in the pockets of the corpse. An expensive kidskin wallet — Larry Stein's wallet with all his identification, credit cards, driver's license, photographs of Emily, and a few worn business cards. There were two tens and a five in the bill compartment. Besides the wallet, there were a leather key case, a black pocket comb, and some loose change. While I was sorting through it, I told Keough about the kidnap case.

"Now it's in our ball park too," Keough said. "We can help you."

"I wish there were a way," I told him. "You'd better phone Chief Gladstone and let him know about this. Maybe he can put a name on the dead man."

"We're never that lucky," Keough said.

Armed with some head shots of the corpse, I drove the next morning to Marlville to talk to Emily. As I was about to turn into the semicircular driveway, I saw a dark blue Pontiac sedan turning out of the other end of the drive onto the street.

When Emily answered my knock, I could see that she was badly shaken. I wished I'd had the presence of mind to jot down the license number of the Pontiac.

"Have you found out anything?" she asked, opening the door wide.

"I'm not sure," I told her, stepping inside. Bruno ambled over and licked my hand. "I'm afraid I have to show you some unpleasant photographs, Emily."

She backed a step, supported herself with exaggerated casualness on a low table. "Not . . ."

"Not Larry," I said quickly. "A man was killed, and Larry's identification was in his pockets. We need to know who that man was."

"Killed . . . how?"

"Shot to death." I removed the photographs from the envelope and showed them to her.

She seemed relieved to find herself staring at a peaceful composed face. "I don't know him," she said. "At least, not that I can recall."

I followed her into the living room, where she sat bent and exhausted on the sofa.

"Do you know someone who drives a blue Pontiac?" I asked.

She used a graceful hand to brush her hair back from her face. "No, I don't think so. Why?"

"I thought I saw one pulling away from the house as I drove up."

Emily shrugged. "He must have been turning around. We're the end house; they do that all the time."

But she had said "he," and there had been a man driving the car.

That night I began keeping watch on the Stein house. And learned nothing. At midnight, when all the lights in the house had gone out, I went home.

The next morning I learned from Keough that the man in the morgue was still unidentified. His fingerprints weren't in the master files, which meant that he had never been in the armed forces or acquired a police record. His good behavior had earned him five bullets — according to Keough, thirty-eight caliber bullets, probably fired from a Colt automatic.

I watched the Stein house most of the next day and that

evening until Emily went to bed at 11:45. Again nothing. Maybe Emily had been telling the truth; maybe the car I'd seen had only been using the driveway to turn around.

But on the way home I saw the blue Pontiac in the Mc-Donald's lot in Marlville. Of course I'd only caught a glimpse of the car at Emily's and couldn't be positive this was the same one, but after writing down the license number I parked in a spot near the rear of the lot where I could watch it.

McDonald's was closing. After a while some of the parking-lot lights winked out and the swarms of insects that had been circling them disappeared.

A man walked from the red and yellow building, munching a hamburger as he strode toward the Pontiac. He seemed to be in his thirties, medium-height, and muscular rather than stocky — a lean-waisted weightlifter's build. He was wearing dark slacks and a blue short-sleeved sport shirt open at the collar. I couldn't see his face clearly.

When the Pontiac pulled from the lot, I popped an antacid tablet into my mouth and followed.

It took him about two minutes to reach Emily's house. As I sat parked up the street, watching, he knocked on the front door. Lights came on, the door opened, and he entered. Twenty minutes later he came back outside, got into the Pontiac, and drove away. I stayed with him.

He drove toward the city, getting off the highway at Vine and turning south on Twentieth. Ten minutes later, he made a right onto Belt Street and parked in front of a six-story brick apartment building just this side of being condemned. We were in one of those neighborhoods on the edge of a genuine slum. As I watched, he entered the building and a while later a light came on in one of the fourth-floor windows.

I climbed stiffly out of the Volkswagen, crossed the street, and entered the vestibule of the building. There was a dim overhead lightbulb and a row of tarnished metal mailboxes. Two of the names on the fourth-floor boxes were women's. 4-D was listed as B. Darris, 4-B as Charles L. Coil.

After copying all the names and the address, I walked back to the Volkswagen, waited until the light had gone out in the fourth-floor window, then drove home weary for bed.

Ten o'clock. I got up slowly, sat for a while on the edge of the mattress, then made my way into the bathroom and under a cool shower. Ten minutes later I turned on the burner beneath the coffee before returning to the bedroom to dress. After a breakfast of grapefruit juice, poached eggs, and black coffee I was sufficiently awake to ask myself what it had all meant last night.

Emily was seeing the man in the Pontiac and wanted it kept secret. Was he one of the kidnappers? Anyone unconnected with the case? A clandestine lover?

The telephone rang and I carried my coffee into the other room to answer. It was Keough. They had an identification on the body in the morgue — Harold Vinceno, 122 Edison Avenue. He'd been reported missing by his wife three days ago and his general description fit that of the dead man. Mrs. Vinceno had made the positive identification this morning.

I asked Keough to get me an owner from Records on the blue Pontiac's plate numbers, then asked him to find out what he could about the car's owner. When he asked me why, I told him it was nothing solid, just a hunch I was following.

By the time I'd finished my coffee and examined the

mail, drops of rain were pecking at the window. Keough might not call back for hours. I went to the closet and put on a lightweight waterproof jacket, then I left to visit Mrs. Vinceno.

Edison Avenue was near the west edge of the city, medium-priced neat tract houses, on small lots with trimmed lawns that were being watered by the steady pattering rain. The Vinceno house was a white-frame ranch with empty flower boxes beneath the front windows.

Mrs. Vinceno answered the door on the third ring. She was a small haggard woman, probably pretty in ordinary circumstances, with large dark eyes that were red from crying.

"My name's Nudger, Mrs. Vinceno. I'm a detective. I know it's an awkward time but I need to talk to you about your husband."

She nodded without expression and stepped back.

We sat at opposite ends of the sofa. But for a new-looking console TV, everything in the small living room was slightly worn.

"I'm sure the police have asked you, Mrs. Vinceno, but do you have any idea what happened to your husband?"

She shook her head no. "When I saw Harold I was — surprised," she said in a husky voice. "Not because he was dead, but because he'd been shot."

I waited.

"Harold left here three days ago with the intention of committing suicide, Mr. Nudger. We hadn't been getting along. We had money problems — personal problems. He left here in one of his rages, saying he would end everything for himself."

I watched her battle the trembling of her hands to light a cigarette.

"Then he called here the next morning and told me our money problems were solved. He said he'd stumbled across a deal that couldn't miss and he'd let me know more about it when the time came. I begged him to come home, but he wouldn't.

"I didn't take his talk about money seriously. Harold was kind of incoherent on the phone, and he was always stumbling into rainbows without pots of gold at the end of them." She bowed her head and her disarranged black hair fell down to hide her face.

It didn't boost my self-esteem to keep at her, but I did. "Did your husband ever mention Larry Stein, the man whose identification was on him?" She shook her head no. "How about B. Darris? Charles L. Coil?" No and no. Her shoulders began to quake.

Driving to my office, I tried to draw some conclusions and only came up with more questions. Was Vinceno one of the kidnappers? Had he actually intended to commit suicide, or had he been playing for his wife's pity? Had he known Emily? The man in the Pontiac? The only person involved in the case I could be sure Vinceno had crossed paths with alive or dead was Larry Stein.

My office is on the second floor of a Victorian apartment building that was converted into oddly shaped bay-windowed offices when the neighborhood declined. It has a certain ornate charm and the exterminator comes every six months.

I was informed by my answering service that Lieutenant Keough had called and left a number where he could be reached. When I dialed the number, Keough came to the phone and told me that the blue Pontiac was registered to William Darris, thirty-four years old, of 6534 Belt Street, apartment 4-D. Darris had a record — B and E, Plainton,

Missouri, August third of '69, placed on probation; armed robbery, Union, Missouri, May seventh of '71, convicted and served three years. There were also a raft of moving traffic violations and a minor drug charge.

"You're from Plainton," Keough said. "Do you know this Darris?"

The name in conjunction with Plainton had already opened a door in my memory. "I know of the Darris family. There were two boys in their early teens when I left. They'd be in their thirties now."

"What connection might they have with Vinceno?" Keough asked.

"I don't know yet. I saw Darris leaving the Stein home late last night. And he was there before, but Emily Stein denied it."

"That's all?"

"All I have."

Keough sighed. "It could mean anything. Maybe we ought to talk to Darris."

"I wouldn't now. If he's mixed up in the kidnapping, we might be putting Stein's life in danger. I think the thing to do is watch him."

"All right," Keough said. "We put somebody on Darris. What are you going to be doing?"

"I'm going to Plainton."

I didn't tell him what I was going to do before I left for Plainton.

When Darris was gone from his apartment, along with his tail, I entered the building on Belt Street and climbed the stairs to the fourth floor. Ignoring my fluttering stomach, I used my Visa card to slip the lock so I could enter apartment 4-D.

The tiny apartment was a mess, the bed unmade, rumpled Levis and a pair of dirty socks in one corner, hot stale air. I knew the places to look and how to look, and I worked hard at looking to stifle my fear.

Within ten minutes I found it, a sealed white envelope taped to the outside of the back panel of a kitchen cabinet drawer. I took it into the bathroom and ran hot water into the basin until steam rose. Then I held the envelope over the rising steam until the glue had softened enough for me to pry the flap open. Inside was five thousand dollars.

Resealing the envelope with the money inside, I replaced it on the back of the cabinet drawer, then, after making sure everything was in the same disorder in which I'd found it, I left.

Plainton existed in reality much as it did in my memory — white frame houses, small shopping area, unhurried pedestrians. I'd taken a flight to Saint Louis and connected with an Ozark Airlines flight to Jefferson City, where I'd rented an air-conditioned Pinto for the drive to Plainton. Now I was driving along the streets where I'd spent my childhood and adolescence, before my family moved to Kansas City.

I parked in one of the angled slots near the sloping lawn that led up to the city hall, fed coins to an ancient parking meter, and left the car in the shade of a huge cottonwood tree.

Benny Shaver was the man I wanted to talk to. We'd been good friends in high school, and now he owned a restaurant on Alternate Route 3, Plainton's main street.

Benny had taken out a liquor license in the twelve years since I'd been through town, and now the sign atop the low brick building read SHAVER'S PUB AND RESTAURANT.

The air conditioner was on high in Shaver's. There was a

155

counter with upholstered stools and a number of tables, each with a red-checked tablecloth and an artificial rose in a tall glass vase. The pub had been added on. There was a door near the counter over which the word PUB was lettered, along with what might have been Benny's family crest. The crest wasn't crossed pitchforks against a field of guernseys; it was crossed swords over a shield engraved with something in Latin, maybe the hours. I walked into the pub and saw a man and a blonde woman in one of the booths, and behind the bar where it wasn't so dim stood Benny. Less hair and more jowl, but Benny.

I walked to the bar, sat on a stool, and called for a draft beer. Benny sauntered over and set a frosty mug on a red coaster, then squinted at me. I noticed that the scar on his forehead from the auto accident we'd had as teenagers was less vivid now.

"God's great acorns, it's Nudger!"

We both laughed and shook hands and Benny reached a beefy arm over the bar and slapped my right shoulder so it hurt. "Twelve years," I told him.

"It is at that," he said, and looked momentarily frightened by the press of time.

After three beers' worth of reminiscence I said, "I need some information on William Darris."

"Is he in trouble?" Benny asked.

"Possibly."

"I haven't seen Billy in about two years. I don't miss him, Alo."

"Why not?"

"He came in here a lot and couldn't drink like he thought he could. This was after he got out of prison and thought he was rougher than he was. I had to break up a couple of fights he got into, mostly over women."

"Married women?"

"Some. Billy claimed he was trying to make up for time lost in prison. I never saw him, though, after he took up with the Colter girl."

"Who?"

"You remember Emily Colter. She was a looker, moved away a long time ago to become a model or something. Well, she was back in town a few years ago to visit her cousin, and she kinda fell in with Billy. About a month after she left town, he left too, claimed he got a job in the East. I wished him luck and hoped he'd stay wherever he was going. He was always in trouble and prison made him worse."

I didn't think Benny could guess how much worse. After declining lunch and saying goodbye, I left town.

I was splashing cold water on my face in the office the next morning when the phone rang. It was Keough.

"Emily Stein got the ransom-delivery instructions in the mail," he said. "They want the hundred thousand tonight."

"I'll bet," I said. My stomach came alive and wielded claws.

"The tail on Darris hasn't brought us much," Keough went on. "He's been getting together with an ex-con named Louis Enwood, extortion and armed robbery. We put a tail on Enwood too."

"Have they been near a mailbox or post office?"

"Nope. I don't think they're it, Nudger."

"Are you going to be in your office all morning?"

"Most of it."

"I'll phone you back later," I said.

I combed my hair, rinsed my mouth with cold water,

157

opened a fresh roll of antacid tablets, and left the office to see Emily Stein.

She was home. Her Mercedes convertible was parked near the garage at the side of the house where I'd seen it before. I walked around to the rear of the house, then returned to the front porch and rang the doorbell. A sprinkler on the wide front lawn was flinging a revolving fan of water with a staccato hissing sound. Bruno was lying in the shade near the corner of the house, staring at me like the good watch dog he was.

When she opened the door, Emily smiled at me. She was wearing a pale-pink dress. Her smile lost its luminescence when she saw my face.

"You heard about the ransom instructions," she said. "I was just on my way to draw the money from the Marlville Bank."

"Why don't you write him a check and give it to him next time he comes by the house?" I suggested.

She stepped back into the cool entry hall, and it was as if she'd stepped across time and aged twenty years.

"You, Darris, and his friend Enwood are in it together," I said.

She turned and walked into the big room with the French furniture and powder-blue drapes. I followed her.

"You called me into it to make it look like an authentic kidnapping and give you an even better excuse not to call in the F.B.I. After all, you didn't have anything to fear if it went right. And at that point you thought everything had gone right."

She sat on the sofa and swayed slightly. The drapes were open, and a pitiless slanted light fell on her.

"You typed and mailed the notes to yourself," I told her, "even the last ransom note. Larry Stein cared about you enough to set out for a lonely meeting with only five thousand dollars when he was sure the extortionists would want something more. Only Larry was smart, and an angle-shooter. Somewhere along the line he ran into Harold Vinceno, contemplating suicide, maybe pumping up his courage over a few drinks. Larry talked Vinceno into delivering the five thousand, maybe offering to pay him a thousand for the job, and they exchanged identification in case the extortionists would check. And Darris and Enwood, who'd never seen your husband close-up, were not only interested in the money but in killing Larry."

"Billy made me do it," Emily murmured.

"No," I said. "He and Enwood wouldn't have killed Larry just for the five thousand dollars. When a married man is murdered, the wife is always at least initially suspected. You needed a cover, like a phony kidnapping scheme complete with notes, ransom money, and a bumbling gumshoe who wasn't much of a threat. Only the hundred thousand wasn't ransom money, it was the final payment to Darris for killing Larry. You probably never really loved Larry Stein, and half his money as he saw fit to dole it out to you wasn't enough." I watched her close her eyes, felt my own eyes brim as tears tracked down her makeup. "When did Larry come back?"

"Yesterday," she said, her eyes still clenched shut, "when he read in the papers about Vinceno being identified by his wife. That's the only time anything about the case got in the papers. Until then, Larry wanted to stay dead to the kidnappers. He was afraid for me."

"And you were afraid of Darris," I said, "afraid he'd think you double-crossed him and he'd want revenge. Darris found out the same way Larry did that he'd killed Vinceno — the wrong man. That's why Darris came here to

159

see you, to demand the hundred thousand, to continue with the original plan."

"I was afraid of him," Emily admitted, opening her eyes. "That's why I wanted you — nearby. I should have known you'd figure it out. You were always smart, you always saw things differently. This hundred thousand, Alo, it's only a fraction of what's left . . ."

"There was only one way you'd be able to mail that final note to yourself," I told her, "and only one more thing I have to know for sure before I phone Chief Gladstone."

She knew what I meant and something buckled inside her. But she had enough strength to stand and walk with me through the house and out the back door into the yard. She waited while I went into the garage and got a disturbingly handy shovel.

Despite everything, I found myself still admiring her. She had masterminded everything, from seducing Darris to hiring me on the recommendation of my noted lack of success. And but for Vinceno's impersonation of her husband, it all would have worked. In this or in any other world, I would never find another Emily.

She was leaning on me like a lover and sobbing as we walked to the dark churned earth of the now meticulously weeded garden, to where the freshly planted tomato vines were flourishing in the hot sun.

The Explosives Expert

Billy Edgemore, the afternoon bartender, stood behind the long bar of the Last Stop Lounge and squinted through the dimness at the sunlight beyond the front window. He was a wiry man, taller than he appeared at first, and he looked like he should be a bartender, with his bald head, cheerfully seamed face, and his brilliant red vest that was the bartender's uniform at the Last Stop. Behind him long rows of glistening bottles picked up the light on the mirrored backbar, the glinting clear gins and vodkas, the beautiful amber bourbons and lighter Scotches, the various hues of the assorted wines, brandies, and liqueurs. The Last Stop's bar was well stocked.

Beyond the ferns that blocked the view out (and in) the front window, Billy saw a figure cross the small patch of light and turn to enter the stained-glass front door, the first customer he was to serve that day.

It was Sam Daniels. Sam was an employee of the Hulton Plant up the street, as were most of the customers of the Last Stop.

"Afternoon, Sam," Billy said, turning on his professional smile. "Kind of early today, aren't you?"

"Off work," Sam said, mounting a barstool as if it were a horse. "Beer."

Billy drew a beer and set the wet schooner in front of Sam on the mahogany bar. "Didn't expect a customer for another two hours, when the plant lets out," Billy said.

"Guess not," Sam said, sipping his beer. He was a short man with a swarthy face, a head of curly hair, and a stomach paunch too big for a man in his early thirties — a man who liked his drinking.

"Figured you didn't go to work when I saw you weren't wearing your badge," Billy said. The Hulton Plant manufactured some secret government thing, a component for the hydrogen bomb, and each employee had to wear his small plastic badge with his name, number, and photograph on it in order to enter or leave the plant.

"Regular Sherlock," Sam said, and jiggled the beer in his glass.

"You notice lots of things when you're a bartender," Billy said, wiping down the bar with a clean white towel. You notice things, Billy repeated to himself, and you get to know people, and when you get to know them, really get to know them, you've got to dislike them. "I guess I tended bar in the wrong places."

"What's that?" Sam Daniels asked.

"Just thinking out loud," Billy said, and hung the towel on its chrome rack. When Billy looked at his past he seemed to be peering down a long tunnel of empty bottles, drunks, and hollow laughter; of curt orders, see-through stares, and dreary conversations. He'd never liked his job, but it was all he'd known for the past thirty years.

"Wife's supposed to meet me here pretty soon," Sam said. "She's getting off work early." He winked at Billy. "Toothache."

Billy smiled his automatic smile and nodded. He never had liked Sam, who had a tendency to get loud and violent when he got drunk.

Within a few minutes, Rita Daniels entered. She was a tall pretty woman, somewhat younger than her husband. She had a good figure, dark eyes, and expensively bleached blond hair that looked a bit stringy now from the heat outside.

"Coke and bourbon," she ordered, without looking at Billy. He served her the highball where she sat next to her husband at the bar.

No one spoke for a while as Rita sipped her drink. The faint sound of traffic, muffled through the thick door of the Last Stop, filled the silence. When a muted horn sounded, Rita said, "It's dead in here. Put a quarter in the jukebox."

Sam did as his wife said, and soft jazz immediately displaced the traffic sounds.

"You know I don't like jazz, Sam." Rita downed her drink quicker than she should have, then got down off the stool to go to the powder room.

"Saw Doug Baker last night," Billy said, picking up the empty glass. Doug Baker was a restaurant owner who lived on the other side of town, and it was no secret that he came to the Last Stop only to see Rita Daniels, though Rita was almost always with her husband.

"How 'bout that," Sam said. "Two more of the same."

Rita returned to her stool, and Billy put two highballs before her and her husband.

"I was drinking beer," Sam said in a loud voice.

"So you were," Billy answered, smiling his My Mistake smile. He shrugged and motioned toward the highballs. "On the house. Unless you'd rather have beer."

"No," Sam said, "think nothing of it."

That was how Billy thought Sam would answer. His cheapness was one of the things Billy disliked most about the man. It was one of the things he knew Rita disliked most in Sam Daniels, too.

"How'd it go with the hydrogen bombs today?" Rita asked her husband. "Didn't go in at all, huh?"

Billy could see she was aggravated and was trying to nag him.

"No," Sam said, "and I don't make hydrogen bombs."

"Ha!" Rita laughed. "You oughta think about it. That's about all you can make." She turned away before Sam could answer. "Hey, Billy, you know anything about hydrogen bombs?"

"Naw," Billy said. "Your husband knows more about that than me."

"Yeah," Rita said, "the union rates him an expert. Some expert! Splices a few wires together."

"Fifteen dollars an hour," Sam said, "and double time for overtime."

Rita whirled a braceleted arm above her head. "Wheee . . ."

Like many married couples, Sam and Rita never failed to bicker when they came into the Last Stop. Billy laughed. "The Friendly Daniels." Sam didn't laugh.

"Don't bug me today," Sam said to Rita. "I'm in a bad mood."

"Cheer up, Sam," Billy said. "It's a sign she loves you, or loves somebody, anyway."

Sam ignored Billy and finished his drink. "Where'd you go last night?" he asked his wife.

"You know I was at my sister's. I even stopped in here for about a half hour on the way. Billy can verify it."

"Right," Billy said.

"I thought you said Doug Baker was in here last night," Sam said to him, his eyes narrow.

"He was," Billy said. "He, uh, came in late." He turned to make more drinks, placing the glasses lip-to-lip and pouring bourbon into each in one deft stream without spilling a drop. He made them a little stronger this time, shooting in the soda expertly, jabbing swizzle sticks between the ice cubes and placing the glasses on the bar.

"You wouldn't be covering up or anything, would you, Billy?" Sam's voice had acquired a mean edge.

"Now *wait a minute!*" Rita said. "If you think I came in here last night to see Doug Baker, you're crazy!"

"Well." Sam stirred his drink viciously and took a sip. "Billy mentioned Baker was in here. . . ."

"I said he came in late," Billy said quickly.

"And he acted like he was covering up or something," Sam said, looking accusingly at Billy.

"*Covering up?*" Rita turned to Billy, her penciled eyebrows knitted in a frown. "Have you ever seen me with another man?"

"Naw," Billy said blandly, "of course not. You folks shouldn't fight."

Still indignant, Rita swiveled on her stool to face her husband. "Have I ever been unfaithful?"

"How the hell should I know?"

"Good point," Billy said with a forced laugh.

"It's not funny!" Rita snapped.

"Keep it light, folks," Billy said seriously. "You know we don't like trouble in here."

"Sorry," Rita said, but her voice was hurt. She swiveled back to face the bar and gulped angrily on her drink. Billy could see that the liquor was getting to her, was getting to them both.

There was silence for a while, then Rita said morosely "I *oughta* go out on you, Mr. Hydrogen-bomb expert! You think I do anyway, and at least Doug Baker's got money."

Sam grabbed her wrist, making the bracelets jingle. She tried to jerk away but he held her arm so tightly that his knuckles were white. "You ever see Baker behind my back and I'll kill you both!" He almost spit the words out.

"Hey, now," Billy said gently, "don't talk like that, folks!"

165

He placed his hand on Sam Daniels' arm and felt the muscles relax as Sam released his wife. She bent over silently on her stool and held the wrist as if it were broken. "Have one on the house," Billy said, taking up their almost empty glasses. "One to make up by."

"Make mine straight," Sam said. He was breathing hard and his face was red.

"Damn you!" Rita moaned. She half fell off the stool and walked quickly but staggeringly to the powder room again.

Billy began to mix the drinks deftly, speedily, as if there were a dozen people at the bar and they all demanded service. In the faint red glow from the beer-ad electric clock he looked like an ancient alchemist before his rows of multicolored bottles. "You shouldn't be so hard on her," he said absently as he mixed. "Can't believe all the rumors you hear about a woman as pretty as Rita, and a harmless kiss in fun never hurt nobody."

"Rumors?" Sam leaned over the bar. "Kiss? What kiss? Did she kiss Baker last night?"

"Take it easy," Billy said. "I told you Baker came in late." The phone rang, as it always did during the fifteen minutes before the Hulton Plant let out, with wives leaving messages and asking for errant husbands. When Billy returned, Rita was back at the bar.

"Let's get out of here," she said. There were tear streaks in her makeup.

"Finish your drinks and go home happy, folks." Billy shot a glance at the door and set the glasses on the bar.

Rita drank hers slowly, but Sam tossed his drink down and stared straight ahead. Quietly, Billy put another full glass in front of him.

"I hear you *were* in here with Baker last night," Sam said in a low voice. "Somebody even saw you kissing him."

"You're *crazy!*" Rita's thickened voice was outraged.

Billy moved quickly toward them. "I didn't say that."

"I knew you were covering up!" Sam glared pure hate at him. "We'll see what Baker says, because I'm going to drive over to his place right now and bash his brains out!"

"But I didn't even see Baker last night!" Rita took a pull on her drink, trying to calm herself. Sam swung sharply around with his forearm, hitting Rita's chin and the highball glass at the same time. There was a clink as the glass hit her teeth and she fell backward off the stool.

Billy reached under the bar and his hand came up with a glinting chrome automatic that seemed to catch every ray of light in the place. It was a gentleman's gun, and standing there in his white shirt and red vest Billy looked like a gentleman aholding it.

"Now, don't move, folks." He aimed the gun directly at Sam's stomach. "You know we don't go for that kind of trouble in here." He looked down and saw blood seeping between Rita's fingers as she held her hand over her mouth. Billy wet a clean towel and tossed it to her, and she held it to her face and scooted backward to sit sobbing in the farthest booth.

Billy leaned close to Sam. "Listen," he said, his voice a sincere whisper, "I don't want to bring trouble on Baker, or on you for that matter, so I can't stand by and let you go over there and kill him and throw your own life away. It wasn't him she was in here with. He came in later."

"Wasn't him?" Sam asked in bewildered fury. "Who was it then?"

"I don't know," Billy said, still in a whisper so Rita couldn't hear. "He had a badge on, so he worked at the plant, but I don't know who he is and that's the truth."

"Oh, no!"

"Take it easy, Sam. She only kissed him in that booth there. And I'm not even sure I saw that. The booth was dark."

Sam tossed down the drink that was on the bar and moaned. He was staring at the automatic and Billy could see he wanted desperately to move.

A warm silence filled the bar, and then the phone rang shrilly, turning the silence to icicles.

"Now take it easy," Billy said, backing slowly down the bar toward the phone hung on the wall. "A kiss isn't anything." As the phone rang again he could almost see the shrill sound grate through Sam's tense body. Billy placed the automatic on the bar and took the last five steps to the phone. He let it ring once more before answering it.

"Naw," Billy said into the receiver, standing with his back to Sam and Rita, "he's not here." He stood for a long moment instead of hanging up, as if someone were still on the other end of the line.

The shot was a sudden, angry bark.

Billy put the receiver on the hook and turned. Sam was standing slumped with a supporting hand on a barstool. Rita was crumpled on the floor beneath the table of the booth she'd been sitting in, her eyes open, her blond hair bright with blood.

His head still bowed, Sam began to shake.

Within minutes the police were there, led by a young plainclothes detective named Parks.

"You say they were arguing and he just up and shot her?" Parks was asking as his men led Sam outside.

"He accused her of running around," Billy said. "They were arguing, he hit her, and I was going to throw them out when the phone rang. I set the gun down for a moment when I went to answer the phone, and he grabbed it and shot."

"Uh-hm," Parks said efficiently, flashing a look toward where Rita's body had lain before they'd photographed it and taken it away. "Pretty simple, I guess. Daniels confessed as soon as we got here. In fact, we couldn't shut him up. Pretty broken."

"Who wouldn't be?" Billy said.

"Save some sympathy for the girl." Parks looked around. "Seems like a nice place. I don't know why there's so much trouble in here."

Billy shrugged. "In a dive, a class joint, or a place like this, people are mostly the same."

Parks grinned. "You're probably right," he said, and started toward the door. Before pushing it open, he paused and turned. "If you see anything like this developing again, give us a call, huh?"

"Sure," Billy said, polishing a glass and holding it up to the fading afternoon light. "You know we don't like trouble in here."

Men with Motives

Lou Cole sat in Dave Dunstan's office, behind Dunstan's desk, in Dunstan's chair. The darkened office was bathed in a pleasant dim glow from the lighted corridor on the other side of the frosted glass with Dunstan's name lettered on it. There was no sound in the building, no movement. Dunstan's partner, Roy Vickers, had said the Dunstan-Vickers Plastic Company building would be empty.

Cole had met Dave Dunstan by bad luck, and Roy Vickers by chance. He'd gotten the word through the regular, secretive channels: "There's a job for Lou Cole." Cole had gone to the innocent looking Star Dry Cleaners and talked to the old man behind the counter.

"Who wants me?" he'd asked Krueger, the old man, and the old man had smiled.

"A man named Vickers," Krueger had said. "You know who he is?"

"Not the Vickers of Dunstan-Vickers Plastic?"

"The same." A hissing sound came from the back of the cleaners. Krueger ran a hand over his sweating bald head. "I thought you might be interested."

"Vickers doesn't know who I am, does he?" Cole asked.

"Of course not. He only knows that you kill people."

Cole's dark eyebrows lowered in a slight frown. He lit a cigarette and decided to go carefully. "Why did you think I'd be interested?"

"Because he wants you to hit Dave Dunstan."

"Why?"

Krueger grinned. "You'd have to ask Vickers that."

Cole drew on his cigarette. It was bad business, stupid business to hit somebody you were connected with, but it had been four years since he'd even seen Dunstan. He turned and looked out the cleaner's front window at the fine rain that was darkening the street. He did want to kill Dunstan. He dropped his cigarette on the dirty tile floor and stepped on it, knowing that he'd always planned to kill Dunstan anyway, when enough time had passed, when the time was right.

Cole looked at the old man. "Where did Vickers tell me to contact him?"

Krueger handed Cole a small piece of paper with a date, phone number and time written on it.

"I thought you'd want to go through with it, " Krueger said.

Cole folded the piece of paper and put it in his wallet. "Stop smiling," he said to Krueger, and Krueger did.

Cole met Vickers by the outside cages at the zoo. Vickers was dressed as described, leaning on a rail and exchanging stares with a spotted hyena when Cole approached him.

"You Roy Vickers?" Cole asked.

"If you're Krueger's man." Vickers straightened and turned to face him. He was a stocky, middle-aged man with a heavily lined face.

"Krueger's my man," Cole said. He extended his hand and they shook. "It's kind of hot here. Why don't we go over to the shade to talk?"

Vickers smiled at him in a way he didn't like. "Don't you care for hyenas?"

Cole shrugged. "They have a sense of humor."

Vickers followed him to the shade of a big tree by the

171

cage of *Canis lupis,* the Gray Wolf.

Cole slouched against the protective metal railing and folded his arms. "Who told you I was the man for the job?"

"A friend's friend."

Cole like that answer. It was comforting to have a client who was tight-lipped, even though the client had as much to lose as Cole.

"This David Dunstan," Cole said, "who is he and why do you want him dead?"

"He's my business partner," Vickers said, "and I want him dead so I can have the business."

"What business?"

"Dunstan-Vickers Plastic Company. We make —"

"I don't care what you make," Cole interrupted. "Why do you want the business for yourself?"

Vickers looked at him strangely. "The money, of course."

"That's all?"

Cole could hear the wolf pacing behind him while he watched Vickers's face redden slightly.

"My wife," Vickers said, sighing. "I think Dunstan's having an affair with my wife."

Cole nodded. "Two reasonable motives."

"Will you take the job?" Vickers asked.

"We haven't talked price."

Vickers pulled a sealed white envelope from his pocket. "How's five thousand dollars?" he said, holding the envelope out for Cole. "Half now, half later."

Cole took the envelope and put it in his own pocket. "Where can I get Dunstan alone and when?"

"I'll let you know as soon as I can," Vickers said. "There's a phone number in the envelope where you can reach me, Mr. . . . . ."

"You'll recognize my voice," Cole said.

172

Canis lupis scraped the wire of his cage with a gray paw as they walked away.

Cole went from the zoo directly to the Last Stop Lounge where he had some drinks, a bit too much to drink. Vickers didn't know him from Adam, he was sure. If you wanted a swift, professional job in this town and were willing to pay for it, the right inquiries would eventually lead you to Lou Cole, or him to you. So Vickers knew Dunstan was playing with his wife, but he didn't know that five years ago Dunstan had stolen Lou Cole's wife, stolen her and left her dead from an overdose of sleeping pills in a Texas motel.

Cole ordered another drink. For the first time since he'd entered "the profession" he felt a deep desire to kill the man his client had paid to have destroyed. He felt good about this, and yet he felt uneasy. It was a serious breach of ethics to hit anyone but a complete stranger. There was no doubt that eventually the police would get to Cole in their investigation, even though his motive was five years old. That's why half the money he'd receive from Dunstan's death would go to establish an alibi. Cole had paid for these alibis before, and they were tight and reliable.

Finishing his drink, Cole leaned forward over the bar with his eyes closed and listened to the music blaring from the jukebox. He thought about what it would be like to kill Dave Dunstan, and for the first time in years he let himself really think about his dead wife Laurie. He wanted another drink, but he realized he'd had enough so he left.

Skillfully striking a match with his rubber-gloved fingers, Cole lit a cigarette and leaned back in Dunstan's desk chair. While the flame was still flickering he used it to check the time on his wristwatch, then he slipped the burnt out match into a breast pocket. From another pocket he drew a small blue steel automatic with a silencer, checked it and laid it before him on the desk. In the light from the hallway, Dunstan would make a perfect silhouette target when he opened the door to enter the darkened office.

Vickers had come up with the means for a very safe murder plan. He'd arranged for the building to be empty on Friday evening and he'd given Cole a key to a side door. He then drew him a detailed floor plan of the five story building, showing the stairway and elevator, the working area, all of the exits, and Dunstan's office on the fourth floor. At exactly ten o'clock Vickers would call Dunstan and ask to meet him at the office on some urgent pretense. It was ten fifteen now. Instead of Vickers, Dunstan would find Lou Cole.

Vickers was providing himself with an alibi for that evening. He was making the rounds of some night spots with friends. At precisely ten thirty he would slip away and phone Dunstan's office, wait two rings and then hang up. He would call again immediately and Cole would answer the phone and let him know what had happened. Vickers had to cover himself in case Dunstan failed to show up.

It was ten twenty when the phone on Dunstan's desk rang twice. Ten minutes early. A vague apprehension stirred in the back of Cole's mind. When the phone rang again he picked it up and said nothing.

"Lou Cole?"

Cole stiffened. Vickers didn't know his name.

"I know it's you, Cole." There was humor in the voice that was not Vickers's. "This is Dave Dunstan, Lou. I guess you're wondering what's going on."

Cole gripped the receiver harder. "I'm wondering."

"Well, I'll explain," Dunstan said cheerfully. He was

174

always so damned cheerful, Cole thought with a twinge of hate.

"You're sitting on the fourth floor of the Dunstan-Vickers Plastic Company, Lou. You know what we make?"

Cole was silent.

"We make all kinds of things," Dunstan said. "Just the other day I had a clock made all out of plastic. Imagine that, Lou, the whole thing plastic!"

Cole listened to his own hard breathing while Dunstan gave him adequate time to imagine.

"Now why a plastic clock, you ask," Dunstan said. "Of what use? To collect insurance, Lou."

Fear grew a cold knot in Cole's stomach. For all his cheer Dunstan was a dangerous man.

"What kind of insurance?" Cole asked. He knew he should hang up the phone and get out of the building, but he was somehow unable to move.

"Why, fire insurance," Dunstan said. "For two partners who want to get out from under a failing business. And there's only one other person who'd burn down the business besides us, Lou, and that's you. You have enough motive to kill me, so you sure have enough to destroy my business. I knew you'd have killed me eventually, Lou. This way I'm one up on you."

"Listen, Dunstan. . . ." Cole was suddenly cold but he was sweating.

"The plastic clock is perfect," Dunstan continued casually, "Because it can be the timing device on an incendiary bomb and then melt into nothing. In fact, as of five minutes ago the building should be on fire. We put a bomb in the elevator shaft and on the stairway landing on the floor below you. You can't go downstairs, Lou, and it's a long way from the roof."

Dunstan was still talking as Cole dropped the receiver and bolted for the door. "You have the motive, Lou, and you can't very well have been somewhere else when they find your remains in the ashes. You know, dental records and all that. . . ."

There was a thick grayish haze in the hall. Cole ran along the echoing tile floor to the elevator and pressed his hand to one of the metal doors. It was almost too hot to touch. Smashing his fist into the door, he wheeled and ran for the stairway, but the smoke was thicker there, and when he looked down he could actually see the flame walking toward him. Coughing violently, he dropped to his knees and began to crawl.

". . . And it's a long way down from the roof," Dunstan's voice was cheerfully repeating on the phone, and then the line went dead.

Twice Removed

My name is Lockwood. I'm a realist. I have to be, where I'm going. Ackerley has hired me to do this sort of thing before, but my instincts tell me that it's never been as important as this job.

Don't ask me why the job is necessary. Don't even ask me who I'm working for. Oh, sure, Ackerley hired me, but I don't know who he's working for. So I'm twice removed, you might say, from the source of my instructions. Considering the nature of my work, it's better that way.

The DC-10 touches down on the runway with a faint screech of rubber, and within minutes I've deplaned and am walking through the terminal building toward the baggage claim area. When I've picked up my tan leather suitcase with its brass locks, I carry it in one hand, my attaché case in the other, and make my way outside where I can get a cab.

After checking into a midtown hotel under an assumed name, I unpack, pour myself a drink from my silver travel flask, then sit down to examine the contents of the envelope in my attaché case. Some brief typed instructions are in the envelope, along with some added bits of information that might be useful. There is even a key to Garth's apartment. The people I work for are unfailingly thorough.

Garth is a fry cook at a small hamburger joint in the downtown area. His hours are from noon until nine o'clock, taking in both the lunch and supper crowd. He won't be home now. I leave the hotel and take a cab to within a block of his apartment, then walk the rest of the way.

The building where Garth lives is large and in bleak disrepair. There is a child's rusted tricycle near a heavy wood door with a cracked circular window. As I climb the concrete steps toward the entrance, I see that some of the windows in the looming brick face of the building have been boarded up, and most of the other windows display only lowered yellowed shades. The neighborhood, the building, is inhabited by people who prefer that their misery be private, who neither ask nor answer questions. Doubtless, this is one of the reasons Garth was chosen.

The vestibule is profaned by crude graffiti. No one sees me as I walk up the stairs to the fifth floor, down the long faded hall to apartment 5-E, and push the button beside the tarnished doorknob. There is no answer; the bell tolls inside like the muted distress signal of something lost. After a few silent minutes, I unlock the door and enter.

The apartment consists of a living room, bedroom and small bathroom. It conforms exactly to the floor plan I memorized. But the floor plan didn't show the filth, the many empty beer cans, the stacks of newspapers, the moldy bread on the sink counter, the unmade bed with its soiled sheets, the disarray of paperback books in a corner. On a stand, near the foot of the bed, is a small portable TV with a long kinked antenna, like that of an alert insect. My teeth are tightly clenched as I begin to look around more closely.

Most of the paperback books are of a sociological nature. In a shallow desk drawer are dozens of newspaper clippings concerning Daniels and the campaign. On one of the bedroom walls is stapled a lewd poster of a young blonde, and next to it on the wall are scrawled the words KISS, KISS in what appears to be black crayon.

Then I make my most important discovery: a diary.

Almost every page is filled, in the same childish scrawling as the letters on the wall. It is quite a personal diary. I get out my instant-developing camera and photograph each page, then take a few shots of the apartment. After making sure that everything is as I found it, I leave and return to my hotel.

At midnight, I dial Luther Garth's number. He answers sleepily after the tenth ring.

"This is Mitchell," I say. "I wrote another letter last Friday but the time for threats is past. The time for action has arrived."

There is a low gasp on the other end of the line. "Who is this?"

"It's us. We know it's kill or submit, kill or submit, kill —"

"Who *is* this?" Fear makes Garth's voice small.

"Time for a noble act, a healing act, a glorious act —"

Garth hangs up.

I replace the receiver in its cradle and light a cigarette. The call is a good beginning. I know my job; I've been carefully briefed by the psychiatrists. Mitchell is Garth's middle name.

The next day, I again let myself into Garth's apartment. Under yesterday's date, I make a few brief entries in the diary in Garth's crude and childish scrawl.

That evening, I have supper at the diner where Garth works, and as I eat my hamburger and french fried potatoes, I catch sight of him in the kitchen beyond the serving shelf. He is a slender young man, with a shock of reddish hair and small, bewildered blue eyes. To a stout man, who is obviously the diner's owner or manager, I complain quietly about my hamburger being burned. I hear him pass the complaint on to Garth in the kitchen. Voices are raised, and

179

the stout man calls Garth a psycho. Beautiful!

"He called us a psycho," I say to Garth on the telephone that evening, at midnight. "I could kill the fat scum, but why should we? He's nothing — the symptom, not the disease."

Garth doesn't hang up. He can't. I hear his breath hissing into the receiver. Like escaping steam under great pressure.

"The blonde girl spat on us," I say. "She could have refused me politely, but she laughed and then she spat on you. We won't have to remember *that*. Or have you already forgotten? We'll write it down then forget it. She's like the rest of them who laugh at me, who underestimate us. But they'll find out they're wrong. Soon."

"I want to know who this is!" Garth cries, in a tight, pleading voice.

"The only cure for some diseases is to kill them before they spread."

I hear Garth sobbing quietly.

"There are certain people who are like individual cancerous cells."

The sobbing continues. Deep sobbing, punctuated by choked inhalations.

"There is a limit to what we'll take, to how much contagion you'll put up with before we do something noble, something healing, something glorious."

There is a click on the other end of the line and the connection is broken. I listen for a few seconds to the lonely, static sound in the receiver before hanging up.

Within less than two weeks, Garth actually comes to accept "Mitchell's" late night calls as routine, sage communications from his other self, the self who wrote in the diary and sent letters and thought the secret thoughts. The psy-

180

chiatrists were right when they told Ackerley that it would be easy, that it would be inevitable. It dismays me, somehow, that anyone can know that about a man, even so obvious a psychopath as Garth. But Garth is mine now, and I know what to do with him.

On the thirteenth of the month, he is fired from his job. Apparently something was bothering Garth. He appeared tired all the time, was irritable and too preoccupied to perform his work. Hamburgers were burned; orders were confused. The stout man had to pay him off and tell him not to return. The dismissal is an unexpected development that will make my own job easier.

I have only two more days.

When Garth goes out for lunch the next afternoon, I let myself into the apartment and make lengthy, incendiary entries in the diary. I pin several of the newspaper clippings from the desk drawer over the poster of the blonde, then cross out each letter S in the words KISS, KISS and replace each with an L scrawled in black crayon. Then I lay the untraceable .38 Smith & Wesson revolver on top of the diary.

I phone Garth that evening and talk about us buying the gun. At first he doesn't remember, doesn't know what I'm talking about. Then he does recall buying the revolver, and remembers why we bought it.

I phone him several times in the early hours of the next morning.

At noon, I pack, check out of the hotel, and take a cab to the airport. There is nothing I can do now but wait and see if I've succeeded.

By the time the plane lands, the news is out. Senator Bradley Daniels and his pretty blonde wife, Gloria, have been shot and killed at a shopping center political rally, where the senator was trying to muster support for his campaign for the Presidency of the United States. The assassin, Luther Mitchell Garth, is in custody, claiming that he has been used and was the pawn of a conspiracy. At this point, however, officials have no reason to believe that he hasn't acted alone. The evidence is overwhelming that Garth is, not surprisingly, insane, and that his denials of sole guilt are nothing more than the ravings of a madman, perhaps a multiple personality. His apartment, the venomous entries in his diary, seem to confirm this. His is a classic case.

A week has passed. Ackerley is pleased. His employer is no doubt pleased. Whoever clandestinely chose Garth's letter, from the many threatening letters Presidential candidate Daniels routinely turned over to the authorities, must be pleased. And why not? It was a professional job, and on a rather grand scale.

I'm waiting now, in the usual place in the park, for Ackerley to pay me. And here he comes, a tall man with one shoulder noticeably higher than the other, walking with his customary, unhurried, deliberate gait. But there is someone with him this time, a short man in a light tan jacket. It isn't like Ackerley to bring company. I am curious, and slightly annoyed.

When the two men draw nearer, I see the way the man in the tan jacket is looking at me — warily, yet with a total disregard for how I am looking at him. Almost as if I'm inanimate. Fear drops through me like a wedge of ice.

"Congratulations," Ackerley says. "You have moved history." He is carrying the leather briefcase from which he usually pays me.

I nod, watching the man in the tan jacket watch me.

Ackerley sighs sadly, the sigh of a man taking a regrettable but necessary precaution. The short man draws a silenced automatic from beneath his jacket.

"Mr. Lockwood," Ackerley says, "there is a darker history of this world that must never be written."

I attempt to shout, but the silenced automatic jumps twice in the short man's hand, making two quick coughing sounds, like strangled laughter.

As I lay dying, watching the two men walk away, I concede through my agony that my killing was a neat, professional job. Ackerley must be pleased.

And no doubt his employer will be pleased.

Winds of Change

"Last night when I was with my wife I accidentally spoke your name."

Alison didn't answer David immediately. Slanted sunlight blasted from between the clouds in the California sky and glinted off the highly polished gray hood of her 1936 Chevy convertible. Tommy Dorsey's band was playing swing on the dashboard radio. The car was five years old, but Alison regarded it as if it were the newest model. She had only recently been able to afford such a luxury.

"What was your wife's reaction?" she asked at last, shifting gears for a steep grade in the twisting road.

David threw back his handsome head, his blond hair whipping forward in the turmoil of wind, and laughed. "None. She didn't understand me, I'm sure. There's so much she doesn't understand about me."

Alison didn't caution him to be more discreet, as she usually did. She seemed lulled by their motion through the warm, balmy evening. Her long auburn hair flowed gracefully where it curled from beneath the scarf that covered her head and was knotted beneath her chin. She knew that she and David were an enviable young couple in her sleek convertible, speeding along the coast road in mountainous Big Sur Country, with the shaded, thick redwood forest on their right and the sea, charging the shore and crashing sun-shot against the rocks on their left.

He extended a long arm and languidly, affectionately, dragged his fingertips across the shoulder of her wool sweater. She felt her heart accelerate at his touch.

"My wife doesn't know you're a spy," he said.

Alison turned her head toward him and smiled. "Let's hope not."

She braked the convertible, shifted gears again, and pulled to the side of the highway. Then she drove up the narrow, faintly defined dirt road that led to their usual picnic place. Within a few minutes, the car was parked in the shade of the redwood trees of smaller variety that grew in that wild section of California.

She got out the wicker picnic basket from the trunk, watching David's tall, lanky frame as he quite carefully spread the blanket on the grass. David was a methodical person, which was why he was good at his job; he had a talent and fondness for order. Alison stopped and deftly straightened the seams of her nylons, then joined him.

Alison Carter and David Blaine both worked at Norris Aircraft Corporation just north of Los Angeles. Alison was a secretary and David the chief of security. The people who were paying Alison for information about the top-secret XP25 pursuit plane had advised her to strike up an acquaintance with the plant security chief. If she were caught, the relationship would be a valuable insurance policy.

Of course Alison had followed their advice. She believed everything they told her. She had been barely eighteen when Karl Prager had first approached her, had first become her lover. Nineteen when their affair was over and she was in too deeply as an informer ever to hope she might get out.

Not that it had bothered Alison to sell "industrial information." Oh, she knew she was working for the Germans, actually, but what difference did that make? It wasn't as if America was at war. Politics didn't interest Alison in the slightest, and the money Karl paid her more than doubled her meager salary earned as a secretary.

Alison hadn't had to think of a way to meet David. Her rather extravagant habits, considering her salary, prompted him to ask her some routine questions one day. When she'd told him she was the beneficiary of her late father's will, he'd believed her.

They'd seen each other again, after business hours, despite the fact that David was married. Apparently he and his wife Glenda were having difficulties. For Alison, the business of seducing the shy and precise David Blaine quickly became pleasure. And by the time he found out she was violating company rules, he was willing to overlook her transgressions.

On Saturdays, David would often give Glenda an excuse, that probably even she didn't believe, and he and Alison would drive up the coast road in Alison's convertible and picnic with sandwiches and champagne in their private, lover's hideaway.

Alison sat down beside David on the blanket. She untied and removed her head scarf, plucking out the bobby pins helping to hold it in place. Through the trees, the undulating blue-green sea was barely visible, but she could hear its enigmatic whisper on the rocky beach.

David paused in unwrapping the sandwiches. He dug into his shirt pocket and handed Alison a folded sheet of paper patterned with scrawled numbers. "Here," he said casually, "these are the performance specifications you asked for."

The figures represented the date on the experimental plane's latest test flight. Alison accepted the paper with a smile and slipped it into a pocket of her skirt. She knew that David took the business of revealing company information no more seriously than she did. He didn't know to whom she was giving the information — probably he assumed it was a rival aircraft manufacturer — and he didn't care. It was his love affair that was important to him, that had consumed his very soul, and not dry columns of figures that meant nothing except to an aeronautical engineer. He knew he'd be fired if the company found out about Alison and him, but he could always get another job of some sort. And he'd still have Alison.

After they'd eaten the ham sandwiches and finished the champagne, David looked at her with his level blue eyes. His head was resting in her lap, and she was stroking his fine blond hair that was just beginning to thin at the crown of his head. Alison had thought the first time she saw David that he looked very much like movie star Richard Widmark.

"There's so much I want to say to you today," he told her.

"Not now," she said, bending her body and kissing him on the lips. "Let's not talk now."

As usual, David saw her point of view and agreed with it.

An hour later, in the purpling twilight, Alison lay on her back and watched a plane drone high overhead in the direction of the sea. A U.S. Navy plane, she noted, on a routine nighttime training mission.

David was asleep beside her, his deep, regular breathing merging with the sounds of the plane and the eternal sighing of the sea. Though her body was very still alongside his sleeping form, Alison's mind was tortured and turning.

Not that she had any real choice. Her time of choices was over. She wished David had never told her about speaking her name in front of his wife. But he had. And Alison knew that he might speak her name again in the wrong circumstances, even if tomorrow he still saw things her way.

Quietly, she rose from the blanket and fished in her straw

purse for her key ring. She walked to her car, the tall grass tickling her bare feet and ankles, thinking *tomorrow, tomorrow . . .*

She unlocked and opened the car's trunk, and left it open as she returned to stand over David. She was holding a small revolver that she'd gotten from the trunk, the gun they had given her.

Alison didn't want to miss where she was aiming, didn't want to hurt him more than necessary. She did love him.

She knelt beside David, placing the gun barrel inches from his temple, and glanced in all directions to make certain they were alone. In the sudden chill breeze rushing in from the ocean, she drew in her breath sharply and squeezed the trigger.

The crack of the gun seemed feeble in the vastness of mountains and sea.

Alison sat with her eyes clenched shut until the sound of David moving on the blanket ceased. Then, still not looking at him, she returned to the car and got a shovel from the trunk.

She wrapped David's still body in the blanket and dragged it deeper into the forest. She began to dig.

In a very few hours, halfway around the world, a signal would be given, and the Japanese would attack Pearl Harbor. War would immediately be declared, not only against Japan but against Germany and Italy as well. The rules of the game Alison was being forced to play would abruptly change. Who knew if David would have been willing to continue to play if the stakes were real? Who could say what else he might have accidentally let slip to his wife? Alison knew that much more than her job, and perhaps a criminal record, depended on David's silence now. Her survival was at stake.

As she cast loose earth over the huddled, motionless form in the blanket, Alison didn't realize she was burying a ring in David's pocket, the engagement ring he had intended to give her when he awoke. The ring with her initials engraved inside the band. The ring wrapped loosely in a copy of the letter he had written to his wife, confessing everything and explaining why he was leaving her.

Alison worked frantically with the shovel, feeling her tears track hotly down her cheeks. At least David's war was over. He was at peace. Her war was just beginning, and look what it had already forced her to do.

She would be one of the first to realize why hers was a losing cause.

The Lemon Drink Queen

She almost begged to be kidnapped, so I intended to oblige. Thana Norden was her name, the wife of Norman Norden, the millionaire lemon drink king. Old man Norden — about seventy years old — kept to himself in their big house on Florida's ocean coast, while his young wife Thana kept the bartenders busy in the big hotels up and down Collins Avenue.

Norman Norden worshipped his wife, and in the news releases concerning his civic activities, and in the society page write-ups, he never failed to mention the fact. "Worth all my money," he had said of her in one TV interview. That had stuck in my mind.

Thana acted the part of something worshipped. She was a very well-built brunette, of medium height and weight, about thirty, with large, slightly tilted brown eyes, long legs and a flaunting elegance about her. Her specialty, the way I heard, was to lead men on and then not deliver. She might not have been rare that way, but she was rare in a lot of other ways, and she loved to bring it to everyone's attention. I sat and heard her hold court with her bought friends in a lounge one evening. "My jewels . . . my car . . . he'd do anything for me . . . flying to Paris next Tuesday . . . why, he'd give a fortune to kiss my hand . . ." Those were the sort of remarks that dotted her conversation.

After watching Thana for a few weeks, I found that her favorite pastime also fitted in with what I had in mind. She liked to take long, solitary walks on the beach. I'd sit concealed in my old car and watch her stroll in the moonlight, and I'd consider the possibilities. I was almost forty now; the big break had never come. Everything I'd ever done had always started sweet and ended sour. Was I considering something stupid out of some mounting desperation, or had I realized finally that I had to take a chance?

I can't say I made up my mind all at once, or even consciously, but one day I realized that I *had* made up my mind.

So that night I took one final draw on my cigarette, took one final look through the windshield at the small figure of Thana Norden below me on the beach. She was walking barefoot in an evening dress, about to disappear around a gentle rise of sand. A long swelling wave rose from the dark ocean and rolled toward her to sigh and splay gently about her feet. In the moonlight she glistened like pure gold.

The kidnapping itself would be the easiest part; but where would I hide a package like Thana Norden?

I figured the answer to that would have to come later. The thing for me to do now was to learn all I could about Norman Norden himself. That way I'd know better how to proceed, and how much to ask for ransom.

It was easy to find out what I wanted to know about Norden — so easy it kind of scared me. He was more important than I'd thought, worth more than I'd thought. He'd inherited over a million dollars and the Norden Lemon Drink Company from his father, Milton Norden. Then, with the increasing popularity of concentrated frozen lemonade, he'd built his father's business to ten times its former size and branched out into manufacturing other food products. Alone, without an heir until Thana, Norman Norden had acquired a huge home in New England, a plush New York town house, two swank penthouse apartments in

191

Miami and a vacation "cottage" in the Bahamas. He spent ninety-nine percent of his time in the sprawling mansion in Miami Beach, and from his office there he conducted his vast business.

On a particularly broiling, humid afternoon I lay on my back in bed and decided after some deliberation to ask $250,000 ransom for the precious Thana. With that figure in mind, I fell asleep listening to the rain begin to fall.

That evening, before it began to get dark, I had a quick snack, then drove to look over Norden's Miami property. I'd learned that both penthouses were used for business purposes only, and that they were seldom used at all. If someone very important came to town on Norden business, the larger penthouse with its pool atop the Brently Building was opened and put at the client's disposal.

I parked near the Brently Building and looked up at its top floor. According to the business-magazine article I'd read at the library, this, the more used of the two penthouses, was occupied for only a few weeks out of the year.

Squinting up into the sunlight, I could make out long rows of draped windows. A little casual conversation with the doorman told me the penthouse was unoccupied now, and the tiniest seed of an idea began to sprout in my mind.

When I saw the site of the second penthouse, smaller and less expensive than the first, on the top of the twenty-story Martinaire Hotel, that seed took root. The Martinaire was part of a section of older buildings, onetime fine hotels that depressed economic conditions were forcing out of business. What interested me most about the old but stately Martinaire was the vacant west wing. That wing, I discovered, was being remodeled to contain fewer but larger rooms. The front of the building was a sheer twenty-story rise, but the west wing rose only twelve stories to stair-step

192

into the main section of building. I investigated further, then walked back to my car, smiling.

I had everything planned and was ready to act two evenings later. I tried to make up my mind when to perform the actual snatch, and as I followed a slightly drunk Thana Norden out of a bar that night about eleven o'clock, I decided then was as ripe a time as any if she were heading for her late walk on the beach.

Thana must have been even drunker than usual, for I had some trouble keeping my old sedan up with her fast and reckless driving. She pushed her little red sports car so hard it was almost suicidal, her dark hair whipping behind and around her in the wind. She was something, Thana Norden was, like a heroine from a book.

Finally she parked the car where she usually did, ran down to the beach and bent gracefully sideways to remove her shoes. I parked down the road about a hundred yards in the direction I knew she'd be walking and sat waiting, my hands clenched on the steering wheel.

After what seemed a long wait, I saw her below, walking slowly and carrying her shoes in one hand, looking out as she often did to the rolling dark sea. I got out of the car, shutting the door softly behind me, and watched her walk past before I started down toward her.

The sighing of the waves kept her from hearing me as I approached from behind, and when I touched her shoulder she whirled with a startled look in her pale face. "Thana Norden?"

"Yes . . . ?" she said, frowning as if I'd interrupted her from complex thought. "What do you want?"

"You're coming with me," I said, watching her eyes for the fear that would allow me to manage her; but there was no fear — only annoyance, indignation.

"You must be out of your mind!" she snapped.

"*You* must be. A solid-gold girl like you, in the habit of walking alone on the beach at night. You were bound to be stolen."

"Stolen?" Now she looked at me curiously. "You're *kidnapping* me?"

"You've guessed it."

"You're serious?"

I nodded, drawing the small .32 revolver from my belt.

She looked up at the stars and laughed. "All right," she said when she was finished, "I'm kidnapped. You go ahead and call the shots."

"Walk along with me," I said, motioning with the revolver, and side by side we began the walk toward my car. Thana didn't seem frightened at all, didn't even seem nervous, though in a way she seemed excited, almost like a pretty girl embarking on a much anticipated date.

When we reached the sparsely grassed earth we stopped so she could put her high-heeled shoes back on. Then I prodded her ribs with the gun and we walked on faster toward the car.

I let Thana drive while I sat beside her with the revolver leveled at her side. I was glad to see that in the confines of my car she seemed more frightened than before.

"Back to the city," I ordered her.

"My makeup is in my car," she said as we passed her parked red convertible.

"It stays there. It won't matter what you look like for the next few days."

She drove on, staring ahead at the curving dark road.

"How much ransom are you going to ask?" she said after a while.

"More than you're worth."

194

"I'd like to say you can't get away with it, but you probably can. My husband will pay plenty to have me back."

"Thanks for the moral support. Now be quiet and drive."

"I'm not stupid, you know," she said lightly, "even though I am beautiful. I know I'm worthless to you dead, so don't bother with your threats."

"A lot can happen to you without your dying," I told her. That seemed to get to her, and I saw her jaw muscles tense as she tried to concentrate on the road.

"I said I wasn't stupid," she remarked after a few minutes. "After you get the ransom money I will be worthless to you, and you've let me see your face. You know I'll be able to identify you."

"Sure you will, only you'll never see me again, and I can change myself enough so no one will be able to identify me from your description." What I told her was true. Acting had been one of my many short-lived careers that had turned out to be something other than I'd thought, so the art of altering my appearance wasn't new to me. My normally sand-colored hair was dyed black now and combed low over my forehead, and the shape and thickness of my eyebrows were subtly changed by dark pencil. The fashionable dyed mustache I wore could also go when the time came. Naturally I wouldn't be seen anymore at my usual haunts, because my old life as a self-described beach bum would be over.

A tractor-trailer whined past us with difficulty, doing over seventy. I cautioned Thana to stay below the speed limit. Death-defying driving seemed to be a habit with her.

When we reached the Martinaire Hotel I had Thana drive around the block and park in the alley alongside the vacant west wing. I moved quickly, with the smoothness and economy born of careful planning.

After reaching into the back seat and grabbing the duffle bag I'd brought, I shoved Thana roughly from the car, followed her with the gun pressed against her. Through a lockless wooden door I took her inside the empty wing to a small room that probably had been used to store linens or cleaning equipment. A light in that room couldn't be seen from outside, and by the glow of my flashlight I bound Thana tightly to a metal support and pressed adhesive tape over her mouth. She sat limply without a suggestion of struggle, and her dark eyes were trained on me as I took one final look at her by the flashlight beam, then walked from the room and closed the door behind me.

Within twenty minutes I was back, and when I opened the door to the small room and switched on the flashlight, Thana was looking at me as she had when I left. I'd parked my car ten blocks away in the garage I'd leased and taken a cab back to within two blocks of the Martinaire Hotel. From there I'd walked the rest of the way.

I untied Thana but left the tape across her mouth, and jabbing the small of her back with the gun barrel, marched her outside again into the alley. With one deft toss I looped a thin, weighted rope about the bottom rung of the counter-balanced steel stairs of the old fire escape and pulled them down. Then I slung the duffle bag over my shoulder and motioned Thana to climb ahead of me.

It seemed like an hour, that climb. We passed darkened window after darkened window as we rose. During the day this part of the building would be teeming with workmen, but at this time it was completely deserted and ideal for my purpose.

We were both breathing hard when we reached the top window. I'd taken care of the latch earlier, and I slid the

196

window open and pushed Thana inside, cursing softly for her to be silent. I used my flashlight with a dark handkerchief over the lens to guide us, but I knew where we were going, could have stage-directed the whole thing in my mind even in the dark. I let Thana, struggling for air, lean against the elevator well as I pressed the button. She didn't seem afraid, and from time to time her frantic breathing even seemed to take on the aspect of exhilarated laughter behind the adhesive tape.

Now the riskiest moment: we had to negotiate a short stretch of hall that passed occupied rooms.

The elevator doors slid open onto the empty hall, and we moved through the door at the end of the hall and up the narrow, steep stairway to the roof. Now I felt sure we'd make it as I gripped Thana's elbow and walked with her across the tar and gravel roof of the twentieth story of the Martinaire Hotel, the roof of Norman Norden's penthouse apartment. Near the center of the roof, we stopped.

I bound Thana's hands behind her, and crossed her ankles and bound them tightly. Then I took a longer piece of rope from the bag, looped it beneath her arms and tied it behind her.

I'd already forced the lock on the small opaque skylight to Norden's apartment, and I raised it and propped it open carefully. After dropping my duffle bag through the opening, I gently lowered Thana into the darkness below. The lack of vibration in the rope told me she was completely relaxed and cooperative. I tucked my flashlight downward through my belt so I could see below, then hung by my hands from the skylight for a moment before dropping to crouch beside Thana on the floor.

I'd brought it off! It would have been impossible to get into the penthouse unseen through the main part of the hotel, past doormen, guests and an army of bellhops. Yet here I was, in the least likely spot. While Norden fretted and sent out his private searchers, or even if he called the police, here I would be above it all in the plush penthouse of the lemon drink king himself. The irony of it really got to me, made me feel terrific. I almost laughed out loud as I straightened and moved the soft beam of the shielded flashlight about the room. Thana was sitting awkwardly cross-ankled, staring up at me, her idle hands still bound behind her.

After making sure the heavy, lined draperies were completely closed, I turned the lights on low. Very, very nice. The large living room we were in was furnished modern and plushly carpeted in beige, with a jagged stone fireplace on one wall. The whole thing was in the subdued taste of extreme wealth.

I walked over and untied Thana's ankles, then helped her to her feet and removed the long rope from beneath her arms. After promising to knock her unconscious if she screamed, I peeled the tape from across her mouth.

"Ever been here before?" I asked her.

She nodded her head yes, working her lips together to ease the sting from the peeled-off adhesive tape. "A few times."

"Plush," I said admiringly. "And private."

"Now what?" Thana asked, walking as if to loosen a stiffness in her legs, moving her slender shoulders as if they ached. "Am I supposed to spend the next several days with my arms tied behind me?"

"Not if you behave."

"It would be foolish of me even to consider misbehaving."

"I'm glad you see it that way," I said, but I wondered if

she really did. I couldn't trust her.

I walked around, getting the layout of the apartment set in my mind: two gigantic bedrooms, two baths, a large kitchen, a dining room with an oversize chandelier, and the room we were in, spacious and glassed-in on three sides hung with heavy draperies.

I untied Thana and told her to sit on the long, modern sofa. Then I disappointed her by showing her the simple device I intended using to limit her movements: a pair of handcuffs I'd bought at a magic shop. I snapped the cuffs about her right wrist and a polished wood arm support of the heavy sofa. Then I removed her gold wedding ring and dropped it into my shirt pocket.

"I have some gold fillings, too," she said.

"I'll remember." I patted my pocket and walked over to slouch in a soft chair.

In the early-morning hours, after tying Thana firmly to the sofa and gagging her, I climbed back up onto the roof and left the same way I'd gotten into the Martinaire. I wore dark overalls now, lettered 24-HOUR SERVICE across the back, so I'd attract a minimum of attention and be difficult to remember if someone in the hotel did happen to glimpse me.

From the phone booth on the corner I made the call to Norman Norden's residence. At first, whoever answered wouldn't put me through to Norden but when I mentioned Thana's name and said it concerned her safety, Norden was on the line in ten seconds.

Norden sounded anxious, overwrought. When I told him I was holding Thana for ransom he let out a long, old-sounding sigh, as if he'd expected something like this to happen and now his fears were realized.

When I told him how much it would cost to get her back,

he simply said, "Very well," without even hesitating. I admired him then, and felt a little sorry for him, until I thought about his money. He asked me how he could be sure I had Thana. I told him not to worry, that I'd prove it to him, then contact him later. The agreement was the standard one, that he wouldn't call the police and I wouldn't harm Thana. He wanted to talk some more, get more assurance that his young wife wouldn't be touched, but I hung up on him to keep the conversation short. After slipping the gold wedding ring into the stamped envelope I'd prepared with Norden's address typed on it, I dropped the envelope into a mailbox near the phone booth. I bought a detective novel from a big all-night drugstore across the street, then went back to the dark alley fire escape of the Martinaire Hotel's west wing.

Thana was awake and uncomfortable. When I removed the tape from her mouth it released a stream of curses and complaints.

"Take it easy," I said. "You wouldn't talk to me like that if I had a million bucks."

"You'd need two million!" she told me, chopping the words off angrily. "What did Norman say?"

I looked up at her as I was untying the rope around her ankles.

"That *is* where you went, isn't it? To telephone your demand for ransom?"

I nodded, unwinding the rope and standing. "Your husband's worried about you, and he didn't seem to think a quarter of a million was too high a price to get you back."

"Just the way you planned, hmm?"

"Just," I said, untying her arms, then handcuffing her right wrist to the sofa arm in such a way that she could stretch out and sleep.

"Don't think I'm not aware of what else you plan." She was glaring up at me with a dark, almost-a-dare defiance in her eyes, and I realized what she meant. "After all," she said, "rape carries the same penalty as kidnapping."

"Maybe you're flattering yourself," I told her.

"I know better!" she spat out at me. It was almost as if she were trying to argue me into it to prove she was right.

I stood looking down at her and she met my gaze without blinking. "You're a means of making a quarter of a million dollars," I said. "You don't have to worry about being molested by me — if you *are* worried."

I walked to the other side of the room where slanted morning light was beginning to edge in around the heavy draperies. When it was light enough out, they could be opened. That shouldn't be noticeable or remarkable from twenty stories below in the street, and I was beginning to feel like a prisoner in the apartment myself. Thana had been right to an extent. Desire for her would intrude itself into any man's mind after a while. However, one of the main reasons I never actually considered touching her was that I knew if I did, Norman Norden would never rest, would never let himself die, unless I'd preceded him. The money he could spare and forget, but I knew he had to have his wife back "as was."

I stretched out in one of the bedrooms and slept for a few hours. Afterward, I arranged things in the apartment so Thana would have a little necessary freedom of movement. First I closed and locked the kitchen and bedroom doors, then I checked in the hall bathroom and removed anything she might use for a weapon, then broke the lock on the polished gold doorknob. The telephone was my big worry; Thana had only to lift the receiver from its cradle to indicate to the hotel below that someone was in the penthouse.

The phone was on a very long cord, though, so I set it high up on the top wall bookshelf where she couldn't reach it. I fastened the receiver down with adhesive tape so that even if Thana pulled the phone down by the cord it would hold firm. She thanked me when I freed her from the sofa and let her walk about with her wrists handcuffed before her.

Most of the day she just roamed around the apartment, sitting now and then to read part of the paperback detective novel I'd bought. I watched her try and fail to concentrate on the book.

"You have lousy taste in literature," she said at last, giving up and throwing the novel across the room.

"I bought it for you," I said, getting up and walking to the long window overlooking the street. The draperies were open more than halfway and the view of the city was impressive. Below me I could see the ant-like cars feeling their way through heavy traffic to the stop sign at the intersection, where they paused and seemed to consider which way to go next before moving on straight or turning.

"This is intolerable," Thana said behind me.

"Be quiet and I'll fix supper," I told her without moving.

"Fix what for supper?"

"Bologna sandwiches."

"That was lunch."

"It'll be breakfast too," I said, and it was.

I listened to Thana complain the rest of the next day, then late that night I bound her to the sofa again and went out to make my second telephone call.

Norden had already received the wedding ring in the mail.

"I want this to be over with," he said in a shaky voice. "I have the money ready in small bills. I took the liberty of assuming you'd want it that way."

"And the police?"

"I swear I haven't talked to them, to anyone!"

"Tomorrow night," I told him, getting to the point to shorten the call, "send your chauffeur in your blue limousine, carrying the money packed in one suitcase. Have him turn north on Route Seven from Highway Y at exactly eleven o'clock, and tell him to drive at exactly forty miles an hour. When he sees the flash of a blue light, he's to pull to the side of the road immediately, dump the suitcase and drive on. Understood?"

"Understood," Norden said "What about Thana? Is she —"

"She's fine," I said, "and if everything goes right she'll be back to you in no time. *If* everything goes right."

"You can trust me," Norden said. "I swear it. But you mustn't harm her."

"I don't want to, Mr. Norden," I said, and hung up.

Of course it was true, I didn't want to harm Thana; and for some reason I believed I *could* trust Norman Norden not to bring in the police at this point. The old man, in my brief but tense conversations with him, had shown an admirable self-control and concern for the safety of his wife. I guess you'd say, a certain class.

I got back to the penthouse and untied, then handcuffed Thana to the sofa so she could sleep, and so I could sleep without worrying about her getting to the telephone or hurling something through a window at this stage of the game.

"I think our worries are about over," I told her. "Your husband's going to pay off tomorrow night."

She sneered up at me. "Did you think he might not pay to have me back?"

"Not for a second. I'm beginning to think I should have asked for more."

"You underestimated my value."

"Or Norden overestimates it."

She spat at me then, but I moved back and she missed.

"How's it feel to be set up for life with millions of dollars?" I asked.

"It feels great! It's a feeling you'll never know."

"You sound like you're trying to convince both of us."

She laughed, a quick humorless laugh that was more a reflex from a touched nerve than anything else. The swiftness of her mood changes was startling, though for some reason the changes seemed to be only on the surface.

"You're partly right." She lay back and rested her head on the sofa arm. "It gets boring after a while . . . like anything else. You might find that out. You're the same unhappy you, with or without money."

"But it beats starving," I said.

Thana shrugged. "I guess anything beats that. Except maybe sleeping stiff as a board on this damned couch."

"One more night," I said, "and you can be free to recuperate on your yacht."

I turned my back on her and went into the bedroom where I began going over the way I had things planned for the next night's pickup. I'd turn north onto Route Seven two minutes after Norden's chauffeur had entered it, and drive the legal limit of sixty. Route Seven wasn't heavily traveled at that time of night, and if I did pass any cars between us I could look them over to make sure they weren't police. Our respective speeds would bring the cars together at the right spot. Then I would accelerate close to the limousine, blink my blue-lensed flashlight through the windshield and drop back to wait for the chauffeur to pull to the side and dump the suitcase. I'd park well back of him with my headlights on, and when the limousine drove off I would speed forward, pick up the money, and a third of a mile down the road turn onto the cloverleaf and maze of roads at the heavily traveled state highway. A quarter of a mile from that cloverleaf was another one. If anyone were trying to trace me he'd have to reckon on the possibility of me traveling in any of eight directions, and Norden's chauffeur wouldn't even be able to identify my car. I wouldn't return to the penthouse. I'd check the money, then phone Norden and tell him where to find Thana. It seemed foolproof; as foolproof as you can make something like that.

As the next day dragged by, the waiting began to play on my nerves. Still, there was that feeling of anticipation — a good anticipation — because, unlike so many of my schemes, I was somehow sure the whole thing would work as planned.

Thana's nerves seemed to be wearing thin, too. She paced the large, luxurious living room, absently raising and lowering her handcuffed wrists before her as if completely absorbed in whatever she was thinking. The way she was acting kind of surprised me. I was sure she was convinced I didn't mean to kill her when I had the ransom money. She should have been feeling a pleasant anticipation too, an anticipation of freedom.

I tried to ignore her endless pacing, tried to ignore my own nervousness, and I made a good try at reading the paperback novel I'd bought three nights before, but the words were only words, nothing more. I set the book aside and checked my watch. Five o'clock. I decided it might be a good idea to try to get whatever rest I could before tonight's activity, so I handcuffed Thana to the sofa arm and slouched on the other end of the sofa myself. After what seemed like an hour, I dozed off lightly . . .

"Who the devil are you?"

"I'm his prisoner! He's kidnapped me and he's holding me prisoner!"

The question, asked in a man's incredulous voice, stirred me from sleep. The answer, screamed in Thana's shrieking voice, made my eyes open with a start.

There were two men, an older man in a well-cut, dark suit, and a short, mustached man in work clothes, carrying some kind of long metal toolbox.

I stood, not really knowing what to do, and I saw that I'd drawn my revolver and was aiming it unsurely at them. They both backed away slowly, then the mustached man suddenly hurled his toolbox at me. I raised my hands but not in time. The heavy box struck me full on the chest and I staggered backward. The gun roared in my ear and I found myself sitting amidst wrenches and lengths of cut pipe, the toolbox open and lying across one of my legs. The two men were gone.

I kicked the toolbox away with a clatter and stood up, trembling, wondering what had happened, how it *could* have happened. Thana was staring up at me from the sofa, her features set in a strange-looking sort of defiance.

As I walked toward her I saw blood on my hand that was still holding the gun. Something had cut my arm badly and the blood was running down in a thick, red current.

"Who were they?" I asked in a shaken voice, but Thana only stared at me with that same rigid look on her features. I backed away from her and went toward the bathroom to wash some of the blood from my arm and try to stop the bleeding.

Halfway down the hall, I knew.

I heard it first, rather than saw it. Then I stopped and

looked down at the inch-deep pool of water I was walking in. I sloshed the last ten feet to the bathroom door and went in.

The cold-water tap in the wash basin was barely turned on, the water running silently in a twisting, steady stream that had filled the washbasin and caused it to overflow. As I went to pull the plug I saw that toilet paper had been stuck into the overflow drain at the back of the basin. Thana had engineered this earlier in the evening to signal for help. The water had finally run through to the floors below and was brought to the attention of the hotel management, who had brought it to the attention of a plumber.

Cursing the first time I'd ever seen Thana Norden, I splashed water over my throbbing arm, ripped off my shirt sleeve and made a tourniquet of it that helped slow the flow of blood from the jagged cut near my elbow. I'd known from the beginning there wouldn't be time to descend twenty stories to the street if the police were called, and as I walked back into the living room I could already hear the screams of faraway sirens.

Thana was sitting on the sofa calmly now, staring up at me with certainly more defiance than fear.

"You fool!" I almost screamed at her. "Why did you do it? You knew it was almost over, you were almost free! Why did you mess up the whole thing?"

Her face shone with intensity. "Did you think I believed what you told me about not killing me? Believed anything you said?"

"It was true! I thought you knew it was true!"

The sirens were much louder now, and some of them stopped directly below. I ran to switch off the lamp in the corner near the fireplace, and the room was snapped to near total darkness.

The telephone rang. I walked to it, my numbed legs

moving jerkily, and untaped and lifted the receiver.

"I advise you not to harm the girl," a slow but tense, deep voice said in my ear. "Have you?"

I waited a long time before speaking, listening to the even breathing on the other end of the line. "No," I said. "She's all right. I was never going to harm her."

"Then you're smart. You should be smart enough to know the only thing for you now is to come down unarmed and turn yourself over to us."

I thought about that while I squeezed the receiver so hard my head ached. The penalty for kidnapping was death; I could be turning myself over for death.

"The building and the entire block are completely surrounded," the voice said. "There's nothing else for you to do but surrender, it will go easier on you since you haven't harmed Mrs. Norden."

I hung up.

There had to be something I could do. *Something!* Escape down the fire escape would be virtually impossible — but what else was there? One other possibility: I could use Thana as a hostage and make them let me out, make them give me a car and a head start.

Yet I knew that was almost no possibility at all.

Powerful spotlight beams hit the windows then, bathing most of the room in a chalky white light, changing night to fierce day outside the top floors of the Martinaire Hotel. The draperies were opened wide, and I moved along the wall to their edge and stared down, but all I could make out were the incredibly bright lights aimed up at me.

"Your whole idea's turned rotten on you, hasn't it?" Thana said behind me.

The telephone rang again, and I went quickly to answer it.

"I thought you were smart," the voice said. "Do the smart thing now."

"Maybe I'm not as smart as you think," I answered. "And I wouldn't try to come up if I were you. Mrs. Norden might get hurt." I knew that Thana was my only card left to play. If the little fool hadn't blown everything . . . just when I'd almost brought it off!

"Hello . . ." It was another voice on the phone, a familiar voice.

"Norman Norden?"

"It is," the voice said. "Listen to me before you do anything else. Will you agree to that?"

"If you talk fast," I said.

"Fast and to the point," Norden answered. There was a decisiveness in the aged voice that hadn't been there in our earlier conversations. "We both know your situation is almost hopeless; your only chance of escape is to use Thana as a hostage, and that would be a slim chance. A deal is what I offer. I have money, power, influence — you have my wife. If you bring Thana down, unharmed, and release her, I'll see that you get a car and four hours of immunity from the law."

I tried to consider the angles to that sort of offer, but my arm was bleeding again and I felt faint. It was hard for me to concentrate on anything.

"I can offer something else," Norden said, taking my hesitation for consideration. "If you are apprehended later, I'll pull every string to see that you get off lightly."

"Why would you do that?"

"Why shouldn't I? I'm considered by some to be a mercenary man. In my youth I was even more mercenary. I can understand what you did and why you did it, so I bear you no personal animosity. And I've never broken my word on a

209

business deal. My only concern is for my wife, can't you understand that? Please bring her down safely and I'll see that you're given a car, four hours, a chance! Please!"

"Can you really do it?"

"Of course I can. Thana's safety is the prime concern of the police, too. If I effect a deal to get her back unharmed, they'll go along with me."

I was sitting on the floor now, looking at Thana and thinking more clearly. "I want something else."

"Something else . . . ? All right, yes, you have it. I intended giving it to you for Thana in the first place. It was the hotel manager who recognized Thana and called in the police. The money will be in the car."

"Along with an electronic device so the police can trace me."

Anger and frustration welled up in Norden's voice when he answered. "Isn't there anything I can do to get you to *believe* me?"

I was surprised myself to find that I did believe him, that I trusted his word. I believed he'd do anything for Thana, and he and I both knew that what he offered was my only real chance.

"How soon can the car be here?" I asked.

"It's already here and waiting for you. The money will take half an hour."

"We have a deal," I said, and hung up. I made it to my feet and said to Thana, "I wish I had your kind of luck."

"What does that mean?" She was sitting very straight, glaring at me contemptuously.

"It means you're part of a trade. Your safety for mine. Your husband's down below worrying about you."

Thana didn't bother to answer, just stared at me for a long moment, then turned her head to watch the slight play of the bright spotlight beams over the wide windows.

I went into the bathroom again, found some gauze and bandaged the cut on my arm. Then I washed my face and hands in cool water and fixed my rumpled and bloodstained clothes so they looked almost passable. Then I waited for everything to develop.

A half hour hadn't passed when the telephone rang again. I got assurances from everyone: Norden, the hotel manager, the police captain in charge of operations below. A gray car with its motor idling would be parked directly outside the lobby entrance.

I told them I was coming down, and went to get Thana.

"Come on," I said, unlocking her handcuffs and holding her by the wrist. "We're going downstairs." As I pulled her to her feet her face was impassive, her body tense.

"Do you really think I believe you're turning me free?" she said. She gazed out the windows again at the brilliant white light sent up from the scene of excitement and turmoil below. As I saw the glazed shine in her dark eyes I knew for the first time that in a way she was enjoying being the center of it all.

Suddenly, with more strength than I thought she had, she jerked her wrist loose and was free of me. She snatched up a long-necked glass vase from a coffee table and backed away.

"Listen," I pleaded, "there's no reason for this now. What I told you is true. You can talk to your husband on the phone if you like."

"It's a lie! It's all a lie!"

"Don't be crazy." I moved toward her, not understanding why she wouldn't believe me. "It's over. You're safe. You're going home."

She slashed the air with the long vase and I stepped

211

back. We were near the windows now, and I had to shield my eyes from the light. I could hear Thana's breath hissing through her teeth. Then, when I saw the glinting, half-secret grin on her face, I realized that she *did* believe me.

I drew the gun from my belt. "No games now," I said, waving the barrel at her. "There isn't any reason to be afraid. All I want to do is take you downstairs. Now walk to the elevator." I motioned with the gun toward the entrance to the private elevator, but Thana moved the other way.

I lunged then and grabbed at her wrist, grasped it for a moment. She lashed down at me with the vase and I raised my other arm in defense. The vase glanced off my shoulder, and at the same time Thana twisted, twirled from my grip. I grabbed at her waist, felt the smooth material of her dress slip painfully from my fingers as she hurled herself out into the blinding light beyond the glass that had shattered behind her.

After the sound of splintering glass came her scream, a long, shrieking scream, a scream of terror to others who might have heard it. From where I stood paralyzed, however, the sound was different: it was a high, triumphant scream, a scream of deliverance.

In the echo of that scream I suddenly understood about Thana, about the reckless way she lived. I understood her fast and dangerous driving, her relentless drinking, her long nighttime walks looking out to sea. Yet here, twenty stories high and the focal point of concern, excitement, a thousand upturned eyes and dozens of brilliant, probing spotlights, I was the instrument she'd chosen.

I meant her no harm at all; I'd have done anything to save her and myself. That's the way it's been all my life. They say you learn from experience, but sometimes the trouble with that is, by the time you've learned, the experience is over and it's too late.

The arrest, the trial, the sentence — I went through the whole formality in a kind of detached haze. The upright citizens of the state would execute me a dozen times if they could. Murder, kidnapping, and the wrath of Norman Norden — I had about as much chance of surviving as Thana Norden did after flying through that plate of glass into the sultry Miami night sky. So the electric chair's waiting for me, and I'm waiting for it. I'll have to agree with the judge that in the penthouse that night a murder was committed, only there's some confusion in my mind as to who was the victim.

Police Commissioner Lyle Brell was early, and not without reason. He took the long flight of steps to the renovated three story brownstone with the feigned vigor of a middle-aged man who fancies himself still in shape. Absently he brought up his right hand in purposely casual movement and smoothed his graying but full head of hair. Early as it was, there might be a stray camera or two here.

He rang the doorbell and waited. If there were a camera or two about, the tall brownstone building, converted from a six-family apartment, offered a flattering backdrop. The hedges were neatly trimmed and the porch and window frames were freshly painted. In one of the worst sections of the city, the building shone like a testament to what could be done if only the residents cared. The most impressive thing was that the ex-convicts had done all the work themselves.

Ben Wert, the notorious paroled safecracker, opened the door for him.

"Afternoon, Ben." The commissioner was careful to shake hands for the possible camera.

"Commissioner Brell! We weren't expecting you for a while." Wert was a sharp-eyed, grinning man who always appeared to need a shave.

"I thought it might be wise to drop by early," Brell said, "before the press and all the television boys show up."

"And I'd call that a sound idea, Commissioner." The voice belonged to Reverend Callahan, founder and manager of Care Halfway House. "It's no secret you're running for Congress later this year, as well you should. Can't blame you for wanting to see that things here go smoothly."

"It's not so much that, Reverend Callahan," Brell said, "as it would be good for Care Halfway House to make a favorable impression on the people of this city through the media. After all, you depend entirely on donations."

Reverend Callahan, a small, white-haired, blue-eyed man with an oft-broken nose, gave the beautiful smile that had evoked many a donation. He was a mail-order reverend, as everyone knew, but no one cared. It was results that counted. "And your consideration is appreciated, Commissioner," he said, "as much as the generous check from Citizens Against Crime."

Citizens Against Crime had grown into a large organization in the past few years, its membership swelling with the city's rapidly rising crime rate. Reverend Callahan had spoken a few times at their meetings. Since the organization's donation was a sizable one, and since the commissioner *did* intend to run for Congress, and since such donations were the lifeblood of Care Halfway House, it had been decided that it would be advantageous for all concerned if Commissioner Brell would present Reverend Callahan with the check in a ceremony before the press and TV cameras.

"What you've accomplished here is both useful and impressive," the commissioner was saying. "These 'halfway houses' to help ex-convicts adjust to their freedom and stay out of prison are nothing new, but I'd feel safe in saying that yours is the most successful such venture in the country." *And if it helps drop the crime rate,* the commissioner added to himself, *it will help me to become a Congressman.*

Callahan beamed. "An exaggeration, Commissioner, but it makes me proud nonetheless."

215

"You *should* be proud," said the fat, red-faced man who had slipped through the still-open door.

"If it isn't Murphy of *The Times*," Callahan said with a warm smile.

"Would you put your arm around the reverend?" Murphy asked Brell, readying his camera.

"Proud to," the commissioner said, as his arm snaked about Callahan's shoulders and his teeth flashed.

There would be no time now to make sure things went perfectly, the commissioner thought, but it probably didn't matter anyway. The check presentation should still result in plenty of votes.

The rest of the press was arriving now in droves, fifteen minutes early to get the candid, human side of things as the enterprising Murphy had done. A microphone was thrust before the commissioner's face.

"How would you sum up the success of Care Halfway House?" the reporter asked.

"What Reverend Callahan has accomplished here is both useful and impressive," the commissioner said, smiling. "I'd feel safe in saying that it's the most successful such venture in the country."

"Do you plan to toss your hat in the ring for Congressman later this year, sir?"

"At this point, no. But the future is uncharted territory to us all, Tom."

The reporter seemed flattered that the commissioner knew his name. Commissioner Brell kept up on such things.

Another microphone, and a TV mini-camera from Channel Seven Eyespot news.

"Commissioner, could you tell me the significance of this donation?"

"Our alarming crime statistics are a matter that should

concern us all, Bill, and while organizations like Citizens Against Crime are alerting people to that fact, establishments like Care Halfway House are doing their share on the front lines, so to speak."

"Do you intend to run for Congress, Commissioner?"

"There is a bridge —"

"I think they want us outside," Reverend Callahan said. "Mrs. Dunhaker has arrived with the check."

Indeed, on the front porch of the neatly trimmed brownstone stood the redoubtable stout form of Mrs. Irene Dunhaker, president of Citizens Against Crime. Several reporters were talking with her while a knot of neighborhood people and a few minor city officials gathered at the base of the steps. A microphone had been set up, Commissioner Brell saw, as he and Reverend Callahan stepped outside. Television cameras from all the major channels were on hand.

Both Reverend Callahan and the commissioner shook hands with the smiling Mrs. Dunhaker for the press, then the commissioner stepped nimbly to the microphone.

"It's all there in the statistics," he said, when at last he got to the point. "In this age of 'revolving door' courts and prisons, we have here an example of what can be done to help sincere men regain their honesty and self-respect — for their own good and the good of the community. In the past four years a mere six percent of the ex-residents of Care Halfway House have been arrested for a serious offence. And this during a period when our city's crime rate has risen forty-eight percent!

"Some of the men who've passed through this building I have known personally as habitual criminals and thought to be incorrigible. I'm happy to say that Reverend Callahan has proved me wrong! The once-familiar names no longer

217

show up on the police blotters, in the statistics. I can think of no better place for the earnestly donated funds of Citizens Against Crime." With an elaborate gesture Mrs. Dunhaker handed the commissioner the $5,000 check. Without looking down at it, the commissioner passed it on to Reverend Callahan.

"I'm pleased," Reverend Callahan said, stepping to the microphone and smiling his beautiful smile. Flashbulbs popped. "Pleased for myself and for my boys . . . the fellas who have succeeded against odds that had overwhelmed them before. I'm happy for all of us . . . and all of us thank you." He kissed the smiling Mrs. Dunhaker on the cheek and shook hands with the smiling commissioner. Flashbulbs popped again. End of presentation . . .

From a third floor window Reverend Callahan looked down at Commissioner Brell's taxpayer-purchased sedan as it slowed briefly for the corner stop sign, then made a left turn. Members of the press and Mrs. Dunhaker had likewise departed. A few area residents stood below, enjoying the sunshine and chatting. Then, still talking, they began to walk slowly toward the corner.

Reverend Callahan turned away from the window, toward Willie Clark, a short, sad-faced man who had recently been released from an eight to ten year sentence for bank robbery. Despite his plea of not guilty, there had been little doubt of his guilt — no doubt at all in the minds of the jury — as he had been surprised inside the bank's vault after closing time. He was the latest to be recommended to Care Halfway House.

"I'd like you to meet Ben Wert," Reverend Callahan said, nodding toward where the ex-safecracker sat in a corner with his legs propped up on a footstool. "He's something of an expert in your field and a member of our guidance staff."

"I know him by reputation," Clark said warmly.

"Then I'm sure you'll listen to what he has to say and accept his help."

"You got caught on that bank job because you used too much explosive on the safe and somebody on the street heard," Wert said with something like condescension. "And you left a window open where you'd shorted the alarm and entered. What you'll learn here is not only everything about safe-cracking, but about breaking and entering as well.

"A good safe man needs some of the skills of a good house-breaker. Another staff member will instruct you in that." Wert let his legs drop from the footstool and sat up straight. "You've got to listen close here, Clark. We teach you everything you need to know, but then it's up to you."

"What he's saying," Reverend Callahan said with a reassuring smile, "is that when you leave here, we don't want you to become the wrong kind of statistic."

King of the Kennel

With his eyes still focused on the girl on the other side of the restaurant, Alex Goodnight watched the waiter approach, a mere shadow figure in the corner of his vision.

At precisely the right moment he turned and addressed the waiter. "Just coffee, please. Black."

Alex's voice was slightly but not very noticeably slurred. He sensed rather than saw the waiter nod and leave. Again Alex focused his attention on the girl, and again the gold ball point pen between his large fingers moved occasionally with surprising speed and deftness. The small notebook before him on the table, inconspicuous behind the sugar container and salt and pepper shakers, was a maze of shorthand.

The girl looked up for a moment and caught his gaze and he moved his eyes away casually, waiting a full half minute before daring to look again. When he looked back she was no longer interested in him, but was still talking animatedly to the man across the table from her.

Alex's sad but alert blue eyes watched her. She had well formed and mobile red lips across even teeth, rather pretty lips, easy lips for a deaf man to read. He watched the slight stretching motion of the *e*'s, the rounded, almost pouting *o*'s and the delicate touch of her tongue on the tips of her even teeth for the *th*'s.

Whenever she said something that might be of interest, or mentioned one of the names Alex had been told to watch for, his gold pen moved idly but with nimble speed across the note paper.

The waiter arrived with the coffee, and Alex's fingers flipped the page of the notebook to reveal harmless looking business notes. The waiter left, the page was flipped back and Alex nonchalantly sipped his coffee from the cup in his left hand.

The girl looked up and noticed him again. She looked away quickly, placing widely spread fingers in her short blonde hair in an unconscious gesture of distress.

"Don't turn now," Alex watched her say, "but do you know the man at the table by the window?"

Alex didn't give the man a chance to turn and look. He glanced at his watch, gulped the last of his coffee and stood. Without looking back, he placed the money for his bill on the table and walked out of the restaurant.

As soon as he entered his fourth floor efficiency apartment Alex removed his shoes and lay down on the bed. Lying on his back, he lifted his legs one at a time and peeled off his socks. He rested there for about ten minutes before rising.

Alex was still barefooted as he walked to the refrigerator, got out a frozen dinner and put it in the oven. Going without shoes and socks when indoors was a habit he'd acquired long ago.

As he walked about the apartment, feeling the cool tile of the kitchen floor, the softness and contrasting hardness of where the living room rug met the hardwood floor, he felt all the subtle vibrations of the tenant-crowded building below him. Perhaps it made him a little less lonely.

While waiting for the dinner to heat, Alex opened the case of his portable typewriter and sat down to transfer the shorthand in his notebook to conventional English. He typed smoothly, with the speed and accuracy of a professional.

After dinner he watched part of a baseball game on television; then he went for a long walk, came home and went to bed.

Early the next morning Alex was driving his small car up the winding dirt roads that led into the hills above the city. He turned off onto a narrow white dirt road and followed it until it became too narrow even for his small car.

Alex twisted the ignition key, feeling the engine stop, then he walked the remaining hundred or so yards to the gate in a high chain link fence.

As he approached the gate he could see the roof of the expensive but secluded house built into the hillside among the trees. When he wasn't traveling, this was where Walther lived.

When Alex was within ten feet of the fence Walther's companions and servants, three large black German Shepherds, ran and hurled themselves against the chain link gate.

They backed off, barking loudly, and with teeth bared hurled themselves again and again.

A tingling sensation ran through Alex's head as somewhere a high frequency whistle was blown. Immediately the dogs became calm, and in unison they turned and trotted off toward the house. Alex waited patiently, and in a few minutes he felt the second tingling sensation that was his signal to enter.

Alex walked up the driveway to the low brick house and entered a side door. For the first time in his life he felt a twinge of apprehension at what his orders would probably be, an apprehension he didn't understand. He walked down a hall and through an open door that led into Walther's office.

Walther was sitting behind his marble-top desk, methodically spelling out words with a tape gun. He had a fondness for labeling things, and Alex had seldom seen him behind the marble desk top when he wasn't turning the alphabet dial and squeezing the plastic trigger to indent the adhesive metal tape with classifications for file folders, personal or business possessions.

Walther finished the word he was working on, looked at the tape with satisfaction and squeezed the separate trigger that snipped it off. The tape fell face up on the desk, but Alex was too far away to read it.

"About the Joyce Chambers woman," Alex said in his slightly slurred voice as he laid his typewritten report on Walther's desk.

Walther nodded and smiled. He was a thin man, with even, angular features and a small but sparkling diamond ring on his little finger. He read through the pages swiftly while Alex waited, then he set the papers on a corner of the desk and looked up at Alex.

"Make yourself a drink," he said silently, pointing toward a small corner bar, and he watched as Alex did so.

Alex was one of several employees in Walther's small but unique and profitable "contracting" business. Like his fellow employees he had been adopted from an orphanage for handicapped children when he was very young, and an old German couple who was in the pay of Walther had raised him. And since Walther paid well, they had raised him to Walther's specifications.

Alex had been tutored to get along in the world as unobtrusively as possible. At the same time he'd been taught to place very little value on any kind of life, human life in particular. He had begun by killing dogs and rabbits by hand when he was nine. His job was still to kill with his hands, but no longer dogs and rabbits.

But the main thing that had been drilled into Alex's head since childhood was the thing that held Walther's operation together — loyalty, complete and unquestioning. All Walther's employees had that in common, from Alex Goodnight to the blind man in London who could study the Braille blueprint of a building and find his way unerringly through darkness to a safe, then open it with the delicate touch of his fingers.

But the deaf ones, like Alex, with their one useless sense and their overdeveloped four others, must be the most loyal of all, for they were the most dangerous.

One of the prerequisites for Walther's employees was intelligence, and because of this intelligence they sometimes began to question, to wonder why. Usually by that time they were too deeply embroiled in what they were doing to protest too much, even to themselves. But at this crisis some of them did balk, and their loyalty could not be taken for granted.

When this happened there was no alternative but to destroy them. A million-dollar operation could not be jeopardized. Of course the one trouble with that drastic precaution was that able replacements were very rare. It was, Walther often mused, an age of specialization.

Alex had finished mixing his diluted Scotch and water, the only thing he drank, and returned to sit before Walther's desk. Walther began to spell out something on the tape gun again, and he had his head bowed so that Alex had to watch closely to read his lips.

"You will have to kill the Chambers woman," Walther said, twisting the alphabet dial. "Get her alone. Do it simply and quickly, as with the man in New York."

"Yes, sir," Alex said almost by reflex.

Walther looked up and smiled rather broadly. "When

you're through with this one I think you'll deserve a nice vacation, say in Miami Beach."

Alex nodded. "That would be very good."

"Fine," Walther said. "I'll watch the newspapers and contact you when it's done." He turned his attention back to the tape gun and Alex stood and walked out of the office and back down the short hall. He knew that Walther had the dogs roaming the grounds only during night interviews.

As Alex neared the high gate he could feel Walther's eyes on him through high powered binoculars. Once before he had gotten this feeling and turned to see the glint of sunlight off the lenses behind a window, and the next time he'd visited the office Walther had purposely laid the binoculars with the personalized red name tape label out where he could see them.

Latching the gate after him, Alex caught a glimpse of the dogs up near the house, running toward him through the sparse trees. He walked toward his car, his shoes crunching evenly on the small white stones, and he didn't hear or bother to turn when the dogs hit the chain link fence behind him.

Alex was waiting the next evening when Joyce Chambers came home from work. From his small car across the street he watched her enter her apartment building and saw the light come on inside the third floor window. She'd taken off her thin, stylish coat, and her slim figure was silhouetted for a moment as she walked to the window and pulled the drapes closed. Alex waited patiently.

Two hours later she came out of the building, walking sprightly in a bright yellow dress through the near-arch formed by the large, untrimmed hedges on either side of the door. She got in her car and drove off quickly. As soon as she'd turned the corner, half a block up, Alex's car made a precision U-turn and followed.

She met the man again. This time at a tavern with outside tables gathered around a small colored fountain. Amber light played over her blonde hair as she sat with the man and they ordered their drinks. Alex didn't bother to watch them this time. Instead he went inside the tavern and sat in a booth near the window so he could keep an eye on her car. He knew that the man never drove to their appointments.

Joyce Chambers didn't leave with the man. Instead she walked across the street and got in her car alone. She walked slowly this time, thoughtfully.

Alex paid for his drink and left. He followed her for a while, until it became obvious to him by her aimless direction that she was driving with no destination. She didn't seem to be checking her rear-view mirror, Alex noted. Of course there was the possibility that she knew she was being followed, or perhaps she was simply driving idly while she thought.

Walther had said to do the job quickly, and it was getting late. There would be little chance to get her alone this way, Alex thought, so he turned his car abruptly and drove back toward her apartment. The entrance vestibule was fairly well concealed from outside by shrubbery and the light was dim. Even if she made some noise he could escape easily without anyone seeing his face. He decided to wait for her there.

She was waiting for him.

As he entered her pale hand touched his arm lightly.

"Please, I want to talk to you —"

He read her lips with difficulty in the dim light.

He stared down at her. There was a softness about her features, a pitiable desperation in her large brown eyes;

Alex's mind raced. "I don't believe I know you, Miss," he said.

The desperation in her eyes shone. "But you do! You've been following me for days!" She looked at him carefully, realizing then, perhaps, that there was something different about him.

His faintly slurred, monotone voice spoke again. "Why would I follow you?"

She knew then. He could tell by the exaggerated enunciation when she spoke, angling her head slightly upward so he could see her lips. "Please don't play games. I only want to talk to you."

He stood thinking for a moment. "Where?"

Joyce Chambers looked around automatically. Even through her desperation there was a touch of self-consciousness. "Upstairs. In my apartment."

It might be better there, Alex thought. Easier, more private, and perhaps it would be a while before the body was found.

He nodded.

She led the way. He watched the liquid, rhythmic motion of her hips beneath the yellow dress as she took the stairs.

Her apartment was small, tastefully furnished, but with a worn, slightly threadbare atmosphere. Furniture that was just entering the last days of its usefulness. Joyce Chambers sat down on the sofa, but Alex remained standing.

Her frightened eyes, which fascinated Alex, grew larger. "I want to appeal to you — to them — for mercy."

Alex felt a twinge of pity. She wouldn't believe him if he told her that he was merely doing his job, that he neither knew nor cared who "they" were.

"I didn't mean to hurt anyone," she continued in a rush of words that Alex could hardly understand. "It started as a

227

silly adventure, a harmless thrill, and then I got in deeper and deeper!"

Alex checked to make sure the drapes were still closed and sat down next to her.

"I'll promise to never talk, to go away —" she was saying, as Alex turned his body to face her on the sagging sofa. Tears glistened on her cheeks as she placed her small hands against his chest, her fingers clawing into the material of his jacket. "I'll do anything! Anything!"

Alex felt a fondness stirring in him, a fondness turning to desire, but a strangely protective desire. He told himself that he would not do this, would not snuff out the light in those beautiful eyes, but the silent voice in the back of his mind gripped his will like iron. Independent of him, his huge hands, his strong hands, rose like separate creatures to her throat and did their usual efficient job. The gouging tips of his thumbs felt no vibrations of a scream.

When it was over, Alex Goodnight bowed his head.

A week, an almost sleepless week after Joyce Chambers' death, Walther contacted Alex with a typewritten, coded letter, and at one the next morning, as a precaution against being seen at Walther's so soon after the murder, Alex was again driving his small car up into the hills beyond the city.

He went through the ritual of the dogs and found Walther behind his desk as usual, idly punching out letters on the tape gun by the shaded light of a desk lamp. Alex got his drink, took his chair in front of Walther's wide desk.

"You did a very good job," Walther said, concentrating on his tape.

Alex sat silently, and after punching out a few more letters Walther raised his eyes curiously.

"I didn't want to kill this one," Alex said slowly.

Walther's eyes narrowed with surprise and a certain

wariness, as if one of his dogs had unaccountably growled at him.

"Well," he said smiling, "a few weeks of fun will make you forget it."

"I want to quit."

"*Quit?*" Walther's voice was amused and incredulous. "But you simply don't *quit*." He shrugged his shoulders as if Alex had suggested defying some irrefutable law of the universe. "You simply don't."

"I don't even want the money for this job," Alex said, "or the vacation."

"I see." Walther looked at Alex for a long time, coolly, appraisingly, a bit sadly. "Would you like to think about it for a while? Let me know later?"

Alex shook his head. "I've already thought. I'm sorry."

Walther sat stiffly, soberly.

"Well," he said at last, with smiling resignation, "perhaps I shouldn't try to talk you out of it."

There was something strange, Alex noted instinctively, about the way Walther was holding the tape gun, the way his finger had slid up the plastic punch trigger, the way he was — *aiming it!* In an instant Alex saw the perforated circle on the plastic front of the gun, exactly the size of a small caliber bullet. Something in his mind flashed an instantaneous message, and without sound or warning Alex sprang.

Alex felt two bullets slice into his body as he crossed the wide desk and his huge hand circled Walther's throat. He felt two more bullets enter as they sprawled struggling to the floor and he looked into Walther's panic-stricken eyes. One of Alex's hands left Walther's throat for a split second, slapped the gun away, and then darted back to its previous position. Alex dug in with his thumbs.

Walther's face became splotched with red, then the red

229

merged with a mottled blue.

And that's when Alex's fingers began to lose their grip. He was bleeding terribly, weakening toward death, and the growing pain in his stomach and chest kept him from tensing and exerting all his power. He saw the glint of sudden hope, of animal cunning, in Walther's eyes as he realized what was happening. Slender fingers clamped Alex's wrists, waiting for the moment when they could push his hands away. Slowly the bluish color left Walther's complexion.

The fingers about Walther's neck were trembling now, losing control. Mustering his remaining strength Alex forced himself to rise to his knees.

Walther lay looking up at him; waiting, watching clinically, almost smiling.

Alex screamed something unintelligible, something scarcely human down at Walther. Then he lunged forward, downward, and with all the viciousness of his death agony sank his teeth deep into Walther's pink throat.

Outside, the dogs were patrolling the grounds.

Abridged

Wallace Deerborne tucked his dark umbrella under his arm and stepped down off the curb. Twenty percent chance of shower, the weather report had said. That was more risk than Wallace cared to chance in anything — his business ventures, his social life, crossing the street or the weather. All in all he'd been seldom rained on.

But into each life . . . as they say. And it was the rain in Wallace's life that caused him to be walking down Twelfth Street this cloudy evening.

He saw what he was looking for and stopped, putting his hands in the pockets of the light topcoat he was wearing, feeling a sudden chill in the dusk air. High above him a street light flickered and came on, and he observed that a few of the cars that passed now had their headlights on.

He breathed deeply, steadying himself, and his cool eyes focused again on the worn, almost unnoticeable sign that protruded over the sidewalk: H. MUDD, BOOKDEALER. Wallace tapped the pointed tip of his umbrella on the pavement and walked forward.

It was a small bookshop, with one narrow unlit display window. The darkened forms of several open magazines, pressed against the glass like huge moths, completely obscured the view inside from the street.

At first Wallace thought the bookshop was closed. But as he turned the knob the door opened with almost alarming ease.

The inside of the bookshop was old but well kept. On

231

Wallace's right a magazine rack ran halfway down the wall and gave way to shelves of paperback novels. On the rear wall were shelves of hard covers behind an old and narrow staircase that led up to a closed door. Behind the wooden counter on Wallace's left the wall from floor to ceiling was one huge bookcase of hard covers, and behind the counter sat the gray-headed man.

The man rose from his chair, which creaked with the sudden absence of weight. At first Wallace thought he was a very old man, but on closer inspection he saw that the man behind the counter was one of those individuals whose age it is impossible to perceive. He could have been fifty; he could have been seventy. The lean, stooped body, the slender, lined face, told nothing.

"Help you?" The gray-headed man asked.

"I'm — uh — looking for a book," Wallace said, feeling immediately that it was a stupid statement. "A particular book."

The lean man's interest seemed to heighten. "Just what sort of book, sir?"

"Mystery," Wallace said. "A murder perhaps."

Dark eyes seemed to draw back in the older man's lined face, then came a guarded smile. "You wouldn't be Mr. Wallace Deerborne, would you?"

Wallace nodded.

"What makes you think you'll find the particular book you want at this particular bookshop, Mr. Deerborne?"

"Telephone calls, Mr. — Mudd, is it?"

"Horace Mudd," the old man said.

Wallace unbuttoned his coat, beginning to feel more at ease. "And you are my anonymous caller, I take it?"

Mudd waved a withered hand to indicate the entire shop.

"You may take anything you want," he said to Wallace,

"as long as you pay for it." He laughed a curious "Eh, eh, eh," that lapsed into a fit of violent coughing.

Mudd swallowed hard, then looked at Wallace just as hard. "You want to kill your wife, don't you, Mr. Deerborne?"

A tremor ran through Wallace's body. He knew it would be useless to ask Mudd where he'd gotten that information. Besides, easily a dozen people knew of Wallace's unhappy married state.

"I want to see one of the books you described on the phone," Wallace said noncommittally. "That is, if you were serious."

"Serious?" Mudd took a handkerchief from his pocket and wiped his lips. "Let me explain the situation to you, Mr. Deerborne. It's important that my clients have complete faith." With a practiced, darting gesture he returned the handkerchief to his pocket.

"Many years ago my father was a guard at a very famous prison, and my father had an idea. For certain favors bestowed on my father, prisoners would get certain favors in return. As my father moved up the chain of prison administration these favors came sometimes in the form of pardons.

"All my father asked in return for these pardons was that the prisoner, always a convicted murderer, write everything about his crime and turn the papers over to my father. Through the years he obtained hundreds of such 'memoirs'."

"And of what use were they to him?" Wallace asked.

"Eh, eh!" There was scorn as well as amusement in Mudd's staccato laugh. "He turned them into a book, Mr. Deerborne, a volume of books, in fact." The seamed face turned to steal a glance at the front door as Mudd leaned farther over the scarred counter.

"As you have no doubt heard, Mr. Deerborne, it is usually one mistake that leads to a murderer's apprehension. The most clever of caught murderers must look back and say, 'If only I hadn't done *that,* or if *this* hadn't happened'. What my father did, Mr. Deerborne, is reconstruct these most clever crimes on paper and carefully point out the pitfalls and how to avoid them."

"An expert's guide for successful murder," Wallace said. There was incredulity in his voice and he was surprised to find that he was breathing rather hard. He removed his hat, revealing thinning brown hair, and set it on the counter. "One thing that bothers me, Mr. Mudd. The co-authors of these books — all of them were failures."

Mudd smiled. "The first time, yes. But after my father saw to their paroles he kept in touch. Almost all of them, with the help of the books, went on to murder again successfully. It gets in your blood, I suppose."

A wistful look came into Mudd's dark eyes. "My father himself had five wives, Mr. Deerborne. He was tried and acquitted two times."

Wallace's heart pounded as he thought of the thousands of injustices he'd suffered living with his ponderous, domineering wife, Hilda.

"Let me see the books," he asked, and there was a pleading quality to his hoarse voice.

"The price," Mudd said evenly, "is a thousand dollars."

Wallace looked into the dark eyes.

"A bargain," he said with involuntary savagery.

Mudd nodded and walked out from behind the counter, his body still stooped in his shuffling gait.

"Upstairs," he said. "Perhaps you could tell me something about your wife, Mr. Deerborne. It might be useful in helping us to select the correct volume."

"She's forty-two," Wallace said, "a nagging, overstuffed harpie who'd rather inflict pain than anything else in this world! A sadistic brute in woman form —"

"Now, Mr. Deerborne," Mudd interrupted, "nobody's as bad as all that."

They began to climb the narrow wooden stairs. "Tell me, does your wife have any serious physical infirmities?"

"A bad heart," Wallace said bitterly, "but a healthy one. Despite her whale-like size."

"Well, I think we'll find a solution to your problem in my volumes."

They reached the top of the stairs and Mudd unlocked the door. He opened it into darkness and his hand darted inside the doorframe and flicked the lightswitch.

The tiny room was unfurnished but for one heavy bookcase, and the ceiling was so low that both men had to keep their heads bent awkwardly. Mudd closed the door behind them and they went to the books.

There were thirty very thick volumes in all. Wallace noted the word INDEX printed on the cover of the first volume, which was also lettered ABD (Abduct) to BLU (Blunt instrument).

"Ah, now," Mudd said slowly and thoughtfully. His thin hand reached for Volume 27.

"There are two volumes devoted completely to wife eliminations," he said to Wallace.

"Excellent."

"The fact that your wife is fat," Mudd added apologetically, "can definitely be worked to your advantage." He handed the heavy book to Wallace. "I'm quite sure you'll find several possible methods in there, and be able to choose the one best suited to your circumstances."

"I'm sure," Wallace said. He looked at the book with something like awe.

Mudd laughed his brittle cackle. "In case you're worrying, Mr. Deerborne, only three sets of books were printed and mine is the last of them. I know for a fact that the others were destroyed over twenty years ago."

"If they're old," Wallace said uneasily, "isn't it possible —"

"Oh, don't let that shake your faith, Mr. Deerborne. Age isn't detrimental to a classic. My father's work has a timeless quality. The books are still quite useful — even more useful now that age has completely obscured the fact that they exist."

As he spoke Mudd opened the door, ushering Wallace out. Wallace tucked Volume 27 under his arm and preceded the stooped man down the stairs.

"About payment," Wallace said as they set foot back on the ground floor.

"As you must have faith," Mudd said, "so I have complete faith in the wisdom of the book's contents. If you follow instructions and use common sense your plan will succeed. So I'll charge you five hundred dollars when you return the book next week, the other five hundred after the murder's been committed successfully. In case of complications, of course, you'll pay after a favorable autopsy, coroner's jury verdict or trial acquittal."

Mudd grinned crookedly. "Let me assure you that is the worst that can happen."

Wallace nodded, running his fingertips lightly over the book's grained cover.

Mudd shuffled back behind the counter.

"Let me put that in a bag for you," he said, motioning

toward the book. "Not that it would appear suspicious anyway."

Wallace handed the book over. Mudd's confidence was beginning to rub off on him and he felt much better. He got his pipe out of his pocket and fired it up as the older man slid the book into a brown paper bag.

"In a week, then," Wallace said around the pipe stem, "I'll return the book here with the five hundred dollars."

Mudd nodded, laying the bagged book on the counter. "If there are customers in the shop just place the book and the money here and leave."

Wallace slipped the book into the broad pocket of his topcoat and put on his hat while the older man came out from behind the counter to see him to the door.

Wallace paused out on the sidewalk and turned.

"I wonder," he asked casually, "just out of curiosity's sake, how did you come to be in such an unusual business? I mean, a bookshop that rents — right here in the center of town."

"I inherited it from my father, Mr. Deerborne." There was a faint movement, like a change of light, in the dark eyes. "He died quite a long time ago. Suddenly."

Wallace Deerborne closed the apartment door behind him. He placed his umbrella and coat in the hall closet and walked hesitantly into the living room. Hilda was sitting in her favorite easy chair, her slippered feet propped up on the footstool. She looked up coolly from the pages of the romance magazine she was reading and her red, petulant lips opened with surprising mobility as she spoke.

"Damn you, you're late!"

"Work," Wallace said. He slumped into the attractive but uncomfortable modern sofa and tried to relax.

"You never worked before on Thursdays, Wallace."

Wallace bent over and loosened his shoelaces. "Well, you know that Miss Bibsly who works at the office?"

"Tall blonde thing with bangs?"

Wallace Deerborne nodded. "I was at her apartment making love to her."

Hilda's mouth opened wide and the magazine slipped from her spacious lap. "Hah! That's a laugh and a half. A girl like that wouldn't touch a forty-five-year-old has-been like you with her gloves on! You can't *do* better than me, Wallace!"

"I suppose not," Wallace said.

Hilda replaced the magazine on her lap with an aggravated glance at Wallace as if he were to blame for its falling.

"Supper was ready an hour ago," she said haughtily. "You didn't expect me to keep the meat and potatoes warm for you while you were working over those silly reports at your office, did you?"

"No," Wallace said. "I'll eat it cold."

"You'll eat it not at all," Hilda said. "I ate it. Things aren't going to go to waste around here just because you don't give a damn enough to even try to come home on time."

"All right," Wallace said wearily, "I'll fix something later."

"You will is right! I guess you've forgotten this is the night of my sister's bridge club. I'm late already!"

"You're right, dear. I had forgotten. It won't happen again."

"Damn you, Wallace! All you think about is that stupid job of yours, or gardening, or your idiot tropical fish!"

"I don't have tropical fish anymore," Wallace said. "You flushed them all down the toilet."

Hilda's eyes shone. "One by one, Wallace! And I enjoyed every minute of it!"

She heaved herself out of the chair, ignoring the magazine this time as it fell to the floor. With a last disdainful look at Wallace she walked toward the bedroom, her chins quivering with each heavy step.

Within minutes Hilda emerged from the bedroom, balanced precariously on high heels, wearing her imitation fur stole.

"I'll be back at eleven," she said. "What are you going to do after supper, Wallace?"

Wallace ran a hand through his thin hair, idly considering Miss Bibsly as he never had before.

"I think I'll go to bed," he said. "I think I'll go to bed and read before I go to sleep."

Wallace did read, for hours, and even that night he chose a plan from Volume 27. It seems there is a deadly poison that can be made from very common ingredients and the sappy substance from a tropical plant. This same substance, however, can be extracted from a very common American plant and used to make the poison.

This was the discovery of the murderer who wrote so long ago for Volume 27. He'd administered this poison to his aging brother and it had worked beautifully. Within a half hour the brother had died, with symptoms exactly duplicating those of a heart attack. Only the most careful and expert autopsy could detect the poison, and even then the doctor had to know what he was looking for.

The long ago murderer's mistake was that he'd recently returned from doing medical research in the tropics, and as luck would have it one of the examining doctors had heard of the rare poison. This known familiarity with the tropics, combined with the fact that the dead brother had no history of a bad heart, aroused enough suspicion for the careful autopsy that was necessary.

But other than that, Wallace thought, as he hid the book in the back of one of his dresser drawers, it would have worked. Wallace closed the drawer and smiled. Volume 27 had some very good suggestions to avoid the few possible pitfalls of the plan, and Wallace had never been to the tropics.

It was definitely better than the meat cleaver and police dog plan, Wallace thought as he climbed back into bed. He was still smiling as he fell asleep.

Three days later Wallace Deerborne returned the book to Mudd, along with the five hundred dollars. There was a customer in the bookshop at the time, an old lady, so Wallace just set the brown paper bag containing book and money on the wooden counter and nodded at Mudd. The nod was returned by a slight smile over the old lady's shoulder and Wallace left the shop.

As the door closed behind him the thought crossed Wallace's mind that he didn't really *have* to pay Mudd the second five hundred. After all, they didn't have a written contract. For that matter, he hadn't really had to pay the first half of the money.

Wallace shook these ideas off, however, shuddering at the thought of how Horace Mudd might collect.

Wallace began the preliminary phase of the plan that very night, seeing that a magazine containing an article on the relationship of obesity and heart trouble fell into Hilda's hands. During the next few weeks this subject cropped up with mysterious coincidence many times, and when the seed of anxiety was firmly planted in Hilda's mind Wallace made his first important move.

It was a small dose, far from lethal, and Wallace waited the necessary half hour or so after lunch for it to happen. He'd placed the poison in her strawberry shortcake. Her only comment was that the whipped cream topping tasted a bit flat.

And then it happened, just as Volume 27 said it would. Hilda suddenly gasped and clutched at her chest, leaning forward and supporting herself with her other huge arm on the table. As Wallace rose to help her he noted that her complexion was flushed and splotchy.

Great concern was expressed — Wallace called Hilda "dear" as often as possible in the presence of others — and before the doctor left he recommended an electro-cardiogram and thorough examination, even though Hilda seemed to have recovered nicely. A coronary stroke, however mild, was something that must be looked into.

The results of the examination were what Wallace expected. Hilda's heart showed some very minor and temporary damage from her recent stroke, but other than that she seemed healthy. She would have to try to reduce, the doctor said, for her overweight was probably what caused the mild attack. Hilda was released from the hospital with that caution, and a history of heart trouble was established.

Only Wallace knew that three weeks later a massive heart attack would take the life of his massive wife.

The funeral was small and touching. ". . . A woman dearly loved . . ." Wallace heard the minister say, as the mourners bowed their heads for the eulogy. There had been no trouble or suspicion; the same doctor who had conducted Hilda's examination had also signed the death certificate.

As Wallace stood there foremost among the knot of mourners and listened to the women's stifled sobs he actu-

241

ally felt a bit sorry for Hilda, wondering for the first time if perhaps he should simply have asked for a divorce. But no, he thought, she would have caused all the trouble possible and milked him dry of everything the courts would allow. And even if she wouldn't have contested the divorce the effect on his business career would have been disastrous.

With his head still bowed Wallace unobtrusively leaned forward and peered down to make sure the grave was deep enough.

". . . Like a light gone from our lives . . ." the minister was saying.

Hilda's bridge club sobbed louder.

". . . Sadly missed by us all . . ."

Wallace fought back a yawn.

". . . Amen."

It was only the morning after the funeral when the knock came on Wallace's door. Wallace tied the cord on his red terrycloth robe and crossed the living room. As he opened the door he heard a familiar sharp laugh, and there was Horace Mudd, standing in the hall with his hands on his hips, looking admiringly at the black funeral wreath that hung on the door.

Wallace recovered from his surprise. "Mr. Mudd," he said and stepped back, "come in."

"I dropped by to offer my condolences," Mudd said as he shuffled awkwardly past Wallace.

"For my wife's death, you mean?" Wallace closed the door.

"In a manner of speaking."

Something very unpleasant stirred in the back of Wallace's mind.

Mudd sat in the chair that had been Hilda's favorite. "I also came by to tell you about the deletion."

"Deletion?"

"Yes," Mudd said, "you see, my father made one major change in all of the volumes. He eliminated that piece of advice most often quoted by murderers."

"Which is?"

"Always murder alone, Mr. Deerborne. Never confide — in anyone."

"But I did do it alone," Wallace said uneasily.

Mudd smiled and shook his head. "You confided in me, Mr. Deerborne."

Dizzily, Wallace sat down on the sofa.

"There is one thing you're forgetting," he said in a high voice. "Because I did confide in you, you're my accomplice. You're equally guilty in the eyes of the law."

Mudd looked amused. "Law?" He started to laugh and coughed violently, dabbing at his lips with a dirty white handkerchief. "Why, there's nothing against the law in renting you a book, Mr. Deerborne. How was I to know you'd take it seriously? If everyone did that, mystery novels and authoritative books on crime would have to be taken off the market. And I don't recall giving you a receipt for the five hundred dollars."

Wallace stared intently at the floor.

"I know what's going through your mind, Mr. Deerborne, but you'll find that it would be disastrous for you to harm me. There are records that would be revealed in the event of my death. Why, one of my ex-clients recently paid all my hospital bills for a major operation, so concerned was he with my survival."

Mudd smiled his seamed and crooked smile. "No, Mr. Deerborne, you don't want me to die; you want just the opposite." He drummed his thin fingers on the arm of Hilda's chair. "Still, while I'm alive, there's always the possibility of anonymous telephone calls to the police, the exhumation of

243

your dear wife's body . . ."

Wallace suddenly felt very weak.

"Blackmail," he said in a hoarse, trapped voice.

"Business, Mr. Deerborne." Mudd stood with great effort and moved slowly toward the door. He turned before leaving. "Like any good business, I'll bill you for the remainder of the payment on the book."

"At the end of the month, I suppose," Wallace said miserably.

"At the end of every month, Mr. Deerborne." Mudd folded the stained handkerchief carefully and tucked it into his pocket. "For as long as we live."

Mail Order

Angela lay quite still. I watched her sleep. About her blonde-streaked locks wound the black lace contraption that was supposed to protect her hairdo as she slept. An elastic chin strap was relentlessly working to keep her double chin from growing. Dark eyeshades covered the upper part of her face to keep the morning sun from waking her prematurely. I knew that beneath the special Thermo-weave blanket was an intricately designed sleeping bra the purpose of which was to preserve her bosomy uplift. At the foot of the bed a wire framework beneath the covers lifted them tentlike eighteen inches above the mattress to prevent them from causing pressure on the toes that would lead to ingrown toenails and later serious foot problems. Lying open across Angela's softly heaving chest was the latest Happy House mail-order catalog, its colorful pages riffling gentle in the soft breeze from the air-conditioning vent near the bed.

Angela was a mail-order maniac. Almost every day some item featured in one of dozens of catalogs we regularly received would find its way into our mailbox or onto our front porch, while the checking account struggled for survival.

I had talked to her, explained to her, argued violently with to her. What was the use? Like many other women, her mail-order addiction was too strong for her. The miniature watermelon plants, the inflatable picnic plates, the battery-heated ice cream scoops and countless similar mail-order items continued to pour into our household. Angela was incurable and I was slowly being driven mad.

245

The electric scent dispenser that emitted a pleasant-smelling antiseptic spray every fifteen minutes hissed at me from my dresser as I bent down to lift the Happy House catalog from Angela's sleeping form. Through some cross-up in the mail due to our having moved three times during the past two and a half years, this Happy House catalog that had arrived two weeks ago was the only one we'd received during that time.

I don't know if you've ever seen what happen when you haven't ordered from one of these catalogs for a long time, but they become quite adamant that you should continue to buy from them. This one contained a particularly strong though typical warning printed on the back cover with our family name typed in to make it seem more personal — or more ominous.

"Final warning:" it was very officially headed. *"It comes to our attention, Mr. and Mrs. Crane, that you haven't ordered from our catalog for the past two years. This is to warn you that we must have an order for at least five dollars from the Crane family NOW in order to maintain your account. Remember, Mr. and Mrs. Crane, this is your last chance — it's up to you!"*

As I was lifting the catalog lightly, the doorbell rang, and I lowered the open pages again onto Angela and crossed the room to climb into my pants. Almost midnight, I noticed with a glance at the imported family-crest clock as I tried to locate my slippers. I didn't know who could be on the porch, but I hoped they'd refrain from punching the doorbell again before I could reach the door. Even through her special sleep-aid earplugs the sound of the loud bell might wake Angela. As I straightened and buckled my belt I almost struck my head on the portable TV aerial attachment that allowed clear, free reception in any weather, then I hurried from the bedroom and down the hall to the front door, my slipper soles padding noisily across the carpet.

Just as I reached the foyer the bell clanged again, and I angrily flipped the night latch and opened the door.

They were in uniform. One of them carried a flashlight that he shone onto a little note pad as if double-checking the address.

"Mr. Harold Crane?" the tall one asked. He was trim and broad-shouldered, with clean, anonymous features and short-cropped hair. His partner with the flashlight was much shorter, heavyset, with a blank moon face and long blond hair that stuck out from beneath his high-peaked black uniform cap. Their uniforms were completely black; they wore gloves and black leather jackets with insignia on the shoulders.

"I'm he," I said, rubbing my eyes. I'd been sleeping on the sofa before going into the bedroom and my mind was still sluggish.

"Come with us, please," the taller man said in a clipped, pleasant voice.

In the moonlight I saw the initials P.D. on the short man's shoulder patch. "Are you police . . . ? Come with you . . . ?"

Both men took me gently by the upper arms and I was led toward a small, dark-colored van parked at the curb in front of my lawn.

"Just cooperate, please," the round-faced blond one said, lagging behind for a moment to close the front door softly behind us.

"Now, wait a minute . . . !" But the van doors were open and I was pushed gently inside. The two men climbed in behind me and closed the doors. The tall one tapped on a partition with his gloved knuckles and the van pulled away.

"I'm not even dressed," I objected. I was wearing only

my pants, slippers and pajama top.

Neither man answered or even looked directly at me, only sat on either side of me on the low bench as the van sped through the dark streets.

We drove for almost an hour, and gradually, my eyes became accustomed to the dim light in the van. I studied the uniform of the man on my left. He wore two shoulder patches on his black leather jacket, one of them a red circle with the yellow P.D. initials that I'd noticed earlier, and below the circle a blue triangular patch containing a white cloud and the initials H.H. I studied the black square-toed boots, the brass studwork designs on their glossy outer sides. I didn't have to be told that the P.D. on the patches didn't stand for "Police Department" as had originally run through my sleep-filled mind. I wasn't sleepy now.

"A kidnapping?" I asked incredulously. "You must have the wrong victim."

No answer.

"You'll find out," I said. "It's a mistake . . ."

"No mistake, Mr. Crane," the tall one said without looking at me.

The van suddenly braked to a smooth halt.

I could hear the crunching of footsteps on gravel as the driver got out and walked to the rear of the van. The van was opened and I was led quickly into what looked like a motel room, though in the darkness it was hard to tell. The closing of the room's door cut short the high trilling of crickets. The van driver, whose features I had never clearly seen, stayed outside.

The inside of the room was neat and impersonal, clean and modern with a small kitchenette. I was led to the kitchenette table and both men forced me down into a chair. The tall one sat opposite me across the small table while the pudgy blond one remained standing uncomfortably close to me.

"I'm Walter," the tall man said. "My partner's name is Martin."

"And you're not police," I said, braving it out despite my fear. "Just who the hell are you?"

"Police . . . ?" Walter arched an eyebrow quizzically at me from across the table. "Oh, yes, the P.D. on our shoulder patches. That stands for 'Persuasion Department,' Mr. Crane. We're from Happy House."

"Happy House? The mail-order company?"

Walter nodded with a smile. There would have been a suavity about him but for the muscularity that lurked beneath the shoulders of his leather uniform jacket. "We're one of the biggest in the country."

"In the world," Martin corrected beside me.

"This is absurd!" I said with a nervous laugh that sounded forced.

Martin pulled a large suitcase from beneath the table and opened it on the floor.

"Our records show it's been almost two years since your last order, Mr. Crane," Walter said solemnly.

"Actually it's my wife . . ."

Walter raised a large, silencing hand. "Didn't you receive our final warning notice?"

"Warning . . . ?"

"Concerning the infrequency of your orders."

"He knows what you're talking about," Martin said impatiently.

"Yes," Walter agreed, "I think he does. What's been the problem, Mr. Crane?"

"No problem, really . . ."

"But a problem to Happy House, Mr. Crane," Walter politely pointed out. "You see, our object is for our organization and our customers to be happy with our merchandise. And if we don't sell to our customers that's not possible, is it?"

"Put that way, no . . ."

"Put simply," Walter said, "since Happy House has to make a profit through volume to be able to keep on offering quality merchandise at bargain prices, in a way each customer's happiness is directly related to each other customer's continuing willingness to order from us."

"In a sense, I suppose that's true . . ."

"Here, Mr. Crane." Walter placed a long sheet of finely typed white paper on the table before me.

I stared at him. "What's that?"

"An order blank," he answered.

"Since you've been hesitant to order from our catalog," Martin said, "we thought you might be more enthusiastic if we showed you the actual merchandise." From the suitcase on the floor he drew a flat red plaster plaque and set it on the table.

"What is it?" I asked, looking at the black sticklike symbols on the plaque.

"Why, it's your name, Mr. Crane. Your name in Japanese. A real conversation piece."

"Perhaps you missed it in our catalog," Walter said. "Only nine ninety-nine."

"No, thanks," I said, and I didn't even see Walter's hand until the backs of the knuckles struck me on the jaw. I rose half out of my chair in rage only to be forced back down by the unbelievable pain of Martin digging his fingers skillfully into jangling nerve endings in the side of my neck.

"Of course you don't *have* to order the plaque," Walter said, smiling and laying a ball-point pen before me.

I picked up the pen and checked the tiny box alongside the plaque's description on the order form. Martin's paralyzing grip on my neck was immediately loosened.

Martin bent again over the large suitcase and came up with a coiled red wire with tiny brass clips on each end. "Everyone needs one of these," he said.

"I bought the plaque with my name in Japanese," I pleaded.

Walter smiled at me and began to pound his right fist into the palm of his left hand.

"I'll take it," I said, "whatever it is."

"It's a Recepto-booster," Martin explained. "You hook one clamp onto the aerial of your transistor radio, the other end you clamp onto your ear. Your entire body becomes a huge antenna for your portable radio."

"Only five ninety-nine," Walter said. "Two for ten dollars."

"I'll take two," I said, checking the appropriate box on the order form — but not any too happily.

"I thought you'd be receptive to that." Walter smiled.

A gigantic red-handled scissors with one saw-toothed blade was placed on the table next. "Our Jumbo Magicoated Lifetime All Purpose Garden Shears," Martin said. "The deluxe chrome-plated model. You can cut or saw, trim grass or hedges, snip through inch-thick branches. Never needs sharpening. Twenty-nine ninety-nine."

"Twenty-nine ninety-nine!"

Walter appeared hurt. "It's made of quality steel, Mr. Crane." The back of his hand lashed across my cheek and I was the one who was hurt. This time I did not try to rise. I checked the order form.

The gigantic scissors was followed by inflatable rubber shoes over three feet long for walking on lake surfaces, an electric sinus mask, a urinal-shaped stein bearing the words "For The World's Biggest Beer Drinker," tiny battery-operated windshield wipers for eyeglasses, fingertip hot pads for eating toast . . . I decided I needed them all.

"Excellent," Walter said, smiling beneath his black uniform cap. "This will make the organization happy, and since we're part of the organization we'll be happy. And you, Mr. Crane, as one of our regular customers back in the fold, you'll be happier too."

I didn't feel happy at all, and indignation again began to seep through my fear.

"He doesn't look happy," Martin said, but Walter ignored him.

"Mr. Crane, I'm sure you'll feel better after you sign to make the order legal and binding," Walter said, motioning with a curt nod toward the ball-point pen.

"Better than if he doesn't sign," Martin remarked.

"But he will sign," Walter said firmly.

The sureness in his voice brought up the anger in me. "I won't sign anything," I said. "This is preposterous!"

"What about this?" Walter said, and with the flash of a silver blade severed the tip of the little finger of my left hand.

I stared down with disbelief and remoteness, as if it were someone else's hand on the table.

"This is our imported Hunter's Hatcha-knife," Walter was saying, holding up the broad-bladed gleaming instrument. "It can be used for anything from scaling fish to cutting firewood." He wiped the blade with a white handkerchief, slipped the Hatcha-knife back beneath his jacket and tossed the handkerchief over my finger. Martin picked up the fingertip itself and dropped it into a small plastic bag as if it were something precious to him. He

252

poked it into a zippered jacket pocket.

I held the wadded handkerchief about my left hand, feeling the dull throb that surprisingly took the place of pain. There was also surprisingly little blood.

"I'm sure Mr. Crane will sign the order form now," Walter said, picking up the pen and holding it toward me.

I signed.

"Now, how much money do you propose to put down?" Walter asked, and I felt Martin remove my wallet from my hip pocket. I only sat staring at Walter, trying to believe what had happened.

"Twenty-seven dollars," Martin said, returning my empty wallet to my pocket.

Walter turned the signed order form toward him and entered the twenty-seven dollars against the $210.90 that I owed.

Martin gathered all the merchandise I'd purchased and dumped it back into the suitcase.

"So you can carry everything, we'll throw in as a bonus our Traveler's Pal crushproof suitcase," Walter said.

As I stared at him blankly I heard myself thank him — I actually thanked him!

"I'm sure Mr. Crane will be a satisfied, regular customer we can count on," Walter said. "I'm sure we can expect an order from him . . . oh, let's say at least three times a year."

"At the very least," Martin agreed, helping me to my feet.

The ride home in the van was a replay of the first ride, and it seemed like only seconds had passed when I was left standing before my house with my heavily laden Traveler's Pal suitcase. Gripping the wadded handkerchief in place tightly with the fingers of my left hand, I watched the twin taillights of the van draw together and disappear as they turned a distant dark corner.

As I walked up the sidewalk past the trimmed hedges toward my front door I tried to absorb what had happened, to turn it some way in my mind so I could understand it. Had it really happened? Had it been a dream, or somebody's idea of a bloody, macabre joke? Or had it been just what it seemed — the unprovable, ultimate hard sell?

I knew I'd never find out for sure, and that whether or not Walter and Martin had really been from Happy House, the mail-order company could expect my regular orders for the rest of my life.

The Traveler's Pal suitcase heavy in my right hand, I entered the house and trudged into the bedroom, a deep ache beginning to throb up my left arm.

There was Angela, still sleeping in blissful unawareness with her eyeshades and sleep-aid earplugs. The Happy House catalog was lying on her chest where I'd left it, the pages riffling gently in the soft breeze from the air-conditioning vent.

Angela didn't stir as I dropped the suitcase on the floor and the latches sprang open to reveal the assortment of inane merchandise I'd bought. The loud sob that broke from my throat startled me as I stared down at the contents of the suitcase. It was all so useless — all of it!

Except for the Jumbo Magi-coated Lifetime All Purpose Garden Shears. Oh, I had a use for them!

Going, Going . . .

"You'll have to make it fast, whatever it is," Dwayne Darby said, seating himself behind his imposing desk. "I'm a busy man; I don't have much time."

"Maybe even less than you think," Bennet said, taking the uncomfortable hard chair before the desk. With a quick, practiced motion, he reached to his breast pocket and laid a white business card on Darby's polished desk top.

Darby picked up the card and read it in an I'm-a-busy-man glance. "Removals," he said. "What kind of removals?"

"People," Bennet said.

"How and why?" Darby asked.

"A number of 'whys'," Bennet replied, "but there's really only one 'how'."

Darby placed an expensive black-green cigar in his mouth and gave Bennet an appraising look. What he saw was a rather dumpy, going-to-bald middle-aged man with a round, almost doughy face and faded, friendly blue eyes. The gray, off-the-rack suit fitted badly, and the tie was the wrong color for any suit. Bennet couldn't mean what he might mean.

"I'd like to tell you a little story," Bennet said amiably.

"I told you when you came in," Darby snapped, "I don't have much time."

"Oh, it will only take a few minutes," Bennet said with a smile and a gun.

Darby's eyes widened and he pressed back into his chair. The gun influenced him more than the smile. "Take five minutes," he said in a croaking voice.

"I just showed you this so you'd take what I have to say seriously," Bennet said, still smiling and putting the gun back into its small belt holster. "My story starts a long time ago, when, like yourself, I had about my neck an albatross of a wife. No need to tell *you* how miserable she made me. I went to a private detective to have her followed in order to gather evidence for a divorce, but my wife was far too smart to allow that to happen. A divorce on my wife's terms was out of the question so, to put it simply, I had her removed. My not-so-reputable private detective recommended a man for the job."

Now that the gun had been put away, Darby was regaining some of his natural arrogance, but only some. "If you'd please get to the point, Mr. Bennet . . ."

Bennet ignored him. "I was instructed to meet a man at the intersection of Tenth and Market Streets, give him an agreed upon amount of money in an envelope, answer a few questions concerning my wife's habits, then simply go on with my daily life and wait. I was to recognize this man, a tall blond man, by the fact that he had only one arm. After obeying instructions I had only to wait four days before my wife was found slain after apparently interrupting burglars."

Bennet looked at Darby across the desk as if waiting for the vice president of Argoth Industries to understand. Darby only stared at him, waiting for him to continue.

"Do you see?" Bennet said. "It was so easy, so simple . . ."

"I don't intend to hire you to murder my wife," Darby said.

"Nothing so mundane as that," Bennet told him. "To go on with my story, every now and then, for the next four years, I'd see the blond one-armed man seated on the park

256

bench, his 'office', at Tenth and Market, and it gradually dawned on me that crime actually *paid*. Being an enterprising sort, and a businessman by calling, I decided to go into business for myself, bring to the profession a fresh, businesslike approach."

"Killing is hardly a business," Darby said distastefully, "though it might well be profitable. And I thought you told me you didn't want me to hire you for murder."

"That is correct," Bennet said politely. "What I came here for is a bid."

Darby stared at him, the incredulity growing on his stern face. "Bid? . . . For what? . . . Against whom? . . ."

"For my services. And against Mrs. Darby, of course. It's no secret that you despise each other. And it's no secret that you're both very rich. I will accept the highest bid for my services to remove someone's spouse, either yours or hers."

"My wife and I might not be overly fond of each other," Darby said, recovering the old bluster, "but neither of us would stoop to paying to have the other murdered. My bid is zero." He stood to signify the end of the interview. "I'll do you a favor and not call the police."

Bennet smiled patiently. "I'd only deny the conversation."

"We'll both pretend it never took place," Darby said, remembering the gun. "Now please leave my office. And I strongly suggest you don't annoy my wife."

"No need," Bennet said, standing and moving toward the door. "I've already been to see her."

He was almost completely out the door before Darby spoke. "Wait, Mr. Bennet. Come back and sit down."

"Mr. Darby upped your bid by five thousand," Bennet said to Mrs. Darby.

257

Agnes Darby sat fashionably dressed on a fashionable antique sofa in her fashionably furnished French provincial living room. She might have been an attractive woman for her forty-five years had she not been lean and chic to the point of emaciation. On her gaunt, harsh face was a look of pure wrath. "That's just like him!" she said.

Bennet smiled and shrugged. "I told you it was a mistake to start the bidding so low. Not that it matters except that it wastes valuable time, and for one of you time is an increasingly scarce commodity."

Agnes Darby took a sip of tea from a very expensive cup. "Suppose I raise his bid five thousand dollars?"

"Then I'll see if Mr. Darby is inclined to bid higher."

Mrs. Darby smiled toothily. "Is that necessary?"

"It is the way I conduct business," Bennet said with dignity. "Sealed bids make for frayed nerves all the way around, not to mention lower bids. I believe in the end you'll agree that this way is much preferable; everyone knows where they stand."

Crossing spindly legs, Mrs. Darby said, "All right — twenty thousand dollars."

Bennet nodded. "More reasonable, Mrs. Darby, but I must say that few but the semiprofessionals in my business would act for much less."

The very expensive teacup in Mrs. Darby's hand began to chatter against its saucer. "Damn it, it's five thousand more than Dwayne bid! I expect you'll extend to me the same opportunity he'll get to raise the price!"

"Of course. That's my method."

"But this could go on and on! . . ."

"It never does, Mrs. Darby. It works on the bidders until one of them finally says 'enough!' and refuses to bid. Oh, they think they can run, travel, even sometimes evade me by

258

changing their name or their appearance. Nothing has worked for them so far. My work is guaranteed."

"All right, all right! . . ." Mrs. Darby said, setting down her empty teacup.

"I'll see Mr. Darby first thing in the morning," Bennet assured her, rising to leave.

"Twenty thousand dollars! . . . My God, I didn't think she hated me that much!" Dwayne Darby sat red-faced and shocked in his desk chair and stared at Bennet. "The little —"

"I take it you intend to up the bid," Bennet interrupted.

"You take it damned correct!" Darby said "Make it twenty-two five!"

"Things are beginning to tighten up," Bennet said, admiring the etchings on the wall behind Darby's desk.

Darby gave a short laugh, more like a snort. "Why not? You said we were engaged in competitive bidding. Won't I have a chance to top whatever offer Agnes makes?"

"Indeed you will, Mr. Darby. My bidding is every bit as honest and open as the competitive bidding in which your company engages."

"I'm sure," Darby said, looking suddenly worried.

Agnes Darby lit a cigarette from the still glowing ember of one smoked halfway down, then extinguished the shorter cigarette brutally in the ashtray beside her. "Who does that idiot think gave him his start?" she asked, as if Bennet could answer. "If he hadn't married into my money he'd be nowhere! He's got the ruthlessness to stay where he's at, but he'd never have gotten there on his own!"

"No point getting into personalities," Bennet said, trying to sooth her.

"No point hell! Personality is the reason one person

wants to kill another! It's what your business is all about!"

Bennet nodded. "You have something there."

"Dwayne hasn't spent a night here in over a week. Probably carrying on with one woman or another in one city or another. If he thinks absence has made my heart grow fonder he's wrong!"

"Of course he is," Bennet agreed. "Absence hasn't made his heart grow fonder."

"Twenty-five thousand!" Mrs. Darby said.

When Bennet walked into Dwayne Darby's office the next day he saw an impressive stack of crisp green bills in the center of the polished desk top.

"There's 27,500 dollars there," Darby said with authority. He seemed to be stuck on the odd numbers. "It's yours to carry out of here if it's the final bid."

"That," Bennet said, seating himself and lacing his fingers over a knee, "would hardly be honest."

"But *murder's* not honest!" Darby said in a suddenly frustrated voice. "This is a lot of money for anyone! How much more do you want!"

"Whatever the traffic will bear. That's the basis of capitalism."

"You talk like some kind of damned politician!" Darby got a bottle of Scotch from a desk drawer, poured himself a drink without offering one to Bennet. "Listen, suppose we make thirty-five thousand the top bid, a secret bid. That's more than either Agnes or I can afford to pay, but I can get it from company funds. There's no sense taking a month to bid up to it. I'm sure it doesn't make any difference to you which of the two of us you . . . remove. Hell, you're a businessman like me . . ."

"Apparently not like you," Bennet said with distaste.

"Oh, a killer with integrity!" Darby said, tossing down that portion of his drink he didn't spill.

"Exactly," Bennet said. "Is that your bid? Thirty-five thousand?"

"Hell no!" Darby almost shouted, raising his eyebrows. "Not if it's no deal! I offer 27,500 dollars, and that's my final bid!"

" 'Final' is probably the correct choice of words," Bennet said, standing and walking toward the door.

"That's my final bid for today!" Darby managed to say before the door closed.

The tiny teacup shattered into an amazing number of fragments as it struck the wall near the French windows. "In a way it's almost an affront to my womanhood!" Agnes Darby said, pacing and tossing the saucer carelessly onto the thick carpet. "Can I be that bad? Is it worth thirty-five thousand dollars to have *anybody* killed?"

"You must remember that wasn't your husband's initial bid," Bennet told her reassuringly.

"We *were* happy at one time!"

"All things come to an end. One of you will shortly be convinced of that."

"How could it have come to this? How could he have changed so!"

"Mr. Darby says almost exactly the same thing about you," Bennet lied.

"I bid thirty-six thousand dollars!" Mrs. Darby cried. "I'll get it somehow — if I have to steal for it!"

"Now don't consider doing anything rash," Bennet cautioned.

When Bennet arrived at Dwayne Darby's office early the

261

next morning they were both waiting for him. Agnes Darby sat in her husband's large desk chair, appearing very small and frail in contrast, while her husband stood behind her with his hands resting on the chair back.

"We decided to talk to you together," Dwayne Darby said.

Bennet sat opposite him. "Obviously."

Dwayne Darby scowled at him. "We're retracting our bids."

"Retracting? . . ."

"Yes," Agnes Darby chimed in, exchanging glances with her husband, "neither of us bids a dime to have the other removed. We've talked it over."

Bennet looked offended, flicked lint off his trouser leg. "Then things weren't irreconcilable between you."

"You can hire a good marriage counselor for thirty-six thousand dollars," Dwayne Darby said.

"The blond, one-armed man told me when I hired him years ago that success in anything couldn't always be assured. This has happened before, when the bidding has gotten too high."

"Apparently," Dwayne Darby said in a gloating manner, "it became more than the traffic would bear."

Bennet sighed and stood. "If you change your mind," he said, laying two of his business cards on the desk, "call that number and let whoever answers know you want to see me. Or if you have any friends who aren't getting along with their husband or wife . . . you know, word of mouth advertising . . ."

"I'll repeat a suggestion I made earlier," Dwayne Darby said. "Leave my office." Mrs. Darby smiled at her husband then looked at Bennet with complete disdain on her boney face.

"I'm sorry you both feel that strongly about me," Bennet said, turning and walking to the door, the picture of humble defeat. They couldn't see the smile on his face.

It was Mrs. Darby who phoned first. The women usually did. Less than three days after the confrontation in Dwayne Darby's office, Bennet again sat across from Mrs. Darby in her exquisitely furnished living room.

"Ten thousand," she said, exposing her long, even teeth. "Ten thousand and that's that. There's no reason for you to go away empty-handed."

"Speaking of 'handed', don't you think it's a bit under same to contact me without your husband's knowledge?"

Agnes Darby wrung her skeletal hands, two large diamond rings glittering. "I didn't want to, at first. Then I began to think . . . *what if Dwayne contacts you?* . . . I'd never know, never have a chance to up his offer." She looked at Bennet, her blue eyes widening. "Well, what if he *did* talk to you before I had the chance? It wouldn't be fair! Not fair at all! Can you blame me for wanting to talk to you first?"

"As a matter of fact, your husband has already talked to me," Bennet said to make her feel better. "His offer was fifteen thousand."

"Twenty thousand!" Dwayne Darby roared in his office the next morning. "She bid twenty thousand dollars for your services after we'd agreed? . . ."

"It was more of an offer than a bid," Bennet told him. "My divulging the information to you puts it into the classification of a bid."

Darby touched his desk lighter to one of his greenish cigars, puffed smoke furiously in his best dragon-like manner. "So we're back on the escalator! Why of all the! . . .

Who does she think she *is?* . . ."

"Women are the deadliest of the sexes," Bennet said. "Devious and not to be trusted."

Darby was pacing now, clenching and unclenching his huge hands, threatening to bite his cigar completely in half. "To go sneaking behind my back like that! . . ."

"Doubtless not the first time."

"I ought to kill her!"

"That," Bennet said, "is a matter best left to professionals."

Backed into their previous corner, Dwayne and Agnes Darby had a long discussion that evening. It was the next evening that Dwayne Darby entered the house and, standing imperially just inside the door, smiled at his wife.

Mrs. Darby threw out an angular right hip and advanced bonily on him. Dwayne took her famished form directly into his arms, and for the first time in over a year Mr. Darby kissed Mrs. Darby.

"No need for either of us to worry ever again about Mr. Bennet," Dwayne Darby said, petting his wife reassuringly and marveling at the sharpness of her shoulder blade. "His game is over. He won't be back, ever! . . ."

"You're so supremely clever, darling," Agnes Darby cooed, snuggling against Dwayne and beginning already to forget about Bennet. She believed in what her husband said. Hadn't he clawed his way in five years to the vice presidency of Argoth Industries? A man like that never said anything definite unless he knew he was right.

At that same moment Bennet looked up from his newspaper as the door to his apartment opened. The blond, one-armed man who entered smiled and reached inside his coat pocket.

"I've got something for you, Bennet."

"Got something? . . ."

"Sure. Something you should have been expecting."

The plain brown envelope hit Bennet squarely in the lap.

"I managed to get them up to forty thousand dollars," the blond man said. "There's your twenty."

"Forty thousand . . ."

"Darby gave it to me at Tenth and Market today. You must have done some good work on them. He practically begged me to take the job."

"It worked again," Bennet said with his usual wonder, laying the envelope on the table beside his chair.

"Of course it worked," the blond man said, unstrapping his left arm from behind his back and flexing his fingers. "It's worked every year for nineteen years. It will always work."

"Human nature being what it is," Bennet added, somewhat sadly. "I'll have to admit again, you were right."

"I had a hard enough time convincing you of that in the beginning," the blond man said with a chuckle.

"I'll have to admit you were right about something else," Bennet said. "You told me nobody would get hurt, and you were right. In nineteen years, nobody has ever been hurt."

Moon Children

Harold Lamb stumbled into the bathroom. He twisted the chrome handle to run hot tap water and leaned with both hands on the washbasin, looking at himself in the mirror. There seemed to be more wrinkles beneath his eyes; his straight brown hair seemed to be a bit thinner; he seemed to be fading away, morning by morning, before himself in the mirror.

He pushed the absurd thought from his mind and splashed some now-warm water over his face, running wet fingers through his hair. His throat was dry and he felt slightly nauseous, but he always felt like that in the mornings until his coffee had worked its chemical magic. After drying his face with a coarse towel and arranging his hair with a comb, Lamb returned to the bedroom.

The first pair of socks he put on had a hole in them. He peeled them off and flung them back in his dresser drawer. "Darn it, Gilda," he yelled to his wife who was preparing breakfast in the kitchen, "these socks have a hole in them!" The feeble, unintentional pun didn't escape him, as he knew it wouldn't escape Gilda, and he felt impotent even in his anger.

"Which color, dear?" Gilda called back, discreetly ignoring the pathetic humor in Lamb's anger.

"The blue ones," Lamb said. "You know I always wear the blue ones on Tuesday."

"I'll buy another pair today when I shop."

Lamb put on a pair of his green socks, finished dressing

and then went into the kitchen for breakfast. Gilda, in her gray robe and with her graying hair still in curlers, was already seated. Lamb sat across from her and began to eat absently as he scanned the morning paper. It was their ritual to eat in silence.

Lamb noticed that his two eggs, which he always preferred fried once-over-lightly, were not cooked enough and the whites contained pockets of liquid. It was then that he observed, somewhere deep in a corner of his mind, that it was going to be one of those particularly aggravating days.

He expertly turned a page of the newspaper with one hand, and almost instantly the other hand which held his fork stopped in its upward motion toward Lamb's open mouth and lowered an impaled bite of egg back onto the plate.

"Good Lord, what's this?"

"What's what, dear?" he heard Gilda ask from the other side of the newspaper.

Lamb closed his eyes and then looked again, to make sure his senses hadn't deceived him, but the words were the same, in regular, everyday newspaper print that somehow heightened their terrible, unexpected impact: "MOON CHILDREN, JUNE 22 to JULY 21 — Today is the end."

"The daily horoscope column," Lamb said in a choked voice, handing the paper across the table to Gilda.

"I'm Pisces," Gilda said. " 'A good day for organizing money matters in A.M. Be sociable in P.M. and you will meet someone who can help solve that special problem.' "

"Not that!" Lamb said. "My horoscope! Moon Children!"

He watched as Gilda absorbed the fateful words, frowned then laughed. "Probably just a misprint," she said,

267

handing the paper back to Lamb, "or somebody's idea of a joke."

Lamb took a long sip of coffee. "A joke," he said, "or a mistake. Probably, but still it shocks you when you read the column every day and then . . . this."

"You don't really believe in it, do you?"

Lamb toyed with his coffee cup. "I suppose not . . . Or maybe I do, vaguely . . . You'd be surprised how often it's correct."

Gilda merely arched an almost nonexistent eyebrow at him.

"Today is the end . . ." Lamb said softly. "What do you think it means?"

"It could only mean that everyone born in the time period that makes them Moon Children is going to drop dead. And that's not very likely, is it?"

Lamb had to admit to himself that it was not. Then a very unlikely but disturbing thought struck him. "Suppose," he said to Gilda, "just for fun's sake, that this is the only paper with those words in it."

"Then I'd advise you to increase your life insurance," Gilda said. "But that isn't the only paper with those words in it, and you can prove that to yourself easy enough by buying another copy, if you're really going to let such a stupid thing bother you."

"No need for that," Lamb said, glancing at his watch. It was already two minutes past the time he usually left for work. "No doubt it is just a misprint." He stood abruptly to leave and knocked over the salt shaker, spilling white granules over the dark table top. Gilda laughed, but it was a full ten seconds before Lamb started laughing.

Lamb bought two copies of the morning *Globe* at the bus

stop. He waited until he was on the bus and seated before turning to page nine. Of course the words were there, in both papers. He felt immeasurably better. Odd, he thought, how an unreasonable fear can grip a man, and he leaned back in his seat and relaxed completely as the bus wound its way downtown.

The bus braked to a stop at Third Street and Lamb got off. As usual he was the only passenger to emerge from the bus at that stop, and pleasant silence engulfed him as the bus's deep diesel roar faded away down the narrow streets. It was still early, and only a few automobiles passed Lamb as he walked down the uneven sidewalk, squinting into the rising sun to read the sign that jutted out from his place of employment: ORION'S RARE GAMES AND GIFTS.

Lamb entered the front door to the tinkle of the warning bell and nodded to his employer and owner of the tiny shop, Walter Orion.

"Good morning, Mr. Orion."

"*Two* papers, Lamb?" Orion asked, arching an eyebrow exactly as Gilda had done. Walter Orion was a tall, angular man with haughty features that were a true indication of his personality.

Lamb was suddenly aware of the two *Globe*s under his left arm. He began to offer some weak excuse, and then he remembered that Orion was also a Moon Child. They had talked about astrology only last week. Walter Orion, in fact, was a firm believer in the art.

"Something in them I thought you might be interested in, Mr. Orion."

" 'Today is the end'?" the tall man asked with a faint, crooked smile.

"You've read it then."

"Yes," Orion said. "Undoubtedly a typographical error." He turned his attention to what he had before him on the counter. "Come and see this, Lamb. Isn't it beautiful?"

Even Lamb, whose appreciation for artistic beauty was far less sensitive than Orion's, had to admit that it was beautiful. It was a set of chess pieces, every piece made of delicate and intricate fine crystal. The pieces were large but possessed of infinite grace.

"Polish them," Orion said. "And be doubly careful. They're worth a fortune individually but twice that as a set, and as yet they're not insured. A gentleman is coming in tomorrow to inquire about buying them."

Lamb lifted a pawn and held it up to the light. "Such superb workmanship," he said admiringly. "Where were they made?"

"In France," Orion said, "over a century ago."

"Did it give you a shock this morning?" Lamb asked.

Orion didn't answer.

"Our horoscopes, I mean," Lamb said.

"If you must know, it did, momentarily," Orion said. Lamb could see that Orion was oddly annoyed by the fact that he and Lamb were born under the same sign. "Of course," Orion went on, "I realized right away that it was an error or a prank of some sort. Anyway, those mass circulation readings are so general that such a prediction would be impossible."

"Still," Lamb said, "it gave me a start."

The telephone rang and Lamb placed the pawn back on the chessboard. But as he turned to move toward the phone he felt his little finger just barely tick the top of the pawn and he gasped as he heard the crystal bounce on the hardwood floor.

He whirled and stooped immediately to pick up the

270

pawn, but Orion was already there and slapped his hand away. Orion stood and examined the pawn lovingly and said under his breath, "Undamaged." Then he looked up and turned his wrath on Lamb.

"A stupid blunder, Lamb!" he hissed through clenched teeth. "An inexcusable stupid blunder!"

Lamb knew with a flush of shame that Orion was right, but still he didn't deserve to be berated this way, like an errant twelve-year-old. He shrugged hopelessly. "An accident, Mr. Orion. I — I'm sorry."

"You would know what sorry really is if the pawn had broken," Orion said with self-contained fury.

Both men stood looking at one another silently for a long moment, Orion in unconcealed disgust, Lamb in agonized shame. Amidst the shelves and showcases of bizarre game pieces and bric-a-brac a clock ticked loudly. At last Orion, now somewhat more composed, simply said, "Polish them, Lamb," and turned and walked into the back room.

Things kept going wrong about the tiny shop all morning. An almost sure sale of a miniature roulette wheel had fallen through; Orion himself dropped a pair of antique dice and had to search for more than fifteen minutes for the die that had bounced beneath a showcase. Lamb felt rather smug about this, until a customer he'd unavoidably kept waiting remarked on the poor quality of the service and stalked out. It was as if Lamb and Orion were caught up in a strong current of misfortune and unkind fate, and both men sensed this current.

Lamb's lunchtime arrived at last, and it was with a great deal of relief that he left the small shop and began walking the five blocks to the restaurant where he normally ate. The way was lined with tiny shops, somewhat like Orion's only more modern. They sold everything, from gift cards to

271

sporting goods, and their narrow show windows were crammed with displays.

Even in the bright sunshine and among the noonday crowd of pedestrians an odd oppression, an anxiety, hung over Lamb. He stopped suddenly before the outdoor equipment store that he'd passed hundreds of times, and he peered into the window with an interest that he found surprising. "Five dollars down!" the sign said, only five dollars down, and hadn't he always meant to buy one someday, for Gilda to have around the house when he worked late? Lamb peered into the dimness on the other side of the window and saw a smiling clerk beckon him into the interior of the store. Impulsively he entered. Impulsively he purchased the small revolver.

When Lamb returned to the shop Orion was showing a customer some merchandise. The customer made a small purchase and departed, and Orion leaned on the counter and turned his attention to Lamb. Lamb noticed that he seemed to be in a slightly better humor.

"Did you enjoy your lunch, Lamb?"

"Veal Parmesan, Mr. Orion. My favorite."

"Good." Orion straightened and came out from behind the counter. "It might interest you to know, Lamb, that I phoned the newspaper on my lunch hour. That business in this morning's horoscope column was a misprint, something about vandalism or practical joking in the typesetting department." He began rearranging the game pieces on a shelf.

"I supposed it was something like that," Lamb answered, surprised that Orion would bother to check.

"These old gambling chips," Orion said, "aren't they splendidly carved?"

"Yes, indeed, Mr. Orion." Lamb walked behind the

272

counter and began again, very carefully, piece by piece, to polish the crystal chessmen. He had already finished the dark pieces, and as the colored crystal glittered in the bright illumination from the overhead light he was struck anew by their flawless delicacy.

By the time Lamb had finished the pawns the early evening rush hour traffic had started outside. He could have worked much faster, of course, but Orion kept interrupting him with other minor tasks to complete. There was about Orion a nervousness, a coiled uneasiness that became more apparent to Lamb as the day wore on. For Orion, who considered life a game in which he was a master manipulator, this was most unusual.

As Lamb was polishing the crystal king and Orion was standing staring out the window at that area of sunset which was visible between the two buildings across the street, it happened. Lamb was simply standing there, watching Orion unconsciously kneading his clasped fingers behind his back, when the king fell to the floor.

It shattered like a glittering crystal bomb.

Orion whirled, his face incredulous, pained, his eyes blazing in a way that frightened Lamb to the roots of his soul.

"You disgusting fool!" Orion moaned. "Do you realize the worth of the thing you've smashed?" His face became red and the loose flesh beneath his right eye began to tick. "Of course you don't!" He aimed the words at Lamb and spat them out with machine gun rapidity.

Lamb shrugged his shoulders in helpless fright. "Please, Mr. Orion, it was unintentional . . ."

But Orion was moving slowly toward Lamb, his long, taut fingers outstretched and flexing with an insane lust that was soon to be satisfied. Lamb's heart lept, pounded, and he remembered. The revolver was suddenly out and pointed at Orion.

Walter Orion stopped and his hands fell to his sides.

"Please, Mr. Orion! I don't want to use it!"

"But you will, Lamb," Orion said, the flesh still ticking beneath his eye, his body still trembling in uncontrolled hate, "I don't doubt that you will."

Lamb watched Orion walk toward him in slow motion through an atmosphere heavy with fate ". . . *Squeeeeze the trigger*," Lamb remembered the sales clerk telling him, ". . . *'like a lemon*," and the revolver exploded, kicking violently in Lamb's surprised hand.

Orion stood for a moment, still staring at Lamb with infinite disgust, then he crumpled to the floor like a marionette whose strings had snapped.

Lamb slumped against a showcase, realization of the act he'd committed hitting him in waves of impact. *But it had to be that way*, Lamb told himself, *it had to!* and Lamb was also aware of the inevitability of the next thing he must do. His hand steady, he pointed the revolver barrel at his head like a steel finger of guilt. He squeezed the trigger.

Lamb and Orion were on page one, and made much more interesting reading than the item on page nine:

"*The Globe* wishes to apologize for the misprint in yesterday's horoscope column. The error was due to an unfortunate mistake in our printing department, and precautions have been taken to safeguard against such mistakes in the future. *The Globe* assures the followers of the daily horoscope column that it will not happen again."

274

It was Sheriff Sam Ladester on the line. Semloh hadn't seen him in years, since the glass eye affair.

"Bain Semloh?" repeated the laconic, mid-western voice.

"It is, Sheriff Ladester. It's good to talk to you."

"Maybe you won't think so when you hear what all I want," Ladester said. "I need a favor."

"I owe you a few," Semloh said warmly. "Let's see, your re-election's coming up soon, isn't it?"

"I hope. And that's part of why I need your help. I heard you were in the city for the Curious Crime Convention Conference. Thought I'd call you at your hotel to sorta bail me out."

"Trouble in Graham County?" Ladester was the chief law enforcement officer of a small county some distance from the city, the sort of place where an ill-tempered dog would likely be public enemy number one.

"Trouble is right," Ladester drawled. "Has to do with our most famous citizen, Brighton Rank."

"The widely read gossip columnist, eh? I heard he had a home out in the woods. What's happened?"

"He was shot in the back of the head earlier this morning."

Semloh's lazy, almost lizard-like eyes blinked once. He was interested. "Dead?"

"Deader'n a hollered out tree stump."

"That's dead," Semloh said.

"It'd sure help me in a lot of ways if I came up with

something before the big city boys take over the case," Ladester said.

"By 'something,' I take it you mean the murderer," Semloh said.

"That'd be nice."

"I'll be there."

It was quite a house. Bain Semloh had driven for over an hour and a half to reach it. Bleak and impressive, it loomed atop the rise before him, against the climbing-to-noonday sun. There were other large houses half-concealed behind tall trees, owned by wealthy individuals who chose to escape the crime and clamor of the city. Brighton Rank had spent a considerable fortune to have the home built to his own tastes, and Semloh wondered if its darkly ornate ugliness represented its creator's personality.

He maneuvered his rented sub-compact up the long curving driveway lined with poplars and braked before the tall front door. There were three other cars in the circular drive, one of them a dusty tan sedan with a gold sheriff's seal on its side. Without hesitation Semloh climbed from the tiny car, strode up the wide concrete steps and rang the bell.

The door was answered after a pause by a slender man in his early forties, wearing a neat mustache and a rumpled gray suit.

"My name is Bain Semloh. Sheriff Ladester is expecting me."

"Phillip Rank," the man said by way of introduction. "Come right in, Mr. Semloh." He stepped aside as Semloh entered a large entry foyer.

"You are a relative?" Semloh asked as he followed the slender, slightly stoop-shouldered man down a hall lined with oil paintings.

"I'm Brighton's brother."

Suddenly they turned a corner and were in a large comfortable looking room with overstuffed furniture and a high, dark-beamed ceiling. Sheriff Ladester was pacing behind a long beige sofa, and on the sofa, seated perfectly still as wax figures, were two men and a fading but still attractive blonde woman. The trio on the sofa stared expectantly at Semloh, as did a standing, matronly gray-haired woman with a gigantic bosom and red-rimmed eyes.

"Hello, Bain! Been a long time." Ladester almost ran over to shake Semloh's plump hand. The three figures on the sofa were suddenly struck with animation and rose. "You've met Phillip Rank," Ladester said. Semloh nodded and the sheriff turned to the others in the room. "This is Elda Rank, Brighton's wife. On the left Ward Rank, another brother, and on the right Simon Crane, Brighton Rank's secretary. Behind them is Mrs. Drael, a neighbor from across the street."

Ward Rank looked something like his brother Phillip, lean, gaunt-featured, with a wide, flaring nose and thin lips. No mustache, though. Simon Crane was a short man, almost as short as Semloh's five six, only he weighed a good deal less than Semloh, wore high-heeled boots to add a few inches, and there was a compact muscularity to him beneath his well cut suit. Standing, Elda Rank was much more impressive than she'd been sitting down. She was what connoisseurs of blondes described as statuesque.

"The famous detective," Ward Rank said with a hint of cynicism. "At least that's what the good sheriff here tells us. No doubt he could use some of your super-logical deduction."

Semloh didn't like the man's pale eyes. A vicious sparkle in them.

277

"Some small fame is attached to me," Semloh said with a smile. "Professionally useful, at times."

"Mr. Semloh doesn't exactly use super-logic, either," Ladester said.

"In whatever form, your help will be appreciated," Phillip Rank said, though he looked vaguely apprehensive. "We'd all like to see the murderer of my brother caught."

"If all of you would like to see that happen," Semloh said, "I assume you believe an outsider committed the crime."

"Why of course!"

"It's possible," Sheriff Ladester said. "That's part of the problem."

"Suppose you show me the problem," Semloh suggested.

Ladester led Semloh from the room, down the hall to a sweeping staircase and up to the second floor.

"Quite an impressive house," Semloh said, "though a bit baroque."

"Five bathrooms," Ladester remarked lazily. "Who in the hell'd want five bathrooms?"

"I suppose you'd need them if all the bedrooms were occupied," Semloh said.

"Six bedrooms on this floor, and Rank's office and a library." Ladester led Semloh through a spacious hall with a parquet wood floor to a closed, dark stained door. He pushed the door open and let Semloh step inside.

It was a neat workman-like office. Filing cabinets along one wall, a large bookcase, electric typewriter on a stand. Slumped over the desk facing what appeared to be a French window was Brighton Rank, a neat round bluish hole near the crown of his balding skull. In the finger of Rank's right hand was a pencil, the note paper beneath the hand was blank but for a short S-shaped scrawl. On the carpet near the filing cabinets lay a small caliber chromed pistol.

"Don't appear to be any prints on the gun," Ladester said. "Wiped cleaner'n a eye-tooth."

"Clean," Semloh said. "Everything the way it was found?"

"So I'm told. I didn't touch anything."

"Those French doors?"

"Unlocked," Ladester said. "And they go out to a small porch with steps running to the garden below. The killer could have entered and left that way."

"Any sign of that happening?"

"Nope. No sign it didn't happen, either. Ground's hard from a month's drought."

"What are their respective stories?" Semloh asked, pointing with a pudgy finger at the floor to represent the people below. "None of them seem particularly grieved by Rank's death."

"None of them are, I guess," Ladester said. "Rank had the reputation of being a one way S.O.B."

"Who heard the shot?"

"All of them. And Mrs. Drael, who rang the front door-bell a few seconds after the shot, claimed she caught a glimpse of a stiff-legged man running between the trees along the drive."

Semloh raised his almost nonexistent brows. "Stiff-legged?"

"She said he was sort of lurching along. She had an appointment with Rank to try to talk him into giving to some charity or other, and she says she was thinking about that and didn't pay too much attention."

"Where do the members of the household say they were when they heard the shot?"

"Mrs. Rank was in the kitchen preparing a late breakfast;

Phillip Rank claims he was in the bath near his bedroom downstairs shaving; Ward Rank was reading a book in the room we left downstairs; and Simon Crane was in his downstairs office typing some of Rank's dictation for next week's column. Nothing particularly interesting in that column, incidentally."

"Then everyone was downstairs."

Ladester nodded. "Or say they were. The house is plenty big enough for any of them to have shot Rank, run downstairs and pretend to come from somewhere on the ground floor to the foot of the stairs. They all say when the shot was fired they hurried upstairs to Rank's office. Confusion all over the place. The door was open and they barged in and found him dead. Then Mrs. Drael rang the bell and asked who the limping man was. She had an appointment to see Rank at ten o'clock, so apparently the killer didn't."

Semloh walked about casually, examining the corpse and everything else in the room with seemingly passive interest. Then he motioned to Sheriff Ladester that they could go back downstairs.

As Semloh and the sheriff reentered the ground floor room Ward Rank looked up at them with distaste. He was languidly smoking a cigarette in a long pearl holder. Semloh instinctively disliked cigarette holders and people who held them.

"Solved?" Ward Rank inquired.

"Almost," Semloh said. He noticed that Phillip Rank was staring at him, his hands in the pockets of his rumpled trousers as he rocked back and forth nervously on his heels. Elda Rank seemed the most composed person in the room. She was seated next to Simon Crane, who was slumped with what appeared to be absolute despondency in the corner of the large sofa.

"Have you finished with things, Sheriff?" Mrs. Drael asked from where she stood near the window. "I mean is it all right for me to leave, to go home now?"

Ward Rank looked aghast. "You mean you'd walk out in the middle of the act?"

"Why don't you shut up!" Simon Crane said with surprising viciousness from the sofa. "Don't you realize your own brother's been killed?"

"Past tense," Ward Rank observed. "Nothing to be done about it now."

"Do you have any ideas?" Elda asked Semloh. He noticed for the first time that her gray eyes were large and strangely enchanting, and there did seem to be a muted sorrow in their depths.

"Deduce, super sleuth," Ward Rank said. Simon Crane glared at him.

"Mr. Semloh has his own methods," Sheriff Ladester said firmly. "Give him time."

"Oh, I think the facts are becoming murkier," Semloh said, and began to pace absently as he talked. "We will use what I call my process of illogicality. There are very few clues and in all likelihood the murderer was an intruder in the house. If that is true we will probably never learn his identity anyway, so let's discard that possibility and work on the theory that a member of the household is guilty."

"Preposterous!" Ward Rank said, clamping his cigarette holder between his teeth.

Semloh shrugged. "You all have motive: Mr. Rank's money in the instance of his wife. The same motive plus sibling rivalry in the instance of his brothers. As for Simon Crane, he might well be in a position to take over Mr. Rank's column himself. It's done that way I understand, the protégé-secretary filling the breech."

"I don't deny it," Simon Crane said. "I intend to attempt just that."

"What you call your 'process of illogicality'," Ward Rank said disgustedly, "is exactly that. Illogical!"

"Of course," Semloh said. "When a premeditating murderer plans his crime, he anticipates that his pursuers will use logic. Thus he attempts to throw them off the track by arranging circumstances that logically point away from him. He expects logical chains of deduction. Therefore for the sake of this exercise we will assume that what is logical is untrue."

"For instance?" Simon Crane asked interestedly.

Semloh's lips curved up, his mustache down. "Mr. Rank was found dead at his desk, killed apparently as he was beginning to write something. So we will assume he was killed somewhere else."

"Ridiculous!" Ward Rank snorted.

Semloh's smile widened. "Possibly. But who knows where it might lead? We strike what the murderer has fabricated, here and here; and here it crumbles. And the truth is revealed."

Though he still took slow, measured steps, there was something predatory now in Semloh's pacing. "In the back of Mr. Rank's head is a bullet hole, a fired revolver lies on the floor. We will assume he was not shot."

"I still don't understand," Phillip Rank said perplexedly. "Why will we assume that?"

"Because it might well be exactly what the murderer doesn't want us to assume. You see, if your brother wasn't killed in his office, he was killed somewhere else in the house."

"That's logical," Elda Rank said.

"Nothing is perfect," Semloh replied. "If we went right down the line — taking only the illogical alternatives in sequence, there would be a certain consistency and perverted logic of sorts in that."

"True," Simon Crane said, nodding, "I suppose."

"Now why would Mr. Rank have been shot if not to kill him?" Semloh asked himself and the room in general, pacing almost imperceptibly faster. "To make it appear that he was killed from behind, perhaps. Seems reasonable, so we will reject it. Another possibility is that the killer was trying to disguise the nature of the first wound."

"That doesn't seem too likely," Sheriff Ladester drawled. "A bullet wound from that caliber gun is too small to disguise much of anything."

"It isn't likely the death wound would be smaller than a bullet hole," Semloh agreed, "so for the moment at least we will consider that it was. Perhaps an even smaller caliber bullet caused death, though an autopsy would be able to determine that."

"Possibly my brother wasn't killed," Ward Rank said acidly.

Semloh appeared thoughtful. "Possibly not."

Ward Rank waved a hand disgustedly. "This charade isn't getting us anywhere!"

"I've found," Semloh said, "that with my method of counter- deduction, one sometimes arrives at one's destination quite suddenly and unexpectedly."

"Murdered in another room," Ladester drawled reflectively, "then carried to his office, placed in his desk chair, posed in a writing position then shot. It would take a strong man with a lot of nerve to do that."

"Excellent!" Semloh said enthusiastically. "So in all unlikelihood it was a woman. A woman like —"

There was a strangled sob. Mrs. Drael suddenly leapt from the sofa and flung herself at Semloh, clawing and screaming. "How could you!" she shrieked, as Simon Crane caught her waist and pulled her back.

"A moment, Mrs. Drael," Semloh said calmly. Sheriff Ladester moved quickly to stand in the doorway.

Mrs. Drael stopped, stared at the sheriff, then turned to face Semloh, clenching and unclenching her fists. Then something inside her seemed to buckle, and her soft, poised body settled in resignation.

"You were right," she said in a drained voice. "I came secretly up the back way to Brighton's office. He was working, and we went to the library to talk while he did some research. I killed him, struck him with my high heeled shoe as he bent to pick up something I'd dropped."

"Of course," Semloh said. "You're the only one here without apparent motive or opportunity. An ill-conceived love affair?"

"A hate affair. He was going to write about me in his column." Mrs. Drael's pale complexion blanched even paler. "He discovered that I'd been an accessory long ago in a well publicized murder case; he was going to expose me for publicity!"

"So you decided to kill him first?"

Mrs. Drael shook her head. "I was going to try to exchange some other information I had concerning the case for his silence. Only he wouldn't listen so I had no choice."

"Then you carried him down the hall to his office?" Ladester asked unbelievingly.

"I had to leave that way anyway, so I dragged his body down the parquet hall on a throw rug — it's a trick I learned a long time ago. Then I arranged things to make it look like an intruder had shot him at his desk and left, running around the house and ringing the doorbell to place myself outside at the approximate time of the murder. I even pretended I'd seen someone outside just in order to give the police a suspect."

Mrs. Drael's heart-shaped middle-aged face turned suddenly to a mask of fury and her lips drew away from her teeth as she spat the words at Semloh and everyone in the room. "Brighton Rank got exactly what he deserved!"

No one argued with her as the sheriff led her away.

"I don't believe it!" Ward Rank was saying incredulously around his cigarette holder. "How did you do it? It simply defies all reason!"

"Perhaps," Semloh sighed, staring unblinkingly and with vague sadness in the direction the sheriff and his captive had gone. "But then it's an unreasonable world, isn't it?"